# POWER HITTER

Seattle Cascades Book Four

## C.M. KANE

# COPYRIGHT

used without permission. The publication/use of these trademarks is not authorized, associated with or sponsored by the trademark owners.

Editing & book design by Maggie Kern @ Ms.K Edits

Cover art by Golden Czermak @ FuriousFotog

Photographer: JW Photography & Covers

Model: Tanner Snyder

SEATTLE
CASCADES

# DEDICATION

*For the Seattle Pike Place family, and the way they take care of
their own.*

# PROLOGUE

*S*kye…

"Oh! My! God!" Britta said when she opened her door. "I freaking love your hair!"

"Right?" I replied, running a hand over the shorn undercut at the back.

"Guys, look," she said, ushering me into her apartment.

All my friends were there. The ones I'd lost after Dylan had finally isolated me from everyone. Sammi and Amanda were, of course, sitting next to each other, and came up first. The three of them were inseparable. If they didn't look drastically different, you would think they were sisters. Not the bitchy kind, but the ones who were absolutely best friends.

"That'll show him," Amanda said.

She was the one who had hated Dylan from the start. Told me he was worse than trash and should have been left in the club where we met. Oh, how I wished I had listened to her instead of my stupid heart.

"Seriously," Sammi echoed. "I've never understood guys who need to have so much fucking control over their women. Like, we do have our own identity, too."

"I feel that," I said, moving further into the apartment. "Where do you want this?"

"Oh," Britta said. "Here, let me have it."

"You brought some?" Alexis asked.

She was the only one who had known I had chopped my hair off, but that's because she had done it. I had sworn her to secrecy with the promise I would be doing the big reveal soon.

"Of course I did," I said, setting the tins of loose-leaf teas on the kitchen counter. "What kind of a friend would I be if I didn't let you all enjoy the fruits of my labor?"

We were all children of the Market, family who had grown up in and around Pike Place, where folks knew each other, looked out for each other, and fought for one another. Now, though, we were women in our late twenties who continued to stay connected, even though I was the only one still connected directly to the Market.

"I ordered pizza," Olivia said. "It should be here pretty soon."

"I love you," Alexis said.

She loved pizza more than life itself, I swear. I mean, we all loved it, and took advantage of getting it when we could, but she could eat it for breakfast, lunch, and dinner, and never tire of it.

"We need to do this more often," I said. "I really missed you guys."

"All you have to do is ask," Amanda said. "We've got you."

"I know," I said, a bit sad that it took so long for me to realize I needed to ditch Dylan in favor of my friends.

There was a knock at the door, so I went to it.

"Did you already pay?" I asked Olivia.

"Yeah," she said as I turned the handle, but I never got the door open.

Instead, I was blown back by the blast. Wood splintered into my abdomen, and my ears rang with the echoes. I briefly saw a dark figure on the other side of the hole in the door, but then it was gone, fading like my vision, closing into a darkness I had never experienced before.

# CHAPTER ONE

TWO YEARS LATER...

*J*ohn...

"I fucking hate Houston," I said as we boarded the bus at the stadium.

"Right there with you," Hennings replied.

"Come on," Decker said. "It's not that bad. At least we don't have to worry about them cheating again."

"Fuck that," Hennings said. "They'll always be cheaters as far as I'm concerned."

"Yup," I agreed.

We were heading out for the first road trip of the season, and honestly, I was glad to be getting away. Spring Training was a nightmare, and the season wasn't shaping up to be any better. A change of scenery was always good when you were in a funk, and I was glad of that. I just wish it didn't have to be Houston.

The bus took us up to Boeing Field, where our charter was waiting to whisk us up and over the mountains, then down to the big state of

Texas. At least it wouldn't be hot. April was a nice time to go to the state. Any time after late May was miserable, but I could handle April.

"Don't worry about it," Adams said as he sat next to me. "You'll figure it out. We all do."

"Yeah, well, I'd rather not have to figure it out," I said. "Besides, you never seem to go into a slump."

"Just dumb luck," he replied with a smile. "I'm the turtle in that race, slow and steady."

"Why aren't you sitting with Swift?" I asked, realizing for the first time that the two of them weren't together.

"He's being stupid," he said. "Thinks he needs to go solo with a girl for a minute."

"Well," I said, not wanting to yuck his yum.

"I know," he said, reading my thoughts. "Most people don't do what we do. But we work well together. We'll figure it out. We always do."

"You two are weird," I said. "I've never understood how you can do that. Like, how does that even work?"

"You really wanna know?" he asked, and I thought about it.

"Nah," I replied. "That's just a little bit TMI for me."

"Hey," he said, bumping my shoulder with his. "Don't knock it till you try it."

"I think I'll stick with flying solo," I said.

"Whatever floats your boat," he replied.

"Back at ya," I said.

It didn't take long for the bus to get us to the airstrip, what with it basically being just down the road. We all filed off, dropped our bags by the ramp, then headed up the stairs to load up. It was such a normal thing, we just kind of all went on auto pilot, going through the motions, getting things done.

Jonathan having to retire was a blow to the team last year, but we had found a guy who fit right in. Ricky had come over from Indigo City just after the All-Star game, and he had taken to the program nicely. He mostly played infield but had taken a turn or two out in left field already this season and had done pretty well. While he didn't play

4

much, he was always there to cheer us on. He was on the older side, like just over thirty, much like Bridge, and he'd taken over the role of father figure to the younger guys.

Those of us that had been around didn't need someone to keep them in line, but the rookies sure did. Some were even as bad as Hennings was when he first got here. They soon learned that if they fucked around, they would find out what was what. Now that we were into the regular season, a lot of the kids had moved down to Tacoma, and the triple A team down there. Eventually, they'd be back up, or most of them hoped they would. With the way things went, though, they might never see a game at this level, and they had to be okay with that.

"We know you've all heard this before," the flight attendant said over the speakers on the plane. "But we have to give you the safety talk before we can take off."

She then went through the features and what to do if we crashed. Since nearly every guy on the plane had flown around the country together last year, we mostly just tuned it out. I felt more than heard the cargo bay door shut, then the engines started up, and we were taxiing to the runway to take off. The surge of the engines, up into the air, wheels pulled up inside, and we were off.

Now that we were up in the air, we had four hours to chill until touchdown and a bus to the hotel. I contemplated checking social media to see what was going on but opted to just try to nap during the flight. Not that we weren't going straight to the hotel to sleep, but it was sometimes nice to get a little catnap in on flights if we could. We'd won the game, so at least the rest of the team was in good spirits. I just knew I had a ton of shit to get figured out, and not a whole lot of time to do it if I wanted to stay relevant.

I must have dozed off, because I felt the plane begin its descent, that surge noise they get when they start falling. When I first started, flying freaked me the fuck out. Now, though, after several years of doing it, both with this team, and the ones I'd played with before, along with all the minor league trips, I was pretty much a pro. I tucked my phone into my inside jacket pocket and settled in for the landing.

With the whole team, plus the coaches and medical staff, along with the rest of the folks that worked behind the scenes, our plane was fairly full every time we went anywhere. The airline we flew with sponsored the team, so they probably didn't have to pay for the full fare for everyone to go places, but I was sure it was still a pretty penny to get us places. Thinking about how things were even fifty years ago, I'm sure the players would have loved to have a private plane. Bet they'd be jealous of our lifestyle we were afforded for playing the game. But we worked hard, did our best, and busted our asses for the team, so we should be compensated.

"Ladies and gentlemen," the pilot said over the speaker when we'd touched down. "Let me be the first to welcome you to Houston, Texas."

"Fuck Houston," Hennings said from the seat behind me.

I laughed because he was right. Fuck Houston.

# CHAPTER TWO

*S*kye...
"Thanks for coming in," I said as the last of the customers walked out the door.

It was nearly six, and we had technically been closed for almost an hour, but you didn't throw out paying customers, so I just kept on selling. The tea shop had been here since well before even my parents were a twinkle in anyone's eyes. Miss Sylvie's parents opened it up way back in the late '30s, just after the Depression finally eased up. At first, they weren't accepted as part of the family that is the Market, but after helping several of the shops around them, they were finally thought of as more than just distant relatives who were there for a visit.

Grampy sold flowers from the farm he grew up on. It had been his father's before him, and they were one of the first families in the Market. Grammy had a spot where she sold the honey from the beehives on the farm. The men and women who helped to cut the flowers would man his stall where they were sold, but Grammy sold the honey. She was very particular about how it was described, so she wanted to be the one to do the selling.

Dad had wanted to follow in their footsteps, but Grampy and Grammy insisted on higher education and a proper job, not that he

7

didn't help out when the need arose. When Dad met Mom in college, though, it was a whole different ballgame for them. She was from the strait-laced type of family that saw what my grandparents did as less than. The fact that they raised my dad and his brother up in a house they paid for by working the Market didn't seem to matter.

My parents bought a house out in Redmond and raised me with the thought that I would do what they did, proper jobs with proper paychecks. Instead, though, I'd found my way to Grampy's flowers and learned how to tend the bees when I was barely in school. When Joey was born, though, they gave me the freedom I needed to find my own way.

It wasn't that they ignored me. They just realized that I was never going to be the settled kind of person they were. No, I was much more like Grampy in that regard. Give me fresh air, some flowers to tend to, and bees to ensure that everything kept growing, and I was a happy girl.

I was twelve or thirteen when I started coming to the Market with Grammy to help out. She introduced me to everyone she knew, which was basically everyone in the entirety of the small city that was the Pike Place Market. I especially liked Miss Sylvie. For some reason, I was drawn to her like none other. She was closer to Grammy's age than even my parents, but we didn't really have a grandparent to grandchild relationship, more a friendship born of the love of all things spooky.

The tea store that she had on Post Alley was my haven when I wasn't helping in the family stalls, and I would listen to Miss Sylvie spin ghost stories of those who remained around the area, even when their corporeal forms had left this planet. It didn't take long for me to learn the tales, and the tours she would give. When I was fifteen, she offered to take me on as an apprentice, to teach me not only the ghost stories, but the tea business as well.

I jumped at the chance and had been her loyal companion in her shop for years. She taught me not only what was needed to do the tours, and sell the tea, but how to run the business, how to make sure she had the right products available, and even had me help her write her book about everything involved. As she grew older, she gave me more and more responsibility, and when she began to fade in her later years, she sold me the shop for a song. I'm not talking she gave me a huge discount, she literally had me compose and sing a song, and the shop was mine.

When my grandparents were ready to retire, they offered the shops to my dad, but he wasn't interested. My uncle, Marty, was then offered the shops. Since Dad was older, they wanted to give him the first right of refusal, but he knew it wasn't something he could do, and also knew my uncle would be much more suited to taking it over. He always took care of the bookkeeping and had kept it up even after Grammy and Grampy passed away.

Marty always stopped by the tea shop on the way out, just to check on me and make sure everything was going well. I had a couple of young girls who worked for me on occasion, especially during the summer and on weekends when we were busy, but it was mostly just me, so he worried about me. When I'd been with Dylan, he kept a closer eye on me, but now that Dylan was in prison, I was less afraid for my safety.

It was weird that he'd come to attack me at Britta's place instead of waiting for me to be on my way home, or between the shop and her place. He never did say why he'd chosen that location, and I honestly didn't care. I'd recovered, for the most part. I still went to therapy when the need arose, but mostly just hung out with friends who helped me bash him like the giant ass dumpster fire of a human he was.

Uncle Marty had stopped after my usual closing time and I had given him a head nod to indicate that these were my last customers. He'd taken it as a good sign and headed out. Now that the door was locked, and the lights were off, I was in the back office counting down the till and shoving everything into the safe. Hopefully I'd get home in time to see the start of the Cascades game.

Dad had gotten me to love the sport when I was a kid. He'd even pried me away from the bees and flowers to take me to a few games. It was something we bonded over, and I was glad for it now that I'd grown and gotten out on my own. He'd been hesitant to let me take over Miss Sylvie's tea shop, but when I explained that I would have a place to live right above it, he relented and gave in.

After my attack, though, he wanted me back home permanently. It took me a good six months of recovery before I could even handle anything on my own, so I relented and had Uncle Marty help out with my shop while I recuperated. When I was ready to go back, Dad was fit to be tied and tried to get Uncle Marty on his side, wanting me to close the shop, and do something more respectable.

Thankfully, Uncle Marty had made him see reason, and assured him he'd check on me every day to ensure I was safe. That was the turning point, and I was finally able to return to my own place and to work.

I'd finished the receipts, set up the deposit to drop off before I opened, and was done for the day. Setting the alarm on the shop, I headed up the back steps to my apartment to turn on the television and unwind. It was the team's first road trip of the season and they were heading to Houston, which was everyone's least favorite team. It had been a rough start for some of the guys, but they'd pulled out a few wins. Hopefully the change of scenery would do them good, and they'd get themselves back into the form they were showing at the end of last season. It had been close, but we missed getting to the championship series right at the end. Maybe this year we would see Seattle's first step into the World Series. It was what the entire city was hoping for.

# CHAPTER THREE

*J*ohn...

"Let's do this," Adams said as the Dragons took the field.

He was leading off tonight and was pumped. Of course, he had a right to be. He'd been hitting the cover off the ball already this year. Swift was up behind him, and they were talking low as they watched the pitcher warm up.

Once the pitcher had taken his warm-up pitches, Adams headed up to get into the box. I was hitting clean up, so I was ready with my bat. I'd put the helmet on once I went to the on-deck circle. The crowd was already in fine form, the "boo birds" out in force. It didn't make sense that they were mad at us when it was their own team that had been the cheaters. I guess when you cheat to get your first championship rings, how you got there didn't matter.

The first pitch was high and tight, knocking Spencer back on his ass. He got up, and we heard him shouting but couldn't understand him over the roar of the crowd. They were fucking cheering the fact that their pitcher nearly hit our guy. Typical of the Houston fan base, and we were sick of it. One of these days, they'd do something like this and kill a guy, or knock him out of the game entirely. Nearly happened with Hennings a couple of years before.

Coach was yelling at the ump to give a warning, but the ump was playing deaf and dumb, pretending he couldn't hear shit when he knew well and good that this rivalry was hot. If he was good at his job, he'd have given a warning right then, but obviously he wasn't paid enough to have critical thinking skills.

When the pitcher threw the second pitch, Adams grounded out weakly to their shortstop, who threw the ball to first. Two pitches and one out was not the way to start the game. Swift headed to the plate, swinging a couple of times before getting into the box. At least he made the pitcher work for the next out, throwing several balls that he fouled off before finally sending one out to right field.

"Fuck," Adams said as he watched the ball get caught.

"My sentiments exactly," I replied before donning my helmet and climbing up the steps to head to the on-deck circle.

This guy was an opener, one of those that came in to get the game going. Last time they had one, he'd thrown at Hennings and hit him in the head, sending him to the hospital. With him walking up to bat third, I worried he'd be hit again. Fortunately, the pitcher kept the ball in the zone. Unfortunately, Beckett hit a pop out to their third baseman and we were done for the inning. I trotted down the steps and tossed my helmet, batting gloves, and bat into the bin where they lived, and grabbed my hat and mitt to head out to center.

The rest of the team popped out of the dugout before I could get my gear, so I was trotting out to my position when I passed our first baseman, Matsui.

"You good?" he asked as I went past.

"Better when we beat these fuckers," I replied and he laughed.

I played toss and catch with the new left fielder, Tyrone Jefferson. He seemed decent enough but was young. Like, close to the youngest guy on the field. The kid bounced between Tacoma and Arkansas last season, spending more time in Tacoma, though. I wasn't sure he'd make the team this season, but his Spring Training was better than mine, so I guess he earned it.

When the time came, I tossed the ball to Adams who, in turn, tossed it to our bullpen catcher, who took both balls into the bullpen with him. We got set up and ready for Tanner to throw some nasty stuff. He killed it when we played these little shits last season. Something about showing his old team what they missed out on. He'd played well in the spring, too, so we were hopeful he'd keep that up throughout the season.

True to his form, our Australian weapon made quick work of the shitheads that were the Houston Dragons, and we were out of the bottom of the inning in quick fashion. Trotting in, I passed by their shortstop, who looked at me cross-eyed with a smirk on his face. Something about it didn't sit right with me, but it was what it was, and we'd see what was what when I came up to bat first.

Their opener came back out to start the second inning, not something we expected, which made me all the more concerned with the look I'd gotten from their shortstop. I watched the guy take his warm-up tosses and then headed up to the batter's box. Cammy was set to come up behind me, and he'd been watching the pitcher with as much concern as I had. It was like we could feel something coming but weren't sure what it was going to be.

"Let's go," the ump said after brushing off the plate.

I slid into the box, digging my back foot into the back of it practically on top of the line. We all did that, pushing the back of the box line out so we could be deeper to get a longer look at the ball as it came in. The crowd was loud, but I tuned them out, hoping that I could catch something I could hit hard and far. It didn't have to go out, but that would be a bonus.

"Good luck," their catcher said and I kind of ignored it. I shouldn't have, because the next thing I knew, the pitcher wound up and let loose a fastball aimed right at me.

Shifting my body to the side, the ball hit me square in the pocket of my pants, which was probably the best place it could have hit, what with the natural padding I had there. I dropped my bat and turned to head down to first when I heard someone shout from the Dragons' dugout.

13

"Pansy ass punk," was what I heard.

Instead of taking the base like I had planned, I pivoted and stormed straight for their dugout, and fuck the consequences. These little shits had cheated their way into a championship, and I was not about to let them keep on with the status quo. They'd hit Hennings in the head and damn near knocked him out of the game completely, and there was no way I would let them keep on with this shit any longer.

"Who's the chickenshit that doesn't have the balls to talk to me?" I shouted.

"Fuck you, man," one of the players I didn't recognize shouted back.

"Come on out here and say that to my face, bitch," I shouted, surging toward the stairs, and ready to reach in and drag him out.

I felt more than heard more of my teammates come behind me, backing me up in my fight for our right to play ball without having bull's-eyes on our backs. The player who had shouted at me marched up the steps and took a swing. I ducked and came back with a punch to his gut, effectively shutting his fight right down, as he sort of stumbled back down the steps into the arms of another teammate.

At that point it was on, and I was not about to go down without getting my licks in. They'd been doing this for the last few years, and for me, that had been enough. Arms swinging, punches landing, equipment being tossed around, and bodies smashed together as if we were one big blob of humanity ebbing and flowing with the rage that encapsulated us all.

Eventually, the umps and coaches got things simmered down, but I knew I'd landed a good dozen punches and my hand was hurting because of it. I would be tossed, of course, so that didn't really matter. No, what mattered was that we showed these motherfuckers who was the boss here, and it certainly wasn't them.

As we stumbled back to our respective dugouts, someone tossed a whole fucking box of sunflower seed packets onto the field, and the surge returned, all of us going at it again. I mean, if I'm gonna be fined, I'm gonna get my money's worth, that's for damn sure. After it was all said and done, and everyone was separated from each other, I'd been tossed, Hennings, who had been right on my ass was tossed, Coach was tossed, because of course, and Tyrone was out as well.

On their side, the pitcher was out, along with their manager, and the player who egged me on to begin with. They also made the injured player who tossed the box on the field leave the dugout. We got the bigger issue with losing three good players from our lineup, while they basically lost a bench player, an injured guy, and the opener who wasn't going to be in there long anyway.

"Fuck that shit," I shouted as I made my way down the tunnel to the clubhouse.

"Yeah," Hennings said right behind me.

Tyrone was quieter, this being his rookie season and all, and his first real action of this sort.

"Come on, guys," Coach said as he went past us to the clubhouse.

Somehow, in all the action, I'd lost my helmet. I still had my batting gloves on, though, so thankfully my knuckles weren't skinned in any way, but they were hurting like hell, and I wondered if it was worse than I thought. The trainer had come with us to the clubhouse to check things out and make sure none of us were hurt at all, other than minor things.

"Huffman," Coach called from his office.

"Fuck," I muttered under my breath, knowing he was gonna chew me out for not just taking the base.

As I walked into his office, he said, "Shut the door and sit."

I did as I was told, knowing it wouldn't do any good to pitch a fit to the coach. He was on my side, and it wasn't like this wasn't warranted.

"What the fuck?" he asked, and it wasn't like him to swear.

"I'm sick of them getting away with it," I said. "It's one thing to hit me, it's another to call me a pussy from the dugout. They've had a beef with us since we caught them stealing signs and cheating, and we're all sick of their fucking shit."

"We don't escalate like that," he said.

"What was I supposed to do?" I asked. "Let them call us pussies to our faces, and not get their teeth knocked out for it?"

"John," he said, and he had that fatherly tone. "I know they're cheaters in all our eyes, but they stopped. Don't let them pull you into a fight you don't need to be in. Walk it off, take the base, ignore their pitiful attempts to drag you down. You're better than this, and we both know it."

"I'm just sick of their shit," I said. "So is the rest of the team. We've been putting up with this for almost two full years. When is it gonna stop? When is the league gonna crack down on them? When do we get our reward for doing the right thing?"

"I don't know," he said, and he sounded tired. I waited, wondering what he was going to say or do next, but he finally looked at me and smiled. "Did you land anything good?"

Then I realized he was making sure I understood that he knew what it meant to be called out like I was, and that he inwardly approved of my reaction, even if he couldn't actually show it to the rest of the world.

"Yeah," I said. "Knocked the wind out of that first guy right away. Got a few others along the way as well. I'm sure they're not gonna forget me any time soon."

"Good," he said, then turned serious. "You know there will be fines and suspensions."

"Worth every fucking second of it," I said proudly.

"Get out there and have Gryffin check you out," he replied with a smile.

"Will do," I replied, getting up. "And, for what it's worth, I'm sorry it's gonna fuck things up for the team. Not my intentions at all."

"I know," he said, then motioned with his hand for me to get the fuck on out of there.

# CHAPTER FOUR

*S* kye...
  Grammy had introduced Dad to baseball, and he introduced me. While Dad was good at taking me to games growing up, I'd
enjoyed watching games with her on the television, especially in the
summer when I could stay up later than normal. Now that she was
gone, it was my way to commune with her in the evenings. It was as if
I could hear her cheering along with me as the team did well, and
booing the umpires when they missed a call.

I had the television on and was fixing up some of the leftovers I
had when I heard the announcers say something about a player being
hit. Immediately, I turned to see that the big guy who was the
Cascades' centerfielder was storming over to the Dragons' dugout. I
didn't see what led up to it, but he was pissed, and that was unusual.

Huffman was one of the guys I liked because of his calm, cool
demeanor, but something had set him off, and he was out for blood.
The waves of anger were rippling off him like an unseen force, and he
reached the dugout in just a few short steps. One of their players came
up the steps and Huffman punched him in the gut, knocking him back
into the dugout.

After that, it was a flurry of arms and hands and fists all coming together in chaos. I was worried that someone would be injured in a way that'd cause them to miss more than just this game and the few they'd be suspended for after the brawl was over. It wasn't a secret that players got suspended for fighting, but it wasn't something that usually happened. Most of the suspensions nowadays were caused by drugs, and not the kind that made them happy.

Watching everything, I couldn't tell where any of the players were, other than just seeing the black jerseys clash with the bright orange of the opponent. It was a beautiful dance that played out on my screen, the ebb and flow of players who were surging against each other. If it wasn't for the fighting, it might be enjoyable. But I was worried for the guys who may be hurt in a way that could cause them to lose the job they loved.

Finally, after what seemed like forever, things seemed to settle down, only for someone to say something that caused it to start right back up, and they were back in the swing of the macabre dance. Black and orange swirling together in a cauldron of anger, fueled by competition and the need to be better.

When everything finally settled down again, and cooler heads were seeming to prevail, I watched as Huffman and Hennings, the shortstop, walked off the field, along with another guy I didn't recognize. I knew the coach would also be headed for the showers, and sure enough, the announcers made that statement. It wasn't until everyone was off the field that I realized that the Cascades were on the losing end of the deal, what with having three of our guys thrown out while the Dragons only lost their pitcher and coach. Somehow, it didn't seem fair, but that was the way the sport went sometimes. Not everything in life was fair, and I knew that firsthand.

Instead of moping about it, though, I decided to do something. I pulled out my phone and pulled up one of the many social media accounts I had for the tea shop. I hunted around until I found the right account for Huffman and made a post directed to him asking if he wanted me to send him a pizza, using the hashtags that the station recommended to use. I didn't figure I'd get any traction, but instead of just waiting by the phone, I then hunted up some pizza joints near the stadium in Houston. There was a little mom-and-pop place pretty close that had great reviews, so I added to my initial post with the name of the pizza joint I'd ordered from.

Setting my phone down, I went back to finish heating up my leftovers. Before I even got the food plated, my phone started blowing up. Notifications were coming in so fast the dings were right on top of each other. Then my phone started ringing, and I went over to see what was going on. It was Britta calling me, and I was confused.

"Hey girl," I said when I answered it.

"What did you do?" she asked.

"I have no idea what you're talking about," I said, confusion clear in my voice.

"You're blowing up," she said.

"What do you mean?"

"I mean, your mentions are shooting through the roof," she said. "Have you not seen it?"

"I was fixing leftovers," I confessed. "I mean, I did make a post, then added to it, but that just happened."

"Well," she said, and I could hear the smile on her face. "You, my sweet little tea lady, are the talk of the town. Everyone and their brother's cousin is saying something about it."

"Okay," I said, still just as confused.

"I hope you're well stocked up," she continued. "I'm sure there's gonna be a run at your shop because you are all over the place."

"Hang on," I said. "Let me look and then I'll call you back, okay?"

"Sure," she said, and just as I was disconnecting the call, my dad was calling.

"Dad," I said.

"Skye, what were you thinking?"

"I don't know what you're talking about," I said, still baffled as to what was going on that everyone was calling me. Another beep came through, so I said, "Hang on, Dad."

When I looked at the phone, I didn't recognize the number, so I declined the call and went back to my dad.

"Who was that?" he asked.

"Probably a telemarketer," I said. "I didn't recognize the number, and there wasn't a name attached to it, so I just declined it."

"Be prepared to have an influx of customers tomorrow," he said.

"Britta said the same thing," I replied. "She said I was blowing up."

"If I know about it, you obviously are," he replied. "I'm going to ask Uncle Marty to come and bring a couple of folks to help you out the next few days."

"I'm sure it's fine," I replied, still unsure what was going on.

"I don't think you understand," he said, and then I heard what the announcers on the television said.

"*...and has sent a note that she'll send a pizza to the stadium,*" they were saying. "*From the account, it appears to be a tea shop in the Pike Place Market that's been there for years. Who knew tea lovers were baseball fans.*"

"Oh, no," I mumbled. "What have I done?"

# CHAPTER FIVE

*J*ohn…
    "Huff," Hennings called into the showers as I was just rinsing off.

"What?" I asked.

"Get out here," he said. "There's some serious crazy going on."

"Fuck," I muttered, wondering what was happening now.

I dried myself off and wrapped the towel around my waist, meandering back out into the clubhouse toward my locker. Hennings had his phone in his hand, Jefferson was sitting next to him on a bench, and Coach was behind them, reading over their shoulders.

"Get the menu," Coach said, and Hennings started tapping on his phone.

"What's going on?" I asked.

"You're gonna get us all free pizza," Jefferson said.

"Nah," Hennings corrected. "He's getting pizza. We're shit outta luck."

"What are you guys talking about?" I asked, still confused.

"Hang on," Hennings said, then tapped a couple more times on his phone, swiping around it to get to where he wanted to be. "Look," he said when he'd finally done what he needed, thrusting the phone in my face.

Grabbing the phone from his hand, I pulled it a bit away from my face instead of right up in there and looked at a social media platform where someone had sent a direct post to me asking if I wanted a pizza, then another right under it mentioning a local pizza joint down here.

"What the hell is this?" I asked.

"Someone's gonna get you pizza," Jefferson said, as if it was clear as day.

"I can see that," I said, tossing the phone back to Hennings and heading to my locker.

"Don't you want it?" the kid asked.

"I mean, I won't say no to pizza," I said, dropping my towel to get dressed. "But why is someone sending me shit on some social media platform? I don't even know this person."

"Maybe they like you," Jefferson said.

"Or they hate Houston as much as we do," Hennings added.

"Likely," Coach interjected. "They simply saw that you got screwed at the plate and wanted to give you something good."

"It's weird," I said, pulling on my boxers. "Do we even know who that is? It's probably some troll who's out to show what a fucking idiot I am."

"Actually, it's not," Hennings said with a shit-eating grin on his face. "It's one of those little shops outside Pike Place Market. Like, one of the OG ones that's been there since forever."

"So, it's an old lady sending me pizza?" I asked with a laugh.

"Hardly," Jefferson said, the same grin on his face that was on our shortstop's.

"What are you two fools smiling about?" I asked, unsure whether I actually wanted the answer.

"Take a look," Hennings said, holding his phone out to me.

I walked over to them after buttoning my shirt up and took the offered device. The picture they had up was a woman about our age with short blond hair and eyes as bright as the summer sun in Seattle.

She was stunning and I was speechless. How and why did this woman want to send me pizza? It didn't make sense at all to me.

"I think we broke him," Hennings said and I looked up from the phone to see the three men staring at me.

"What?" I asked.

"I have never seen you look like that at anything," Coach said. "The way you stare is with anger and determination, but this," he continued, motioning to me. "This is something else altogether."

"I don't know what you're talking about," I said, tossing the phone at Hennings and turning back to my locker. "How long have we got to stay here? Or can we get a ride back to the hotel?"

"I've ordered a ride for the three of you," Coach said as he was heading back to his office. "Should be here pretty soon. Once it is, you three need to go straight to the hotel and straight to your rooms. I'll make sure they send room service up to you so you don't starve."

"Huffman's gonna have pizza," Jefferson said. "But we'll be hungry."

"Shut up," I said to the kid as I slipped into my shoes.

I didn't dare turn around, though, because they'd have seen the smile on my face. No, I wanted to save that for that woman. For her, I'd smile all day every day.

THEY TRIED TO GET TO ME ON THE RIDE TO THE HOTEL, BUT I'D CHOSEN to sit shotgun and just ignored them. I hopped out of the car nearly before it came to a stop in front of the hotel, not bothering to wait for the other two. By the time the elevator doors were closing, they were too far away to ride with me. That's when I let them see my smile. They just laughed as the doors slid between us.

Once in my room with the door firmly closed, I flopped onto my bed after kicking off my shoes. I opened the app where she'd posted and saw that several people were making note of what I should order. Instead of reading those things, I went to the profile to find out more about her, and her shop, which led me to her website. Hennings was right in that it was one of the original shops in the Market area. The girl who ran it now didn't seem to be related to the ones who opened it, but I could've been wrong, too. She had that striking blond hair and the brightest blue eyes I'd ever seen. Not something you see very often, but they just pierced through my soul.

She had teas from all over the world and had lots of information on how to make tea properly, what foods to pair the teas with, and even had shipping available for people who either lived out of the Seattle area, or just didn't want to get lost in the hustle that was that area of town. There was also a section on her website that had tours for folks to go on. Most of them were ghost tour type things, which was not something that interested me in the least, but if it let me be around her, I might just make it happen.

When I got to the bottom of the website, I realized that it had just her first name on it, as well as an email address and number for the store itself. Nothing about who she really was, or whether she was married, or in a relationship or anything. I never did anything with anyone if they were already hooked up, even just a one-night stand. No, if you're in a relationship and want to step out, that's on you. Don't bring me into the mix, 'cause I ain't doing that.

Contemplating what I should do, I heard the guys walk down the hall, laughing as they passed my door. I was surprised it took so long for them to get to the floor, and guessed they stopped in the bar to grab a drink, something I could probably use right now if I were telling the truth. Instead, I just kept looking at this woman who had taken it upon herself to let me know she was thinking of me in my mess.

I went back to the app with the post, and replied to her saying a pepperoni pizza would be perfect, but that she wasn't obligated to send it if she really didn't want to. Then, instead of just leaving it there, I also sent a message to her to let her know as well. My phone was already blowing up from the original post, so I just muted that shit so I could get away from it.

Normally, the spotlight didn't suit me, and I avoided it like the plague. I never liked being the center of attention, even when growing up. Hell, my birthday parties were mostly just family insisting they come over to give me shit. I'd have rather spent the day at the batting cage hitting ball after ball after ball, and not being around people. My brother was the complete opposite, though, loving the spotlight any chance he got.

Now, though, I couldn't get the image of her out of my head, and it was making things hard in more ways than one. I'd take the spotlight if it meant I got the chance to meet her. Instead of just letting shit go, I pulled the image on the website up again, and really looked at her. I'd put her mid to late twenties at most with eyes that just drew you in. Some of the older pictures on both the website and the social media page had her with long hair, and I wondered what made her chop it off when she did, and not sooner. Nothing wrong with long hair, but it really didn't fit her.

There was a big gap in the posting on the page that coincided with shortly after she'd cut her hair, and I wondered what had gone on during that time. It wasn't like nothing was posted, but it wasn't the same type of thing. It was as if someone else was running it for that time, and then she picked it up again. The pictures of her with long hair were also not exactly right. Like, something was wrong, but she didn't want the world to know, and it was all in her eyes. With the most recent photos, though, she was bright and beautiful, and I couldn't help but be drawn into her.

"Fuck," I said as the guys started banging on my door.

"Hey, Huffy," they called in high-pitched voices.

"Go away," I growled.

"Why?" Hennings said, still in that high-pitched tone. "You busy busting a nut to the internet?"

They laughed after that, and I just growled more. I set my phone down and went to the door, wrenching it open. Both of them jumped back, shocked that I'd done it, I guess.

"Leave me the fuck alone," I said, and it was probably louder and harsher than needed.

"Okay, Geez," Jefferson said, holding his hands up in a surrendering pose.

"Come on, Huff," Hennings said. "We need some sort of entertainment."

"Find it somewhere else," I barked, then slammed the door in their faces. "Fucking lunatics don't know when to leave a guy the fuck alone."

I flipped the little latch thing that swung over the knob on the door as a safety latch and turned the deadbolt, hoping both noises would indicate that I was done with their shit, and they needed to find another hobby for the night. Then, I took my happy ass to the bathroom, and turned on the water in the tub to let it heat up.

I pulled my shirt out of my pants and slid it over my head, not bothering to unbutton it except at the bottom. Shoving my pants and boxers down, I slid out of my socks as well, then walked naked to the bathroom. I stepped into the tub, and tested the water with my foot, turning the knob to cool it off just a bit before pulling the plunger that allowed water to come from the showerhead.

The burst of cold water was nice, and it warmed quickly enough, which was better. I ducked my head under the spray, and let it run rivers down my back. I didn't mind a warm shower but preferred them on the cooler side. As the water cooled my temper, I imagined the woman from the tea shop. Her hair was short, her eyes were bright, and her smile was infectious.

Then my mind wandered to the pictures of her with long hair. Her eyes were nowhere near as bright, and there was a haunting look in them. She was also thinner in those pictures, whereas she looked more filled out in the ones after. It wasn't that she was fat, but in the first ones she looked sick, gaunt, or starving or something. That thought made me wonder whether she had some sort of ailment of some kind, like she'd cut her hair before it all fell out from cancer treatment or something. It could have been the case, but it seemed like a different kind of something in her eyes.

It was making my head hurt to think about this too much, so I just turned the water off and grabbed a towel. I'd already showered the game off me, so it wasn't like I was in there to clean up, just to cool down, which I'd done. After drying off, I headed back to the bed, slid the covers down and climbed between the cool sheets. I grabbed my phone and opened it with my thumbprint, and it opened back up to her smiling face. Yeah, she was getting to me, and I hadn't even met her. Probably wouldn't, though, unless I made a plan to do so.

Flipping over to the calendar, I looked to see when we'd be back in the city, and fortunately, this was a relatively short road trip, with the three games here in Houston, then four over in Dallas, before heading back home for another week of games against the same teams. Maybe Houston would pull their heads out of their asses and actually want to play ball instead of playing pansy with their throwing at us. If the league didn't hand down some suspensions to their team for this, I was gonna be pissed.

Instead of lingering on that shitty thought, though, I let my mind wander back to the beautiful girl who offered to buy me pizza, and planning a way to meet her when we were back home. Yeah, Saturday would be a good day to do it. Busy enough downtown that I could blend in, but not so horrible that I would get that claustrophobic feeling of the pressing crowd. Hopefully I wouldn't be recognized either. Otherwise, that stealth watching that I wanted to do would be fucked up beyond anything I wanted.

Drifting off to sleep just as the rest of the team came rolling in, I was met with blue eyes like pools in the mountains of my home state of Colorado when the spring leaves were reflecting in their mirrored surfaces, giving me the desire to cool myself within them, and find the solitude I always loved.

# CHAPTER SIX

*S*kye...

I'd had to shut my phone off because it just kept going off, and it was all too much for me. Instead, I turned the television off as well, made a cup of some chamomile and lavender tea with some mint thrown in, then proceeded to draw a bath of very warm water, dropping one of the lavender bath bombs I'd gotten from Sammi when I was in the hospital into the tub. She'd been adamant that I have several and use one when I felt stressed.

All my friends had been amazing to me. Not just the night I was attacked, but throughout the entirety of my healing process, and with the trial afterward as well. Honestly, I probably wouldn't even be alive if it weren't for them, and I would never be able to repay them for the love and caring they showered me with. How I'd ended up with such amazing people in my life, I'd never know. But they were there for me at my lowest, and never gave up on me.

Slipping my sweater dress over my head, I dropped it onto my cedar chest, then pulled my bra off and placed it on top. I then slid my leggings down and placed them into the hamper. My panties went in with them, as well as my socks. Padding into my bathroom, the aroma from the bath-bomb was filling the space with its special scent, already helping to calm my nerves. My teacup was on the stool next to the tub, along with the book I'd been reading. Instead of reading, though, I wanted to just not think, and not deal with anything other than letting my body relax, and ready itself for sleep.

Dimming the light in the bathroom to just barely there, I stepped over the lip of the tub, and slid down into the warm water, shutting the tap off along the way. The rest of the house was quiet, and my phone was plugged into its charger next to my bed. I did turn it back on as soon as I plugged it in but turned on the do-not-disturb feature to keep it from going off while I tried to unwind before placing it face down on the nightstand. My alarm would come on in the morning, so there was no need for anything else to be disturbing my night.

As I slid into the water, I could already feel my body beginning to calm, the aches that I had because of Dylan were eased by the warmth, and the smells from the bubbles just made it that much better. I closed my eyes and inhaled the rich woody scent, letting it fill me with all that was needed to turn my brain off.

Miss Sylvie had ensured that I would be able to live and work all in one building, and she had spared no expense when it came to making the apartment above the tea shop perfect. The claw foot tub was just one of the brilliant features she'd put in. It was deeper than a standard tub, and wider as well. Although I'd never shared it with anyone, it was definitely big enough to do so, if the right person ever came along. This place was my sanctuary, my quiet place, my secret garden in the midst of the bustling city just beyond the walls.

The fact that I'd been at Britta's when he attacked me was actually a surprise. If he'd done so when I was home, he would have made sure that I died, which had been his intent all along. He was behind bars for the foreseeable future, and I was free to live my life without his inter-ference.

Not that a piece of paper would matter, but I did have a restraining order against him, and his family, who were just as horrible as him. They had tried to say that I was making up everything he'd done to me, that the bruises were self-inflicted, that the bite marks he had left on me were just rough sex, and the fact that he had raped me more times

C.M. KANE

than I could count was just him taking what was rightfully his. Honestly, I was glad to be rid of the lot of them.

I could feel my body tensing up with the thoughts of the asshole that had been my boyfriend, so I shut that train down, and just breathed in the wonderful aroma that surrounded me. Thinking through my day, I contemplated what tomorrow would look like when I opened the shop. Sure, I would have an influx of customers, what with the fact that the announcers on the game actually giving the name of my shop, but it wouldn't be too bad, hopefully. I mean, if it was a lot, I would just have to call in reinforcements in the form of my friends, or call Uncle Marty to send some of his workers over to my place to deal with the rush.

Honestly, thinking about having more customers than I knew what to do with was exhilarating, and I wondered whether the player would swing by at some point. I mean, I did offer to buy him pizza, so I would have to make good on that, but he didn't strike me as a tea kind of guy. None of the players did, really. Whatever happened, I'd deal with it the same way Miss Sylvie taught me, one customer at a time, with a smile on my face and joy in my heart as the register rang in the sales.

By the time my teacup was empty, the water was cooling, and I was about as relaxed as I was going to get. I flipped the little lever to let the water drain, and stood up, pulling one of my giant bath sheets around my body. The soft material felt nice against my cooling skin, and I hooked it on the rack on the wall once I was dry. I left the light in the bathroom where it was, just enough to give me vision in the darkness of night as I climbed into bed, snuggling down under the flannel sheets.

Drifting off, my thoughts ran to the game I'd only seen a bit of, and the player who had been so fierce in his reactions. A man who could likely break me if given the chance. He was terrifying in his size, and his eyes held a determination the likes of which I'd never seen before, except in the eyes of my ex when he was hell-bent on hurting me in any way he could, especially in the ways that were humiliating to me.

Unfortunately, my thoughts ran through to the nightmares that had plagued me off and on over the last year, and honestly well before that, although they'd morphed to one specific thing afterward. A masked figure, dark in the hallway, holding a shotgun out in front of him. The more I tried to run, the closer he got, without him even moving. Nightmares that left me exhausted by the time my alarm blared in the morning.

I sat up and shut the phone off, silencing the buzzing initially, but then it started up again. I looked at it and saw that my dad was calling, so I answered it.

"Hey, Dad," I said.

"Marty said there's already a line at your shop," he said without a greeting.

"Oh yeah?" I asked.

"He said you should get down there to take advantage," he added.

Dad had always been all about the bottom line when it came to both my shop and the flowers and honey that my uncle sold. I think it even dated back to when Grampy and Granny owned their stalls.

"I literally just woke up," I said. "I have to put clothes on and stuff first, but I'll be down there soon."

"Snap to it," Dad said. "Take advantage while you can."

"Strike while the iron is hot?" I asked and he finally gave some emotion with a laugh.

"That's my girl," he complimented.

"Don't worry," I said. "I'll probably have to call Uncle Marty and ask him to send a couple of people over."

"I already suggested it," he said.

"Thanks, Dad," I replied. "Now, if I'm gonna get there, I gotta go."

"Kill it, kiddo," he said, then disconnected the call.

I shook my head and set the phone down, only for it to go off again. This time it was Uncle Marty.

"You would think you guys didn't want me to get to work," I said when I answered.

"Just making sure you were heading in," he replied. "I'm sending a few people over there to get the line organized right now, but you should open soon. I don't know how long they'll linger when you're not open."

"I have to put on clothes first," I said. "Which I can't do when everyone and their uncle is calling me."

He just laughed, said goodbye, and hung up. I set my phone down and threw the covers back, got up, and grabbed a pair of panties before walking into the bathroom to do my daily constitution. Once I was done and washed, I ran a comb through my hair, used my toothbrush, and then went back to my room to dress.

With it still being early April, I knew I'd need to dress at least a little bit warm but wasn't sure whether I needed it the whole day, so decided to layer up. I put on my bra, pulled on a pair of leggings, grabbed a decent shirt from my drawer, and threw an oversized sweater over the whole thing before donning my comfortable boots.

Normally, I'd have gone over to the Market to grab something quick to eat before opening the shop, but when I walked in from the back and got a peek through the front window at the line, I knew I needed to get things moving more than I needed to eat.

Grabbing the till with the cash that was in it, I plopped it into the register, flipped on the lights, and turned the sign on before unlocking the door.

"Good morning," I said to the woman that was at the front of the line.

"It's about time," she said, and I cringed.

Apparently it was going to be a "kill them with kindness" kind of day, and I had one of those kinds of people to get things going.

"Sorry," I replied as I pointed to the door. "I'm actually opening early because of the crowd. Normally it would be a couple more hours before I opened."

The way I said it was polite but firm.

"Haven't you heard the expression that the customer is *always* right?" she asked.

"I have," I replied.

What I really wanted to say was that the customer was right when there was a problem with what happened, not when they were being a bitch. But I held that to myself, and just smiled as I told her in my mind what I thought of her. Uncle Marty had been true to his word, in that he'd sent people over. Thankfully, it was Mai, Rio, and Misaki, who were the three that were closest to my age, and ones I got along well with.

"If you don't want to be polite, then leave," Mai said, and I almost laughed.

"Maybe you should go back to where you're from," the woman said, and that was it.

"You can leave," I said, standing between her and my shop. "No one talks to my friends like that in my store, so I don't need your money."

"It's probably crap tea, anyway," she nearly shouted as she stomped away.

"Holy shit," the woman who was standing behind her said. "I'm so sorry she spoke to you guys that way. That was awful."

"Meh," Mai said. "I'm kind of used to it."

"Well, you shouldn't have to be," she said.

"Thanks," I said, then stepped aside, and let her into the store.

The rest of the line seemed to understand that the woman at the front had been horrible, because every single person who had been standing there was patient with me as I explained my teas, as well as the other things I sold, and were overly polite when asking questions.

I had mostly loose-leaf tea in my shop, not just because that's what Miss Sylvie's parents started with, but also because it made the best tea. We had several different types of tea balls, as well as other ways to steep tea. We had cups and pots, and almost anything you could want to use to brew your tea. I even did hand blending of things to give folks exactly what they were looking for when they asked for something special.

By the time the line that had formed before I had opened had been cleared out, another one had formed, and it kept on going like that for the rest of the morning. I'd barely had time to even turn around since I started, and when it was coming up on noon, I was in serious need of a break.

"Hey, Mai," I said over the handful of people who were currently in the store. "I need to take a quick break."

"No worries," she said. "I got you."

As I ducked into the back to the bathroom I had back there, I thought about the sales from today. I would have to do a quick check, but if I had to bet, I'd say the shop had made more today than it had in the last several days to week. Honestly, it wouldn't surprise me if the total was close to what the last week had been combined.

The unfortunate part of that was that I would need to place an order much sooner than I had anticipated, just to have enough of the regular stuff I kept on hand, which included the accessories. It wasn't that it was a bad thing, just that it would take time to restock, and I didn't want to disappoint customers who hadn't gotten here right away. I guess that would be what was considered a first-world problem, and I laughed as I flushed the toilet and washed my hands.

"Rough problem to have," I muttered to myself in the mirror.

# CHAPTER SEVEN

*J*ohn...

"What time we getting pizza?" Jefferson asked as I boarded the bus.

"You ain't," I said as I walked past him.

I went to an empty seat and sat down, spreading myself out enough that it was clear I didn't want to sit next to anyone else. Hennings, being the dick he is, shoved my leg over, and sat next to me with a smirk.

"Dude," I said, glaring at him.

"Hey," he said. "Just need a place to put my ass until we get to the stadium. Then, I'm gone."

I just ignored him, stuck my earbuds in, and shut the rest of the bus out. The drive wasn't long, and we were soon pulling up outside the stadium. As the rest of the team filed off the bus, I held back, waiting until they were all off, or at least on their way, before standing up. As I went down the stairs, I saw Coach standing there, obviously waiting for me.

"John," he said, and he rarely called us by our first names, so I knew it was serious.

"Yeah," I said, looking at him.

"Nothing's official yet, but there will be a suspension and a fine," he said.

"Knew that was coming," I replied.

"The brass doesn't like that you started it," he began, but I cut him off.

"They started it," I said. "Everyone in the fucking stadium knows they started it. Everyone watching knows it, too. Hell, even you knew it last night. What's this bullshit about me starting it?"

"They wanted you to just walk to first," he said. "Take the base and not make waves."

"Are we fucking pansies?" I asked, much louder than I should have.

"John," he said, his voice low, trying to get me to match it. "They wanted you to do what was best for the team."

"By walking away from a fight?"

"Yeah, John," he said, and sounded disappointed. "Sometimes we have to take one for the team, and last night was your chance to do that, but you didn't."

"I don't walk away from a fight," I said. "Never have, never will. You know this about me."

"I'm not saying I agree with them," he said. "But you need to know which battles to face, and this was one they wanted you to walk away from."

"What are you saying?" I asked.

"Just to watch what you do," he said. "Don't get all hot and bothered every time they do something. It's like allowing a toddler to get their way when they throw a temper tantrum. Just shows that they can keep it up and get what they want. We need to reinforce the fact that we don't give a rat's ass about them, but we will mop the floor with them if they try something."

"That's what I thought I was doing," I said, thoroughly confused.

"Just," the coach started, but then stopped himself. "Honestly, I'm not sure what they want us to do. I don't blame you for it, but the upstairs folks are, so just watch yourself."

"Guess I'll play the little boy who's afraid of his own shadow," I said. "Keep my head down, don't rock the boat, and not do anything to draw attention to myself."

"Honestly, that's probably your best bet," he said. "Now, get to the clubhouse and get on the field. I'm gonna need you while I've got you."

I walked away from him, and down the corridor to the locker room. The space was much calmer than normal, even with it being the beginning of the season. Hennings gave me a nod, more a question as to whether I was okay or not, so I just nodded back, then went to my locker to get ready for warm-ups. We'd lost the game the night before, so that always tended to make things a little more mellow in the clubhouse, but it was more than just that. No, something was off, and it didn't feel right.

By the time I'd gotten ready to head out onto the field, everyone was already out there. One of the stadium people poked their head into the locker room. Since I was the only one left in there, I looked at him.

"Someone sent a pizza for a," he began, then paused to look at the note on top. "John Huffman?"

"That's me," I said, having forgotten all about the night before.

"Ah, okay," he said, coming into the space. "This place has the best pizza around, just so you know."

"Thanks," I said, taking the offered food.

He turned around and headed back out the door he'd come in. I took the food and headed for the field, hoping to cheer folks up. When I walked out of the tunnel, a couple of the guys were still getting their gear ready to head out for batting practice.

"What's that?" Cameron asked.

"Pizza," I said, sitting down on the bench. "Want a piece?"

"Sure," he said, coming to sit next to me. "Where did it come from?"

"Last night someone asked me if I liked pizza," I said. "They offered to have some sent to the clubhouse for today's game."

"Why'd they do that?" he asked after swallowing his first bite.

"No clue," I replied, taking a bite myself. "Damn," I said. "This shit is good."

"Really is," he replied.

Hennings dropped down into the dugout after finishing something up, and reached in to grab a slice himself.

"Hey," Cammy said, chastising him. "It's polite to ask for things that don't belong to you. Were you raised by wolves or something?"

"Matter o' fact, I was," he said, folding the pizza slice and stuffing a giant bite into his mouth. "Holy shit," he mumbled around the food.

"Good, huh?" I asked.

"Shit, yeah," he said. "This is some bomb ass pizza."

He reached for another slice, but I shut the lid on his hand.

"One," I said. "There ain't enough to share for everyone."

"Make sure Jefferson gets some," he said.

"Tell him to get his ass over here," I replied.

As if summoned, he dropped down into the dugout and walked over to us.

"That the pie?" he asked.

"Yup," Hennings said. "It's fucking great, too."

"Nice," Jefferson said. "Mind if I have a piece?"

"See," Cammy said, looking at Hennings. "That's how you're supposed to do it."

"Fuck you," he said, then headed back out to the field with a bat in hand.

When Jefferson took a bite of the pizza, he closed his eyes and smiled, savoring the flavors. Honestly, it was what I'd wanted to do when I took the first bite but didn't want to seem weird enjoying my food that much. Obviously, he didn't care.

"Gonna have to remember this place," he said once he'd swallowed the first bite. "They make some really good pie."

"Yeah," I said. "That they do."

A couple of other guys came into the dugout and took pieces of the pizza, but I saved one for Coach. He deserved it just as much as the rest of us.

"Hey, Coach," I called as the guys started to head down the tunnel toward the clubhouse. "Want a piece? There's one left."

"Sure," he said.

I handed him the box, then headed down the tunnel myself. Not getting BP wasn't a big deal for me, but I made sure to let the coach know that I was guarding his pizza. He'd said he didn't care, just as long as I did what I needed to when it came to the game. Assuring him that I would, he let me get changed for the game. When he came back to the dugout after the exchange of lineups with the other coach and the umpires, he looked pissed.

"Guys," he said, low enough that it wouldn't be heard outside the dugout. "They aren't gonna issue a warning at all. Anything happens, he's throwing people out. That means, keep your shit together tonight. I can't afford to have a dozen guys out."

There was a chorus of comments, some asking why this, others agreeing, and even more asking what the fuck. I was part of the last group, because honestly, that was some bullshit right there. They're the ones that start shit, but we're being told to keep to ourselves, and be good little boys.

"Let's kick their asses," Hennings said, and I couldn't have agreed more.

The rest of the team was under the same sentiment as me, in that we were all gonna go out there and do whatever we could to show these fucking little boys that we were men, and we knew how to play the game.

Of course, as soon as Adams headed to the plate, the crowd goes into the same frenzy we'd seen over the past few years. And, of fucking course, their pitcher, an opener again, decides it's a good idea to plunk him in the back with the first fucking pitch. The crowd went nuts, cheering their team on while the ump moved to between the pitcher and Adams, as our guy walked down the baseline to first. I couldn't hear what the pitcher was shouting, but Adams kept on walking without even acknowledging the guy, which just made him get redder and redder.

The pitcher was thrown out, and so was their manager. While the crowd didn't like it, we were giddy. While Adams got on base the hard way, he was on, which gave us the chance to go up as soon as the second pitch. Hennings was up second, and he was a bit nervous about the possibility of them throwing at his head again, but the first pitch by their actual starter was flat down the middle and he rounded on it and sent it over the fence in right field.

Being the smartass that he is, he did a little bat flip with a fist pump added in, and it would have been all fine if the pansy-assed Dragons hadn't felt that that was an affront to their honor. Instead of Hennings rounding first, he was attacked as the pitcher ran to him, punching him in the helmet. Hennings ducked down, and punched him in the gut, knocking the wind out of him. As we started to come out of the dugout, Coach shouted at us to stay put and went out himself, knocking the pitcher to the ground with one punch to his face. Nice to have an ex-catcher as a coach sometimes.

The trainer headed out right after the coach and was kneeling next to Hennings, checking everything that needed to be checked to make sure he was gonna be okay moving forward. Thankfully, the umpires stepped in, and made sure that no other players were involved in the altercation, but they were a little too late for that. Of course their entire team emptied their bench, but we were all back behind the line, out of the way, and clearly not going to push anything.

Once the umps had shooed their team back to their box, they sent Hennings to round the bases, staying with him the whole way as protection of some sort. Adams had been on third when shit started and had stayed there during the scuffle, so he finished his trip around as well. After that, Coach came back to the bench and started talking to the bench coach.

"What's up?" Swift asked.

"They're tossing me," Coach said.

"That's bullshit," I shouted, pissed that this had all started with me getting plunked.

"It was expected," he said. "That's why I told you all to stay put. I needed to know the team was gonna remain whole. Luis is fine to coach without me. We'd already figured this would happen."

"What are they gonna do about the rest of those fuckers?" Swift asked the question we all wanted an answer to.

"Their pitcher is out," Coach said. "Their manager is out, too."

"Lot of fucking good that does," I growled.

"Hey," he said, piercing me with his stare. "You do *not* retaliate. You do your fucking job, do not try to get even, and you play your asses off. Let the umpires do their job, which they are painfully aware they've been lacking in doing, and things will work out."

"I can't…"

"You will *not* retaliate," he barked at me, clearly telling me that I would have to deal with whatever the league hands down, as well as his own punishment, if I go out there brawling.

"Trust me," he said, looking at the rest of the team as well. "They will get theirs soon enough."

"They fucking better," Hennings said.

"Come on," the home plate ump said near our dugout.

"Give us a fucking minute," I shouted, but the coach glared at me. "Sorry," I apologized. "Just need to get our shit straightened out first."

"I know," he said, and he actually looked like he was sorry about what had happened the last couple of days. "We got a game to get back to, though, so sooner is better."

He walked off after that, and Coach headed down the tunnel. Our bench coach, Luis Rodriguez, clapped his hands a couple of times, and looked at us all standing around.

"Let's go," he said, pointing to Jefferson, who had been in the on-deck circle when Hennings was hit. "Get your ass out there and hit the cover off the ball."

With those words, the team settled back, Jefferson heading out to take the plate, and I grabbed my helmet and bat to stand in the on-deck circle and await my turn at bat. I just hoped I didn't get hit again.

# CHAPTER EIGHT

*S*kye...
      The day went by quickly, with the number of customers reaching nearly four times what I'd normally do on a sunny Saturday during tourist season. I had run out of many items and had been working on figuring out how to get a good supply to the shop as soon as possible.

Right after lunch, I'd asked Mai to hold things down while I did something quick on my phone in the office. She'd agreed, and things had slowed down enough that it wasn't gonna be a problem for me to do what I'd said I was gonna do the night before, which was to order a pizza and have it sent to the stadium in Houston.

I double checked the restaurant and made sure they delivered before ordering. I had to do a quick look to make sure I got the player's name right, but it wasn't like it was hard. I mean, John Huffman is somewhat of an ordinary name. Paying with my personal card, because this was definitely not an expense I could justify, even if it did boost my sales for the day and asked that they make sure they handed the pizza directly to the player, and not some grunt that actually worked for the stadium. I wanted to make sure he got it, and it didn't get snagged as retribution for the brawl that happened the night before.

Once the pizza was ordered, I went to the bathroom before heading back into the store. I walked in just as my Uncle Marty came through the front door.

"Dang," he said, drawing the word out as he looked around my shop. "I guess the rush was for real."

"That it was," I said. "Of course we didn't start out the best way."

"How's that?" he asked.

"Some bitch decided to pull the old 'customer is always right' stint," Mai replied. "You would be so proud of your niece, though. She shut her down and sent her on her way without batting an eye. Worked in our favor, too, because everyone in line was smiling when they came in. It was a beautiful thing to behold."

I laughed at her description. I mean, I was kind of firm, and did send her on her way, but it certainly didn't boost my emotions any.

"Next time, just do the stare," he said, then glared at me in the way my dad would do when I was doing something I knew I wasn't supposed to.

"Stop it," I said, smacking his arm. "Besides, I got more important things on my mind."

"You buy that pizza?" he asked.

"Just did," I replied. "Now I have to figure out how to get resupplied before tomorrow."

"Where have you checked?" he asked, and I knew he had an idea.

"The usual places," I replied.

"Let me make a few calls," he said, then walked out of the store.

Knowing him, he had some contact somewhere that would figure out a way to get me what I needed before I even closed the store for the day. Instead of waiting on him, though, I went back to my search for local places. You had to know where to look, and I did, but finding someone who had stock of what you wanted wasn't always as simple as the point, click, add to cart, and pay. No, these things were more complicated than that. The supplier had to have a good reputation, have quality products, and be able to sell in bulk.

Because of the influx of customers, I'd already gone through the back stock that I had for nearly every kind of blend I sold. Honestly, I was contemplating closing early, and remaining closed tomorrow, because of the lack of supply. It would make sense from a business standpoint. It would be stupid to be open, and not have any product to sell. I mean, there were some things, but most of it was remnants of blends, and a handful of smaller items.

"When are you closing?" Uncle Marty asked as he stepped back into the store.

"When I run out of product," I said. "Or, if by some miracle, I get more product in, I'll close at five."

"Okay," he said, then stepped back out the door and put his phone to his ear.

"Your uncle is wild," Mai said.

"Don't I know it," I replied.

She'd been the only one to stay the whole day. Not that I needed much help, except first thing, but she knew it might pick up at lunchtime as well as the afternoon, so she stayed just in case.

"How much you wanna bet he comes up with some miracle supply chain?" she asked.

"Not a chance I'd bet against him," I replied. "He's way too clever and all in when it comes to this kind of thing. Reminds me of Grampy, honestly."

"I never got to meet him," she said.

"Boy did you miss out," I replied. "He was the Governor of the Market for a while. A really great guy who knew everyone. He's the one who made sure that Miss Sylvie got to keep her shop, too."

"Is that why she gave it to you?"

"Oh, no," I replied. "I worked my ass off to make sure I could get it. Worked for her for almost eight years before she signed it over to me. She just passed away last year."

"I'm sorry," she said.

"Yeah," I replied. "Me, too."

"Okay," Uncle Marty said coming in the door again. "Tell them what you want, and they'll get it here before you close."

"Who is it?" I asked.

"Milligan Fields," he said, and I gawked.

"I can't afford…"

"You're family," he said. "Tell them what you want."

I blinked, looking at him for a moment, likely looking like a fish out of water.

"Skye," he said, shaking the phone at me.

I took it, still baffled, and began rattling off different types of leaves I wanted. I started small, with just a few, but they kept asking what else, and the way my uncle was looking at me, I was bolstered to add on more and more. By the time I hung up, I had ordered a pretty penny of supplies that should last me well into the next week when my regular order could get here.

"You sure you got everything?" Uncle Marty asked.

"More than enough," I replied.

"Good," he said, and took his phone.

"How did you get in touch with them?" I asked, curious as to how my uncle, a flower and honey farmer, was connected to the largest farm that supplied tea leaves in the northwest corner of the country.

"Sometimes it's in who you know," he said with a smile. "And who they know. There are benefits to being the granddaughter of the former mayor of the Market."

With that, he turned and walked out the door, leaving me to stare after him in utter confusion. When he was fully out of sight, I turned and looked at Mai, who was just smiling at me.

"Told ya," she said, and we both laughed.

She was a few years younger than me and had been born here. Her grandparents worked for my grandparents, and her parents had as well once they got old enough. She worked for Uncle Marty when she could but was planning on going to college in the next year or so to study economics. My dad had even offered her a job with his firm once she graduated. It was really nice of my dad, but he knew he was going to be getting someone who had a really good work ethic, as well as the skills to do the accounting type things he required.

"I'm not sure they'll get here before I close, though," I said. "I mean, it's almost three already, so if they got here in the next couple of hours, I'd be shocked.

"Never underestimate the power of Marty Robinson," she said with a smile. "If he can't deliver on a promise, he won't make it."

"That's for sure," I replied.

# CHAPTER NINE

*J*ohn...
    Once the shitshow had ended, we'd gotten back to actual baseball, and we were doing well. It was well into the sixth when I went up to bat and had a brush back from the pitcher. I stood there, staring at the umpire, wondering what the fuck he was doing.

"You're out of here," he shouted, throwing a hand to his side, and pointing at the pitcher.

The pitcher, in turn, shouted back at the umpire, something about the ball just getting away from him. Their bench coach, who had come out of the dugout, was shouting the same thing.

"You wanna go, too?" the umpire shouted at him.

"Fuck you," the pitcher said as he stomped off the field.

"Fucking morons," I said, though my voice was low.

"What did you just say?" the catcher asked, getting up in my grill.

I stood there and stared at him, and the fact that his head was barely at shoulder level made it look like he was a kid trying to stand up to his dad or something, and it was so comical that I just started laughing. I couldn't help it. I mean, I outweighed him by a good fifty pounds, and was at least half a foot taller than him, too, so the thought of him being able to do much of anything was just comical.

The umpire must have heard us and stepped up, sliding his hand on the catcher's chest protector, and pushing him back.

"That's enough," he said. "Don't make me toss you, too."

"This fucker just laughed at me," he whined.

"My God," the umpire said. "Is your ego so fucking fragile that you can't see humor in something? Shut the fuck up and get back behind the plate."

It was actually a good thing the umpire jumped in when he did, though, because I was beginning to think I'd have to actually get physical for the second night in a row, and I didn't want to do that. I walked back to the on-deck circle and stood there with Matsui as we waited for their new pitcher to make his way in from the bullpen.

"What the fuck was that all about?" he asked me.

"I laughed at him," I said. "Apparently, he didn't like that."

Matsui looked at me like I'd said something completely insane, then began to laugh. It was a small laugh at first, but I guess the more he thought about it, the funnier it got. Pretty soon, he was nearly doubled over laughing. It was so ridiculous that Coach Rodriguez came up to the top step to see what was going on.

"What's up?" he shouted, and I walked over to him. I told him what happened and he just shook his head, then said, "Knock it off. We don't need anyone else getting tossed."

I didn't answer, just walked back over to the circle, and waited for the umpire to call me back out to continue my at bat. Because the pitcher was thrown out, the one who came in only got the standard between inning pitches to warm up, which sucked for him, but wasn't my problem.

"Batter up," the umpire called, and I made my way back to the batter's box.

"Better not do something fucking stupid," the catcher said, and I stepped out and looked down at him, then back at the umpire.

"Shut your cake hole, Franklin," the umpire said and I had to hide a laugh.

I stepped back in, gave a few practice swings, and waited for the pitch. They'd only thrown the one pitch so far, and it was obviously a ball, so I had a slight advantage. Add to that the fact that their pitcher didn't get his full warm-up, and I was in good standing to get something to hit well, and when the ball was sent up, slow and lazy in the zone, I put bat on ball and sent it over the centerfield fence.

Instead of doing like Hennings had when he'd been pummeled, I dropped my bat halfway to first, kept my head down, and rounded the bases without making eye contact with any of the players from the Dragons' team. I gave a low five to our first base coach, another to the third base coach, and touched home plate without fanfare.

"Asshole," the catcher said as I passed him at the plate.

"Shut it," the umpire barked. "Or you're gone."

Once I was past him, I smiled and gave Matsui a high five, along with Jefferson, who was in the on-deck circle, and then bounced down the stairs to the dugout to continue the celebration.

"What'd he say to you?" Coach Rodriguez asked.

"Called me an asshole," I said and the coach laughed.

Matsui hit another home run right after me, which put us up by three, and we never looked back. By the time it was all said and done, we'd won by a score of six to nothing, which was very nice, especially after the game the previous day. I was, of course, snagged by the reporter for the local station to answer some post-game questions.

"How did it feel to hit that homer?" Jenn asked.

"Always nice to hit one out," I replied.

"Was it especially nice after last night's fiasco?" she asked.

"Honestly," I said, then paused for effect. "Any home run is nice but doing it against a team who is gunning for you just adds a bit extra to it. Hopefully, this will be the last time we have these issues this season."

"Let's hope so," she said. "Back to you guys."

Once the little red light was off, she looked at me.

"Seriously," she said. "What is with them?"

"No clue," I replied.

"Thanks for talking," she said, and I headed into the clubhouse to get showered.

Everyone was in high spirits when I walked in, and Coach looked at me and smiled. It was nice to be appreciated, especially when I toed the line just like a good boy. I pulled my jersey over my head, dropping it on the stool next to my locker, and grabbed my shower kit. By the time I was done with my shower, the post-game interviews had been completed, and I'd missed them as planned. I'd done my one and was good to not do another one for a week or so.

As we piled onto the bus after the game, I got a notification on my phone. Instead of looking at it, though, I shoved it into the pocket of my jacket and figured I'd deal with whatever it was when we got to the hotel. I was a private person by nature, so keeping my notifications silent was one of the ways I kept the boys out of my hair. Hennings had shown me that keeping my extracurricular activities to myself was important in this line of work. Not that I didn't already know it, but the first year he was with the team solidified my instinct to stay in the shadows with my private life.

When the bus started to empty, I heard several of the guys mention going to the bar, and as I stepped off the bus, they asked if I wanted to join them.

"Nah," I said, walking toward the elevators. "Have fun."

I knew that Adams and Swift would find someone to share, which still freaked me the fuck out. Not sure why Hennings was going in there, but maybe just to have a drink. I wasn't going to stop him, and if his woman was fine with him hitting the bottle, who was I to judge. Jefferson and Cammy also went into the bar, so I guess it was a whole group. Not me, though. No, I wanted to see what the notification was that was blowing up my phone, as well as hit the sack.

Keying my way into the room, I flipped on the light and locked the door behind me. I pulled my jacket off and hung it over the back of the chair at the desk, then kicked my shoes off, and sat on the edge of the bed to finish undressing. When that was done, I pulled my phone from my pocket and opened it up, pulling the notification open to see that the tea shop had sent a private message to me.

*I hope you got the pizza.*

Nice that she checked.

*I did, and it was delicious. Thanks so much.*

While it was good, it was the thought of her sending it that made it special.

*Did they give it right to you? I asked them to make sure you got it.*

I laughed and wondered how she made that request. I'd thought it was odd that the delivery guy actually got into the stadium, but that was all that crossed my mind, so the fact that she'd made that request just hit me some type of way.

*He did. Thanks.*

I knew it wasn't that late back in Seattle, even though it was after ten in Houston. I began to wonder how late her shop stayed open, or if she was even at the shop now while she was messaging me.

*Thanks to you, I had a run at the shop today.*

Wait a minute, what? How did I cause a run at her shop?

*What do you mean?*

Wondering whether I was actually talking to the woman who was on their website, I opened up my web browser and took a look at the shop's site again. From what I remembered, it was a small shop, so how many employees could they have? I guess there could be someone in charge of their social media, but something wasn't adding up. My phone buzzed with a notification, but I wasn't done looking at the site, so I ignored it for the time being.

Poking around, I found a link to the history of the shop, and I clicked to see what was there. It showed a few old photos of years gone by with lots of different folks in them. That's when I saw the woman I'd seen before. She was standing with what appeared to be one of the original owners, or maybe someone from the family. Her smile was bright, eyes nearly glowing with excitement. Reading the caption underneath, I was surprised it said she was taking over most of the ownership tasks for the store, as well as the ghost tours they did.

Maybe she was just in charge of running part of it, but the way she talked in her messages made it seem like the store was hers. Messing around more, I found links with information on when the shop was opened, who had been running it, and more information on their hours and what things they offered. It was mostly loose tea, and things to make tea, like cups and pots and such. I wasn't a tea drinker, but they seemed to have plenty of variety available, so I might have to at least try it out at some point. My phone buzzed again, so I moved from the website to see two messages.

*My post blew up, so everyone and their cousin came in to see what it was all about.*

The message sort of made sense, but why were they buying things from a shop that had been there for decades?

*I guess they wanted to pay it forward, or back, since I sent pizza to you.*

Now that made sense. They weren't coming so much for the tea as to see who it was that sent a pizza to me.

*Then getting hit was worth it.*

The penalties for the fight wouldn't necessarily be worth it, but if I could do something for her, that would. Just had to figure out how to meet her. Maybe when I was serving my suspension, that was sure to come down in the next couple of days, I'd head to the Market for an afternoon and check her out. I really wanted to find out whether she was the owner or just a pretty face they put on their website. It appeared the first thing was the truth, but you never knew in these times.

# CHAPTER TEN

*S*kye...
*Then getting hit was worth it.*
I didn't know whether that was the truth or not, but it had been nice for business today. I'd closed the shop right at five, just after getting the huge order in from Milligan Fields. They really had come through in a pinch, and the fact that they rounded up everything I'd ordered and had it to my shop in just a couple of hours, spoke of their status as the best supplier in the Pacific Northwest.

Mai had stayed after I closed, and helped me restock what we could, and store the rest in the back room for refilling throughout the rest of the week. She had said she was working at the fields at Uncle Marty's the next day but would be back at the Market the day after, and would come in to help if I needed it. After everything had been closed up and restocked, I took time to run the report for sales for the day and took it all up with me to my apartment to work over while I watched the game. Even after I figured in the costs for paying Mai for her work today, and the enormous order from the supplier, I was well above what I would normally have in net profits for the month. The fact that it was barely the start of April said this month would be my biggest one yet, and I wasn't about to complain.

Knowing it was a couple hours later in Houston than in Seattle, I opted to not respond to his message, and just finish up the last bits before jumping in the tub, and then heading to bed. I was definitely tired from the day and could use the soothing heat from a soak. As I had so many times, I steeped a cup of my special tea, then started the tub to fill, adding another of the bath bombs to help me relax. I definitely needed to ask Sammi where she got them, because I was down to just a few.

Just as I had the night before, I set my cup on the stool next to the tub, slid into the warm water, and just soaked. It's amazing how much that little thing can do for a body, and I was very relaxed by the time the water had cooled. I pulled the plug, stood up, and pulled the towel down to dry off. Once I was done, I headed to bed to climb between the cool sheets.

Grabbing my phone, I wanted to check and see if there was anything else going on that I needed to be prepared for. Opening the social media app I'd used to do my pizza thing, I saw that there were nearly a hundred messages within that app alone. I also had a ton of emails for the shop.

"Ugh," I groaned. "Maybe that wasn't such a good idea."

I decided to open the messages first, just to get them out of the way. What I found was a bunch of people being super supportive, congratulating me on getting a mention on the game's broadcast. Unfortunately, there were more messages asking for naked pictures, and at least a dozen dick pics. I just marked everything that wasn't supportive as spam, and reported and blocked the ones that were total trash. Once that was done, I checked to see if there were any more messages from Huffman, but there weren't, so I assumed he'd gone to sleep. Instead of looking through the emails, I decided to leave those for the morning. I could only do so much in a day, and today had already been a lot.

After plugging in my phone so it was ready to go for the next day, I turned off the bedside lamp and snuggled under the covers, hoping to sleep well and be ready for another busy day at the shop. Hopefully it would be as fruitful as today had been.

I WAS RUNNING FOR MY LIFE AND WAS EXHAUSTED. EVERY TURN I made just led to another dead end, and I ended up having to double back repeatedly. Each time I ran back, though, he was closer. It was like I couldn't get away, and he wasn't moving, but still gaining on me. There was no way to tell who it was, what with his black hood up, shadowing his face, but I knew. I always knew it was him. Dylan was there, as he had been for years. Except he was locked up. Somehow, though, he got out and was chasing me everywhere I went. Why couldn't I get away from him?

My alarm blared and rescued me from the never-ending chase, and I was never more thankful than when it happened. I turned the alarm off and looked at the ceiling, wondering whether I'd ever be free from the nightmare that had been my life. My phone pinged, so I grabbed it and swiped the screen to unlock it.

***Hope your day is great.***

Wow. Never in all my life had someone wished me a good day just because. There was always something behind the message, something that they wanted. It made me nervous to respond, but it didn't feel right not to, either. Something that Dylan had instilled in me was that if he sent me a message, I was required to respond. Not that I should, not if I wanted to, but it was required. Whether it was a simple text, a call, or a demand for a picture to prove I was where I said I was going to be. Not that I was really anywhere but the store and my apartment.

He never stayed at my place. I refused to allow it. He'd demanded, but I told him it wasn't going to happen. Staying at his place was a nightmare all on its own, though. He treated me as a bang maid, someone to clean up after him, cook for him, take care of all his needs, and on top of that, be whatever kind of sex doll he desired. It was rough, but thankfully I'd persevered and gotten out.

Then he found me and got his revenge. Unfortunately for him, though, I was much stronger than him, and I just kept on recovering. When the trial happened, I was still in pretty bad shape. His attorney had wanted to ban me from testifying in person, because it would be too much of an unfair advantage in the prosecution's case. The prosecutor insisted that if he hadn't done what he was accused of, there wouldn't be anything wrong with me, so the jury needed to see me in my damaged state. Thankfully, the judge agreed with the prosecutor, which just pushed his attorney to try to get him to make a deal.

Of course, Dylan wasn't one to make deals. He wanted to prove that he didn't do it, even with all the evidence. His attorney tried valiantly but was no match when it came to everything that we had against him. In the end, the jury didn't take but half an hour to convict him and demand that he be sentenced to the maximum jail time allowed. The judge had also put a protective order in place that was permanent. It stated that he couldn't be anywhere near me and couldn't send anything or anyone to me on his behalf. Now that I was a year out from the attack and I hadn't heard a peep from anyone connected to him in a good long while. While I was thankful it was coming up to the actual anniversary of it, and that must have been what was making my brain remember everything and cause me to be in a panic. It was probably nothing, but I did make a mental note to touch base with the therapist the state had on retainer to help me in my recovery. Let's hear it for victims' advocacy, and the fact that it can help. Health insurance was nearly impossible to afford, especially since I had a business that I ran, so I relied on the advocacy system to ensure that I would always have someone to help if anything happened related to the attack.

Rolling out of bed, I sat up and looked at the message again.

*Hope your day is great.*

It was such a simple thing to say, but the impact it had was more than I ever anticipated just a handful of words could have on me.

*Here's hoping.*

Not spectacular, but at least I acknowledged his consideration, and responded. Now, it was time to put myself together, and get out into the real world, which needed to start with coffee. I mean, tea was wonderful, and I loved everything about it, but there were days even I needed something stronger, and today was one of those days.

Once I was dressed, I headed down the stairs to the shop, only to see the line already there. Nope, I was not gonna go through the front door, too many people out there to make it safely to the shop. Instead, I turned the other way and stepped out the door at the back of my shop, and into the strange passageways that were the older buildings in the area. They were hallways of sorts, but not really. The bricks from the exteriors of one building matching up against the wood of another, with just enough space to make it through, and out to First Avenue.

I slipped out the door on that side of the conglomeration of buildings, and set foot into the bustle of the morning crowd. It was unseasonably warm for April, and that always brought more of the locals down during the week. The Market still wasn't as busy as it would be on a weekend, but the number of people was still more than I'd like to deal with, especially with as exhausted as I was. I slipped down the street, then crossed First to go to the Seattle Brew Coffee shop. Everyone always liked to go to the big chains, but I'd found that the smaller places usually had less of a crowd, and sometimes even had better coffee. "Hey, Skye," Reagan said as I stepped in.

"Hey, yourself," I replied.

"That bad of a night?" she asked.

Like me, Reagan had grown up in the Market area, what with her family owning a coffee shop so close. True, she wasn't quite in the Market family, but she was like a close cousin, which was good enough for me. Her family opened the coffee shop in the '60s, which technically made them the earlier company than the one that went wild, but they liked keeping it as a small family shop, so I came here when I could. We weren't quite as close as the rest of my friends, as she hadn't gone to the same school as us, but we were still friendly. She knew of my past, and understood my issues, at least to some degree.

"Never-ending chase is awful," I said, explaining my recurring nightmares.

"Double or triple?" she asked.

"Do I look that bad?" I asked with a laugh.

"I just know you only come in when it's rough," she said, starting her machine to get my coffee going.

"Let's stick with a double today," I said. "I do want to at least try and sleep tonight."

"Anything else?" she asked as my coffee brewed and the steamer foamed the milk.

"I think just the coffee this morning," I said, stifling a yawn. "I should get something with protein to get me through the morning. I already have a line."

"Sorry," she said. "I've got nothing to fit that bill. Maybe down to the cheese shop?"

"I think I have something in the office at my shop," I said, remembering I had stashed away some jerky I'd picked up in the last week.

"Here you go," she said. I pulled out my card, but she waved me off. "Family doesn't pay," she admonished.

"And small businesses go under from treating everyone as family," I replied, and dropped a ten on the counter. I knew it was more than the coffee's price, even at menu pricing, but the extra would be a tip for her kindness.

I headed back out to the street and retraced my steps back to the little door that led to the halls of the secret spaces between buildings, keying my way in. I stopped as soon as the door shut behind me, and took a sip of the coffee, and Reagan didn't disappoint. It was strong, just sweet enough, and soothed my nerves while revitalizing my spirit. Once I'd had my moment, I continued through the space to the back of my shop, opening the door, and turning off the alarm.

The way my shop was set up, I could get to the bathroom and office without being seen by anyone up front. I jumped a bit when I stepped into my office and my phone went off. Pulling the device from my pocket, I saw it was Uncle Marty.

"Hey," I said when I answered it.

"You're not open yet?" he asked.

"Not yet," I said. "I needed coffee first. I just got back and am heading up to open in a minute."

"Mai was worried when you weren't there," he said.

"Was she planning to help today, too?" I asked.

"The line is super long," he said. "Best strike while the iron is hot, and get all that extra flow of money coming in."

"I will," I said, setting my coffee down and picking up the package with the jerky in it.

"Hop to it," he said. "The customers are waiting."

"Thanks," I said, then disconnected the call.

I took a bite of the jerky and let the salty meat soak in my mouth for a moment before continuing to chew and swallow it. Another sip of my coffee on the way to the door and I saw what my uncle was talking about. If I thought yesterday was a busy day, I had no idea what busy was. Stepping to the counter, I set my coffee down behind it on the little shelf, then went to the door, pulled the little string on my open sign, and unlocked.

"You're here," Mai said as she slipped past me into the shop itself.

"Welcome in," I said as I pushed the door fully open to allow the throng of folks to enter. "The shop's small, so there isn't room for everyone. I appreciate your patience with us as we get going early today."

With that, I let the door go, and went back into the store to begin the arduous task of answering the same questions over and over again until I felt like my ears would bleed. It would be worth it, though, because from the looks of things, today would be another banner day in sales, and I was here for it. Hell, I might even have to make another call to Milligan Fields to resupply my store. Such a rough problem to have.

# CHAPTER ELEVEN

*J*ohn...

"Huffman," Coach said as we were loading onto the bus. "Stop in my office after you're dressed."

"Sure thing, Coach," I replied.

I heard him tell Jefferson the same thing, so I guess the fines and suspensions would be coming today. No big deal, though. We knew it was gonna happen, so we just had to wait for the official word. I dropped into a seat near the middle of the bus, sliding over to the window. Hennings sat down next to me, and the rest of the team filed in, and settled down for the short ride to the stadium.

Day games were fucking horrible, especially when we had a late night the night before. While we hadn't played bonus baseball, the innings the night before had been long and arduous, and we weren't planning on any practice before the game, thankfully. Once everyone was on board, and all the luggage had been stowed underneath, we were off on the road to work.

Downtown was a stupid place to have a stadium because of the traffic, but it was a brilliant place to have it for the convenience. Today we were dealing with the extra cars from rush hour, so the bus ride was longer than I would have liked. I'd sent a text to the tea shop before I'd walked out of the hotel room. Since we were a couple hours ahead, I hadn't expected to get a response for a bit, but when my phone vibrated to indicate an incoming message, I couldn't help but open it up, and hope it was from her.

"That the shop lady?" Beckett asked, trying to look over my shoulder.

"Fuck off," I replied, not at all in the mood for his bullshit today.

"Just asking," he replied. "Jesus, fuck, get over yourself."

"Fuck off," I repeated and shoved the phone back into my pocket, not even bothering to open it up.

The message would wait until I didn't have an audience. We were scheduled to fly out to Atlanta after the game, but my guess was that Coach would be telling Jefferson and me that we were going home instead. Or rather, that at least one of us was going home. Probably me, from the way I'd been playing to start the season. I was honestly fine with that prospect. The time off would probably improve not only my game but get my mind back on what's important at the moment, which was everything but the Houston Dragons. Might even give me time to meet the woman behind the social media account that I'd been chatting with.

"I see you thinking over there," Beckett said, and I turned to glare at him. "Don't fuck around with fans. It's not gonna get you anywhere good. Trust me."

I barked out a laugh. How was I supposed to take advice about who to date and how to go about it from this little motherfucker? He was the last person I'd ever take advice from outside of the baseball diamond.

"You laugh now," he said. "But trust me, fans are fucking insane."

"Takes one to know one," I said, still trying to get my laugh under control.

"Fine," he said. "Don't listen to me. See if I fucking care."

Then, as the bus had just stopped, he got up like the petulant toddler he was and stomped off down the aisle to the front. I just shook my head at his antics. As if I wasn't a good six or seven years older than him and had no experience at all in the league and what it meant to meet and hook up with bullpen bunnies. Fucking child.

By the time I got off the bus, he was long gone, and already in the locker room. Not that it mattered, but I was glad he was off sulking. For some reason, that made him hit better. Note to self, piss Hennings off right before a game so he hits like a mad man. Once I was in my uniform, I headed to the coach's office to see what was what.

"Hey, Huff," Jefferson said as he was leaving.

"You good?" I asked, noting his somber tone.

"Just fine and dandy," he said, the fake happy in his tone told me otherwise.

"Sorry about that," I replied.

"Nah," he said, and a real smile crossed his lips. "Nothing wrong with backing a brother, and that's what we are in this clubhouse. Don't you never mind about it none."

"Thanks," I said, glad he wasn't pissed at me.

I walked into the coach's office and he looked up from his tablet, his glasses down on his nose like he was trying not to need them, but really did.

"Sit," he said, pointing the stylus at the chair. "And close the door."

Before sitting, I shut the door, then waited. This was his party, so he was gonna have to be in the driver's seat.

"Penalties came in this morning," he said.

"I figured," I replied.

"You get six games and Jefferson gets four," he said. "Fines aren't huge, so you won't see much reduction in your income, but wanted you to know."

"Can I pay Jefferson's?" I asked. "It wasn't his fault, it was mine, so I feel bad about it."

"You know it doesn't work that way," he said. "But I'm sure he appreciates the gesture."

"When does it start?"

"You good with missing Atlanta?" he asked.

"Yeah," I replied.

"Fine," he said. "You'll go home tomorrow while we go over there. Once your games are done, Jefferson will serve his."

"You not asking me to fight it?"

"I know you," he said. "You don't run away from shit you started, and this is all on you, so no, you aren't gonna fight it, you're gonna serve it."

"Just checking," I said with a smile.

"Get your happy ass out of here and go play," he said with a laugh as I stood up and walked out.

Most of the team was already dressed and heading out to the field, so I grabbed my mitt and headed down the tunnel. As I got closer to the dugout, I could hear some of the guys shouting, so I hustled the rest of the way, coming out into the sunshine to see a mass of black jerseys and orange jerseys shoving just up the top of the steps. Not wanting my boys to fight the good fight without me, I hopped up the steps and dove into the fray just to get shoved back down the steps.

"What the…"

The words died on my lips as I saw Hennings get shoved over the barrier and land on his shoulders on the bench at the top, followed by Jefferson.

"Fuck this," I shouted and pulled Hennings up.

Thankfully, he didn't seem too hurt and just shoved me away. As I was reaching for Jefferson, someone landed on top of me, and I slipped down the step to land on my ass with someone in an orange jersey on top of me. Shoving him off, I clambered to my feet, ready to throw hands.

"Hey," Coach shouted, as he came out of the tunnel.

The Dragons' coach was high-tailing it over from his dugout as well. I shoved the dude who'd landed on me away from me, and he gave me a glare that said he wanted to pound my face in.

"Bring it," I said, my fists up and ready to rock and roll with this punk.

"Huff," Coach shouted and the other guy turned, then backed off.

"That's right," I shouted. "Walk away like the fucking pussy you are."

I wasn't sure if he heard me because he just kept walking. Coach had already made it up the stairs, and he and the other coach were working to get the guys separated. I went to Hennings, who was still on the ground, and checked on him.

"What the fuck happened?" he said as he blinked up at me.

"No fucking clue," I replied. "You good?"

"No," he said. "Something is wrong with my arm."

"Great," I said and looked around to see if I could find one of the trainers. "Hey," I shouted, seeing someone come up from the tunnel. "Come here. Hennings needs help."

The trainer came over and then looked at me.

"What the fuck?"

"Yeah," I said. "Someone threw him over the rail and landed on top of him. Dude was huge, too, so I think that's what the problem is."

"You guys gonna talk about me or fix me?" Hennings gritted out through clenched teeth.

"Right," the trainer said. "Where exactly does it hurt?"

"Elbow," he said and went to move his arm, but the trainer held it firm.

"Let me check a couple of things before we move you, okay?"

"Whatever the fuck you do," he began, "do it fucking quick."

I kinda wanted to stay there, but was also watching the brawl on the field, which had simmered down quite a bit. Instead of doing what I really wanted to do, which was to find the fucker who threw my guy, I stayed with him as the trainer assessed the situation.

"What's going on?" Coach asked as he came down the steps.

"That fucking asshole threw me," Hennings said.

"I saw it," I added. "It was the guy that was down here trying to throw punches."

"Did you get his number?" Coach asked.

"No," I replied. "But I'll know the fucker when I see him again."

"Good," he said, and the look on his face told me he'd be the one throwing hands.

The guys were coming down the steps, and some had already headed into the clubhouse to get cleaned up before the game started.

The trainer had Hennings up and was cradling his arm, pinning it against his chest. Hennings was wincing, and I knew it was bad, because there was no way that kid would even pretend to hurt if he could help it.

"Fucking idiots," I grumbled.

"Everyone in the clubhouse," Coach said, and it was an order that was not to be balked at.

We all headed down the tunnel and by the time we got to the clubhouse, everyone was silent. Not a single word could be heard, just the click of cleats along the cement floor. It was something I'd never experienced before. I wanted to ask what the fuck started things, but didn't want to break the silence, so I just headed to my locker and sat down on the chair in front. Everyone else was doing the same, and we all just kind of sat there, not saying anything, and looking like we were all waiting to talk to the principal at school or something.

After a good ten minutes, right when we were starting to get antsy, we heard Coach coming down the tunnel, the clicking of his shoes different from the players with our cleats. As he walked into the clubhouse, he looked around, and something about his demeanor was off.

"Change for the flight," he said. "We're not playing today."

"Are you fucking kidding me?" I asked.

"It is in the best interest of both teams that we let things go and settle down before we come back together on the field," he said, and it sounded like a fucking script or something.

"This is bullshit," Decker said.

"Absolutely," I agreed, and many of the other players chimed in with their agreement as well.

"Coach Robinson and I have come to the agreement," he said. "And the umpires think it is best as well. They are making the call to suspend this game for a later date. It will be their call to make to the league, and they will say that conditions are not good to play today."

"So, they're treating it like a rain out?" Jefferson asked.

"Exactly," Coach replied. "Now, get changed so we can get the fuck out of here."

With that, he turned and walked into the office, and shut the door. We all looked around at each other, confused but thankful we'd be done early with this fucking city. I stood up first, turned around, and started the process of pulling my uniform off to change back into street clothes for my flight home. I heard the rest of the team follow suit, and just tried to put it all out of my head. When we were on the plane, I could ask Hennings what happened. That is, if he went with me. For all I knew, he'd end up in a hospital down here again like he had a couple of years ago.

"Huffman," I heard Coach shout from his office.

I was already changed and had just finished zipping up my bag for the flight home. Walking to the office, I stepped inside, unsure what he wanted.

"Door," he said, and I shut it. "You should get an email with your flight information. Hennings is going home with you, so I need you to be his valet for the trip. They don't want him to lift anything and have made sure that you guys are in first class with early boarding."

"What happened?" I asked.

"Hyper extended the elbow," he said. "They're gonna run more tests when you guys get home, but they want him there, not here, considering the hostility this city has for us."

"I'm glad," I said.

"He'll meet you there," he added. "They're sending him in a car. You can ride the bus to the airport with us. They'll drop you off before we head to the charter section of the airport. That work for you?"

"Sure thing," I replied. "I need to do anything when we land?"

"He's getting Fi to pick him up," Coach said. "You need a ride, too?"

"Nah," I replied. "I'll just ride the train to the stadium and grab my car."

"Don't think you can," he said. "Stadium isn't usually open when we're on the road."

"Fuck," I said, then added, "sorry."

"I get it," he replied. "I'll ask Hennings to have Fi take you home."

"I'll just get a ride share," I said. "No need for her to be put out. Besides, I live kind of in the opposite direction."

"You sure?"

"Yeah," I replied. "See you when you guys get back."

"See ya," he replied, then I walked out of the office.

Once everyone had changed and we were all ready, we walked out and down to our bus, loading on it to take the ride to the airport. I sat near the front so I didn't have to mess with anyone getting off at the drop off location. They'd stowed my bags up top so no one had to open the big hatch underneath.

After I got off the bus, I walked into the lobby where I could check my bag and wait for Hennings to arrive. It didn't take long before he showed up, and I pulled his bags out, and helped him get it checked. We headed toward security, and while we were waiting in line, someone must have recognized one of us because we started hearing all sorts of shit talk from behind us. Hennings isn't one to take shit like that, but even he recognized that the best course of action was to lie low and pretend he couldn't hear it.

"Next," the agent said to us and we both walked up to him to show our ID. "One at a time," he added, glaring at me.

"I'm helping him with his bag," I said. "He's not allowed to lift anything right now."

"Fine," he said, but certainly didn't sound happy about it.

Once we'd shown our ID's, he motioned for us to move along in the queue and drop our bags and such into the bins to go through the machine. Hennings took his shoes off and I dropped them into a bin where he also dropped his wallet, keys, cell phone, and sunglasses. I did the same with my own bin as he moved to the machine that checked him. I was right behind him in line, and when his turn to go in came up, the agent on the other side glared at him.

"I'm gonna need you to put your arms over your head," she said.

"Seriously?" I asked. "Do you not see the brace and shit he's got on? He's not gonna be able to do that."

"Sorry," she said, but she didn't sound it in the least. "Those are the rules we have to go by."

"Then you better get someone over here who can make a better decision than you," I said. "There's a reason he can't move his arm, which is clearly obvious. Figure another way to deal with it."

"Sir," she said, and there was steel in her voice. "I'm going to ask that you keep yourself in control or we're going to have a very big problem on our hands."

"Chill," Hennings said, and I looked at him. "It's fine, I got this."

I stepped back and let him handle it.

"Ma'am," he said, pulling out some southern accent I'd never heard him use. "I apologize for my companion's outbursts. He's had a rough couple of days and is just anxious to head home."

"So you're together?" she asked, and the disgust was clear in her voice.

"Oh, no," he said, sounding shocked even to me. "We are work colleagues, that's all. He's just helping me with my bags and such because I'm not allowed to lift anything. I was recently injured by being thrown over a fence, and then down a flight of stairs."

While that wasn't technically the truth, it was truthful enough, and since he'd asked that I take a step back and let him handle it, I obliged.

"My fiancée is going to be picking me up from the airport," he continued. "I just need Mr. Huffman to help me through this portion of the travel, and to help me gather my things on the other end. I really do appreciate him helping me and would very much appreciate it if you could find a way to help me through this so I don't have to rely on him more than necessary."

I wanted to fucking punch the little shit, but he somehow convinced the agent at the gate to let him through without raising his hand, then did the whole wand and pat-down thing with him on the other side. Unfortunately, they hadn't liked my attitude, so they decided to do the full pat-down with me as well. Not that I don't mind a little fondling, but I'm not into guys, and they picked the biggest dude they had to do the pat-down, and he was more than a little handsy in places he didn't need to be. Instead of complaining, though, I just decided to ignore it and pretend it didn't matter. Once we got to the walkway toward the gates, I glared at Hennings.

"What the fuck were you doing?" I asked.

"Trying to get us through there as quickly as possible," he replied. "You were doing a bang-up job of making sure we were pulled into a strip search, which is not something I'm at all interested in doing unless it's Fi who does it. I didn't mean to sound so harsh, but I wanted to try to make myself look like I didn't like you any more than they did."

"Well, you did a great job of that," I said, a growl in my voice. "You're lucky I like you, or you'd be doing all this without me."

"Trust me," he said. "I want nothing more than to just get home. I hurt, I'm uncomfortable, and I can't wait to fuck Fi."

"Okay, that's TMI," I said, but laughed.

We found our gate pretty quick, and I settled him down with our bags to go grab something to eat and drink. When I got back, he had a whole bunch of young women standing around him, and he was grinning from ear to ear.

"There he is," he said, and the women turned toward me.

"You're so nice to help him out like this," one of the women said.

"Yeah," another chimed in. "It's so sweet that you gave up going with the team to help him. You're a true friend."

"Uh, thanks," I mumbled, confused as to what the hell he'd told them.

"Can I get a picture with you?" one asked. "You're so big and strong. I bet you could lift up at least two of us at the same time."

Hennings was barely holding back his laughter, and I gave him a look that should have stopped his heart, but it only caused him to struggle more.

"I'm sorry, ladies," I said, trying to pull the same shit he did at security. "I've just got so much to do to take care of him. He's so fragile right now, so I don't want anything to happen while I'm entertaining you guys. You understand, right?"

"Oh, of course," the one who asked for a picture said. "We'll let you get back to your duties. Wouldn't want you to get in trouble for him getting hurt."

"I really do appreciate it," I said. "Between the arm and the other injury, well, let's just say that I've had to be *very* helpful in ways I never expected."

As if they were of one mind, they all turned and looked right at his crotch. I hadn't said anything that confirmed he needed help with his dick, but if he was gonna play games, I'd play right along with him. The look on his face was fucking hilarious, too.

"There's nothing wrong with…"

"Ladies," I said, interrupting him. "I need to get him his medication. He seems to be having some issues with his memory as well. I'm so sorry to disappoint you. Maybe next time we're in town, we can get that picture."

"Of course," the one who seemed to be the leader said. "We'll let you get back to tending to him."

She looked at him again and shook her head, a sad look on her face. My smile was broad and sincere, but Hennings looked like he'd eaten something sour. Once they were gone, he turned on me.

"That was some fucking bullshit," he said.

"Just giving you a taste of your own medicine," I replied. "Besides, what would Fi think of you flirting with all of those women?"

"Fuck you," he said, and I just laughed more.

Handing him the soda and sandwich I'd picked up, I sat next to him to wait for the plane to show up so we could get the fuck out of this town.

# CHAPTER TWELVE

*S*kye...

By the time my day was finally slowing down, I was exhausted again. Coffee could only push me so far before I had to find an alternative boost. Fortunately, it was nearly six, and I would be closing as soon as it hit. For a Sunday, the shop was hopping, and I was again needing to place another order. I'd made the call to Uncle Marty, and he'd hooked me up with Milligan Fields to rush another shipment down to me, but they weren't going to be able to get it to me until the next morning.

Mai had stayed with me the entire day, mostly doing the sales so I could answer questions about teas and accessories. It was nice to see the big bump in business, even if it wasn't something I'd done. My phone had been going off a good chunk of the day, but I was just too busy to answer it, or even look at it. Hopefully, nothing major was going on, and I didn't miss out on something important.

"Have a nice evening," a woman said as she left the store.

"Quick," Mai said. "Lock that up."

I'd already had my key out and was locking it. Once it was done, I pulled the little string to shut the open sign off and turned to look at her.

"How'd we do?" I asked and she shrugged.

She pushed the buttons on the machine to print out our reports. It was old school, but I hadn't bothered to upgrade in the last few years because it still worked fine. It was starting to show its age, though, so I had planned to order an updated system that many of the other shops in the area used. By the time it finished running the tape, she looked at it, then back at me.

"What were yesterday's sales?" she asked.

"Not sure off the top of my head," I replied. "But we can compare."

I walked back into the office, and pulled the report from the previous day, then walked back out to where Mai was still staring at the machine. Handing her the report in my hand, I looked at the one from today, and had to blink a few times to make it make sense.

"How did we sell more today?" I asked.

"Not sure," she replied, looking at the report in her hand. "But we sold a shit ton more, and it's ridiculous. Everyone wanted to tip. Like every single customer wanted to add a tip onto their bill."

"We don't do tips," I said, and it was true. Miss Sylvie always hated the idea that customers should pay more than for their product or for the service of the tours. She never wanted to take tips, and I followed the same mentality.

"Maybe they felt sorry for us," she said. "I mean, look at the bare shelves."

I looked around and she was right, the shelves were again nearly bare. Since Milligan Fields couldn't get to us before the close of business, they were coming bright and early in the morning. At least I'd have something to sell tomorrow once I got everything in. Unfortunately, I'd have to be up super early to let them deliver, which was not my favorite thing to do.

"Why don't you go ahead and head out," I said. "I've got to get to bed early tonight so I can be here when the delivery arrives, so I'm just going to leave the rest of the closing duties for the morning."

"You want me to help you tomorrow?"

"If you wouldn't mind," I said. "But if Uncle Marty needs you, then stay there."

"He told me I'm on indefinite loan to you," she said. "Which, honestly, is really great. I prefer working in here than at the Market proper. Way less crowded."

"Are you saying you want to work for me full-time?" I asked.

I hadn't thought about needing anyone full-time because I was pretty good with doing most everything myself. The only time I usually had extra staff was during the summer when it got crazy, and once the ghost tours opened back up again.

"If you need me," she said. "I'd love to have the job."

"I really would love it," I said. "I mean, right now we're booming, but come summer, with the ghost tours starting back up and stuff, I might need an extra manager type person, and I really would love to have it be you. Especially since you know the shop and the business so well."

"You don't have to make me a manager," she said. "I just wouldn't mind a regular schedule. Besides, this would give you a chance to have a day off at some point, too."

"Hadn't thought about that," I said, and it was true. "But it would be nice to have a day off every once in a while. Not weekends, of course, but during the week it would be nice to not have to be here first thing."

"Besides," she added. "Maybe that baseball player might take you out or something. That would be worth it for me. You need someone good in your life."

"Yeah," I said. "Not looking to date anyone at this point. Would be nice to get a little action, but that always comes with strings, like a body behind it."

"There are alternatives," she said. "You do have a B.O.B., right?"

"A what now?"

"Battery operated boyfriend," she said, as if it were obvious.

"Oh yeah," I said. "Hadn't even thought about that. Just been too busy. That, and it always made me feel icky, but that was all Dylan's doing. He said they were only used by whores, so he wouldn't let me use one. I did get one once I broke up with him, but just haven't felt like using it. That residual mental shit he gave me is real."

"I say it's about damn time you said a big, fat, fuck you to him," she said. "Go and use that bad boy. Make yourself feel good. Show yourself that it is not at all about you, but totally about him and his control. You know that, right?"

"Yeah," I said. "I know. It's just hard."

"Look," she said, and the seriousness in her tone made me look at her. "He's an asshole. Always has been, always will be. He is absolutely not worth losing sleep over, not worth giving up orgasms for, and certainly not worth not moving on for. You are an amazing person, and I swear to God, if you don't get out of here as soon as I leave, head up to your apartment, and use that damn toy to get yourself to feel good, I am going to be so disappointed in you."

I blinked for a minute, really taking in what she'd said, and realizing that I had been letting Dylan run my life for the last several years. Even when he was locked up in prison, I let him rule what I could and couldn't do, especially with my own body. It was one of the reasons I cut my hair as soon as I broke up with him. A way to prove that he didn't have control over me any longer. Now, though, there were still things I didn't do, and they all boiled down to one common denominator, and that was my absolute trash of an ex, Dylan fucking Moore.

"There we go," she said, and I knew she saw the resolve in my face as I'd made the decision.

"You're absolutely right," I said.

"I know," she agreed with a smile. "What else do we have to do before you go get your groove on?"

"Let me see," I said, looking around the shop.

The door was locked, the light was off, I needed to gather up the rest of the receipts, and any cash we had around, and put it into the safe. Everything else could be done later tomorrow, or even after closing tomorrow night.

"I have to be here at seven to meet with the guys from the farm," I said. "Last time it took about an hour to get everything offloaded and into the shop. I'll have a couple of hours after that to finish anything but the absolute necessities, which is getting the till shut down."

"On it," she said, pulling the cash from the drawer, and adding the rest of the stuff into the cash bag. "Get the safe open, and I'll finish the rest of the cleanup out here. Once that's done, you go get freaky. I expect to see you well and truly glowing tomorrow when I get here. Which, by the way, do you need me here to help with offloading?"

"Nah," I said, taking the cash bag from her. "If you wouldn't mind being here by about nine, though, that would be great. We can finish stocking anything that's out, and maybe even open early if there's a line."

"You know there's gonna be a line," she said. "You're famous now."

"Great," I said. "Just what I needed."

She laughed as I went to the back and put the cash into the safe. By the time I got back out, she'd pretty much cleaned up everything else, and was ready to head out.

"See you tomorrow," she said as she stepped out the front door.

Locking it behind her, I closed the gate that went across the door to keep at least some sense of security in place, then shut the lights off, and turned on the security system before heading out the back door to go up to my apartment. Hopefully my little toy was charged because she was right. I needed to get my life back, and satisfaction in the face of what I'd gone through might just be the thing to get me there.

# CHAPTER THIRTEEN

*J*ohn...

"Jesus fucking Christ," Hennings said as we got to the baggage claim area after landing in Seattle. "How long does it take to get our fucking bags here? Don't they have some kind of fucking guarantee for it?"

He'd been going on and on about every little thing that he perceived as being wrong since we were in the air. I'd already given him his pain meds before we took off, and they must have worn off, because he was raging at absolutely everything, and I was honestly getting pretty fucking sick of his bitching.

"Hey," I barked, and he turned to me ready to fight me or something. "You have got to get your shit together. What would Fi think if she saw you acting like a fucking toddler right now? Pretty sure she'd hand you your ass for being such a miserable fucking dick. And she likes you. I'm done listening to you, so if you want me to help you get your bag, you better fucking shut your goddamned cake hole before I shove my fist into it."

Whatever I said, or maybe it was how I said it, finally kicked in and he realized he was being an asshole to the one person who had been helping him.

"Fuck," he said. "Sorry. I just want to get home."

"I know," I replied. "I feel the same way. The bags will get here when they get here. Until then, sit your ass down and wait for Fi to show up. I'll grab the bags."

He didn't say anything else, just walked over to where they had a handful of seats on the edge of the area and plopped down. I followed him and set our carryon bags next to him so I had two free hands to grab our bags. Sure enough, by the time I got over to the carousel, the bags were coming down the chute and tumbling onto the roundabout for folks to pick them up. Fortunately, we both were smart when we did our bags, and had obvious indicators on them, so they were easy to grab. By the time I got back over to him, he was smiling.

"She's here," he said.

"Great," I replied, hooking the smaller bags onto the larger ones so I could wheel them all out with me in one trip.

"Hey baby," he said as he walked up to her car.

"What did you do to yourself?" she asked.

"Got thrown over the guardrail into the dugout," I answered, knowing he'd try to make up some sort of heroic story. "Landed on his arm with the other dude on top of him. It was quite funny, gotta say."

"Shut up," he growled, but Fi was laughing.

"Anyway," I said, rolling his bag out in front of me. "Here's his shit, he's your problem now."

"Gee, thanks," she said, but she was smiling. "You good to get home?"

"Yeah," I said. "Just gonna grab a cab. It ain't far."

"I can give you a ride," she said.

"He's a big boy," Hennings said. "Let him figure his own shit out."

"Pretty sure you're a big boy, too," she said with a smirk. "Did you want him to let you figure your own shit out, too?"

"Fuck," he said. "I just want to go home."

"I'm fine," I said.

"Let me give you a ride," she said. "Please? As a thank you for taking care of my asshole of a boyfriend?"

I blew out a breath, then nodded and she smiled.

"I'm sitting shotgun," Hennings said.

"Asshole," I replied.

Her car wasn't exactly big, but it wasn't that small, either. If he shoved the seat up far enough, I'd have enough room to sit behind him.

"Hey short shit," I said as he got into the car. "Pull your seat up. I'm a real man and need actual leg room behind you."

"Shut up," he said, but he did what I'd asked, and pulled the seat up with his good arm after he got in.

"Thanks, little man," I said as a final dig.

"Would you two grow up?" Fi asked, looking directly at Hennings and not me.

I kept my comments to myself, because my guess was that wasn't the first time she'd told him to grow up.

"What's your address?" she asked, her phone in her hand.

I gave it to her, and she punched it into her GPS. It didn't take but a moment, and we were on our way down the road, and up toward downtown. She had a podcast on when we got into the car, but she switched it to one of her playlists of music once we got going, which I appreciated. Every once in a while the GPS would tell her to turn or get on or off the freeway, and I just sat back and kind of zoned out.

"Where should I park?" she asked, and I looked around, realizing I'd completely missed the whole drive.

"Umm," I hummed. "Just pull up along the curb, and I'll jump out."

She did as I suggested, pulling up along the curb of the apartment building I was in, and I opened the door to step out.

"Here," she said, popping open the trunk, her emergency flashers going on the car.

"Thanks," I said, pulling my bags out. "I really do appreciate the ride, although it really wasn't necessary."

"It's the least I could do," she said. "You had to put up with grumpy pants the whole flight."

"That I did," I said with a smile.

"Thanks for helping him," she said, then leaned in and gave me a hug.

I kind of stood there, just letting her hug me, until she pulled away.

"Guess I better get him home," she said.

"Yeah," I replied. "He probably needs another pain pill. They're in the top pocket of his carryon bag."

"Thanks again," she said, then slid into the car, and shut her door.

I pulled my bags behind me as I went into the building, walking across the lobby to the elevators. It didn't take long for the car to come down, and I stepped inside and pressed the button for my floor. The ride was slow, and the music they piped into the elevator was like a bad cover band playing from memory that didn't actually know the song. When the doors opened, I was glad to get out of there and away from it. Down the hall to my apartment, I pulled out my keys and opened my door, flipping the light on as I stepped inside.

"Fuck," I said, nearly gagging at the smell. "What the actual fuck?"

I looked up at the light above my coffee table and saw something moving inside it.

"Jesus fucking Christ," I said, not even sure what the fuck was going on.

That's when something dripped from the light and landed on the table, drawing my eyes down to it. There, in the middle of my table, on top of the handful of magazines I had, was a pile of something brown and black, and it was moving, undulating with things crawling around it, and I noped the fuck out of there, pulling the door closed behind me and pulling out my phone.

"Harborview Apartments," the woman who answered the phone said. "How can I help you?"

"I'm in apartment 302, and there is something dripping from my light down onto my table in the middle of my living room," I said. "Something must be dead upstairs or something, but I can't go into the apartment without hurling."

"Oh, dear," she said. "I'm so sorry to hear about that. I will have to call a maintenance man to come check it out. It may take an hour or so, though, to find someone."

"Yeah," I said. "I'll just call the cops to figure out what's dead above me."

I hung up before she could answer, and then dialed 911.

"911, what's your emergency?" the guy said.

"I think someone died in the apartment above mine," I said. "Not really sure, but there's something dripping into my apartment, and it looks like it's alive."

"Have you tried reaching out to the apartment maintenance?"

"They said it could be hours until someone can come," I replied. "I've been away for business and came home to this. I'm worried about the neighbor."

"Perfectly reasonable," he said. "Can you give me your address and phone number, please?"

I rattled off the address and included my apartment number, as well as my phone number, then I said, "I don't know who lives above me because my business takes me out of town a lot, and I only rent here, don't own the space."

"I'll send someone over to talk to you," he said. "Will you give me your name, please?"

"John Huffman," I said. "I'd really like to get into my apartment, but the smell is awful."

"You should stay out if possible," he said. "The responding agencies may need to see the space undisturbed. Would you like me to stay on the line until they get there? It may be awhile."

"Nah," I said. "No need for you to babysit me. I'll just head to the lobby of the apartment building and wait for them. Will it be cops that come?"

"I'm dispatching both police and an ambulance," he said. "It could be a medical emergency, and I don't want to delay their arrival."

"Thanks," I said.

"Anything else?"

"Unless you need me, nothing I can think of," I said.

"Then I'll disconnect the call," he said. "If someone doesn't arrive within half an hour, please call back."

"You think it's gonna take that long for someone to come?"

"I'm not sure," he said.

"Okay," I said. "Whatever."

I hung up the call and headed back to the elevator to ride it down to the lobby. The building was six floors high, so there was definitely an apartment above mine, I just didn't know who lived there. I wasn't exactly a normal neighbor, what with my hours being mostly late nights, and add to that being out of town for half the season.

I'd never bothered to buy a place here, though. Never felt the need to set down roots, always planning on being traded at a moment's notice. Some guys were good with that sort of thing, but I didn't want to have to deal with the hassle of selling something when I moved on. I had a home just outside Denver that I stayed at during the offseason, but didn't need one here, too. Not that I couldn't afford it, it just didn't seem necessary.

Now, though, I had second thoughts. I mean, it's not something you think about, having to deal with someone dead above you, but I guess this would be the same situation if I owned a condo. Not a house, but did I really want to buy a house? That really didn't feel right to me, at least not yet. Maybe someday when I felt like I'd be in a particular city forever, or at least for the long haul.

I was coming up to the end of my contract, so my agent should be getting with me to let me know about the goings on for getting signed again. I liked the city, and the team in general, and really enjoyed playing with the group that was the core of our team. Obviously, guys came and went, but there was a decent core that were here for the long haul, at least until they needed to be traded. I'd been with Seattle since I was traded right at the beginning of my career, before I even made my debut in the bigs, so moving somewhere else wasn't exactly what I was looking to do. Since I would be off for the next week or so, I thought I should contact my agent, and get with him to see where things were going to go moving forward.

Stepping out of the elevator, I nearly ran into a couple of cops, who looked me up and down, sizing me up, I guess.

"You guys here to answer my call?" I asked.

"Your name?" one of them asked.

"John Huffman," I replied. "I called just a little bit ago."

"Then you're who we're here to see," the other officer said.

"Would you mind taking us up to your apartment so we can see what we're dealing with?"

"Sure," I replied, stepping back onto the elevator, and punching the number for my floor.

The ride up was silent except for the music coming through the speakers. When we arrived on our floor, I could smell it before we even stepped off.

"Definitely decomp," the first officer said. "Which one is yours?"

"302," I replied. "Do I have to get out?"

"Yeah, we kinda do," the second officer said. "I know it sucks, but just try to breathe shallow or something."

"I don't know how the fuck you do this," I said, wanting to hurl right there.

"Keys?" the first officer asked as we got to my apartment.

I handed mine over, with the one out that would let them in, then stepped back, pulling my shirt up over my nose and mouth. I was never gonna get this smell out of anything in the apartment, so everything was going to have to be scrapped. I mean, maybe some things would be salvageable, but I wasn't sure what. I'd left the light on, and they looked through the door, then shut the light off and closed it, handing my key back to me.

"Any idea who lives above you?" the first officer asked.

"Sorry, man," I said. "I'm not here a lot. I travel for work and work odd hours when I am in town."

"When did you notice this?"

"It wasn't there when I left for work on Wednesday," I said. "That was before nine or so. I got home about half an hour ago, and that's what I walked into."

"You got somewhere you can stay for the night?"

"I can go to a hotel," I said. "Not a big deal. You gonna find out what happened?"

"We have to get the management to open that apartment," the officer said. "Can't really just go breaking down the door."

"So, dude's dead and that's not a reason to open the door?"

"Unfortunately, no," he said.

They retraced their steps and headed back to the elevator, and I followed behind them. Once the door opened, we all got in, and headed back down to the lobby.

"Which way to the office?" one of them asked.

I pointed toward the place where he could find someone, then asked, "Do I need to stick around?"

"Nah," he said. "Your name and number are on the report."

"Thanks," I replied.

"Hey," he said, his partner already across the lobby. "If you need someone to clean the apartment after they do the one above you, you can try these guys. They're pretty good and don't cost a fortune."

"Thanks," I said, taking the card he'd held out to me. "Does that smell ever go away?"

"Not really," he said. "It sticks around for days, weeks, sometimes even years."

"Yeah," I replied. "That's kinda what I was thinking. Wondering if I should just scrap everything and start fresh."

"Wouldn't hurt to contact your renter's insurance," he said. "They may be able to cover some of the replacement costs."

"Never thought of that," I said. "Thanks again."

"No problem," he said.

"You coming?" his partner shouted across the lobby.

"Yeah," he said, then turned and walked away.

I pulled out my phone and ordered a car to take me to a hotel close by. Once I was there, I'd figure out what to do next.

# CHAPTER FOURTEEN

*S*kye...
   I closed my door behind me and looked around the apartment. Not much had changed in the last few years, and honestly, that kind of bothered me. Everything in my living space was connected to the old me, the me who allowed a man to run my life, determine what I could and couldn't do. I wasn't that person anymore, but my space didn't reflect the change. Much as I wanted to get a little bit of sexual release, I needed the mental release of change more.

   "No time like the present," I said to myself and dove right in.

   It looked much the same as when I'd first stepped foot in it so many years ago. When Miss Sylvie lived here, she showed me the space that would become mine once she moved on. You could still smell her perfume, still feel her ghosts, and that wasn't necessarily a bad thing, but it wasn't mine. Maybe I was afraid to change it for fear of fucking it up, but if I wanted to start anew, like I'd done with the rest of my life, then I needed to start all over again from scratch. Well, not quite from scratch, but definitely needed to do the whole, 'out with the old, in with the new' routine to get things going.

   Walking to the windows above Post Alley, I flung the sheer curtains off to the side and opened the glass to let in the fresh spring air. It was still chilly, what with it only being the middle of April, but I needed things moving, needed the air to move and to get these bad bits out so new, good bits could come back in. After all, Beltane was coming up soon, so I might as well get a jump start on the refresh that it brought into my life.

"Music," I said, looking around the space. "Definitely need some music."

I turned my speaker on, pulled up Spotify on my phone, clicked through the ads that came up, then hit my playlist. After selecting the shuffle feature, I closed my eyes, flipped the list to scroll up, then down, and picked a song at random. When Respect by Aretha Franklin came on, I knew the fates were on my side.

Starting with the simple things, like putting away the dishes that were in the rack and wiping down the counters, I continued in the kitchen by checking the fridge to see what needed to be tossed, and boy did that start a whole chain reaction of cleaning both it, and the freezer, including wiping the whole thing down with soap and everything. I also noticed that I'd need to get some fresh fruit and veggies the next day to resupply. Aretha gave way to Linkin Park, which gave way to Green Day, and on to even more, including the newest addition to my list, Living My Best Life by Ben Rector. If that didn't fit the bill, then I was obviously doing it wrong.

By the time I was done with the kitchen, I was feeling a bit hangry, so I opted to head out and grab something for dinner, knowing that I'd need to get it before long or I'd be shit outta luck. I snagged my purse off the rack it lived on, grabbed my keys, and slipped out the door, locking the bolt behind me. Dropping down the stairs to the hallway type of thing that led me out the back of the building, I turned right to go around the building itself to get to one of my favorite little restaurants just down the other side of the street.

The Chinese restaurant on Stewart, just past Post Alley where my tea shop was, had the absolute best General Tso's chicken I'd ever had, and it was always a comfort food for me. Any time I wasn't feeling well, Grammy would pick some up for me, along with their sticky rice. She insisted that I had to eat it with chopsticks and was patient to teach me the proper way to use them. Fortunately, I was able to pick it up quickly, as opposed to my brother, who never did figure it out.

As if it knew what was coming, my stomach growled in anticipation, and I couldn't help but laugh. I pushed the door open and stepped in, smelling all my favorite things. The woman sitting at the register smiled at me, and I returned the smile.

"I'd like an order of General Tso's to go," I said.

"Fried rice?" she asked.

"Sticky rice, please," I said. "And I'll need chopsticks. Mine got lost somewhere."

"Sure thing," she said.

She was on the younger side and didn't have an accent that I could distinguish. I wondered whether the restaurant had changed hands since I'd been in last. Had to think on that, but I probably hadn't been here since well before I broke up with Dylan, so probably a couple of years. A lot can change in that time, so I hoped I wouldn't be disappointed when I got my food.

I paid for my food and sat in one of the chairs near the front door to wait. Fortunately, it didn't take long, and I was soon on my way back to my place. As I crossed over Post Alley, I looked down to see what was going on at the pub next to my shop. I could hear the music, and it was really a nice place to go into if you had the time. They had good food, too, but I was in the mood for this, so opted to skip the pub. Besides, if I ended up in there, I wouldn't get anything done in my apartment.

Just as I turned my head away, something caught my eye. There, just in front of my shop, was a guy with a black hoodie, the hood up on his head, hands stuffed into his pockets. My heart pounded as I thought it must have been Dylan, but then my brain reminded me he was in jail. Unsure who this guy might be, and whether he was there to cause me harm or not, I scooted up the hill and around to the front to slide back down the little hallway to my back stairwell. I didn't want to have this guy see me, especially if he meant me harm.

My hands were shaking by the time I got to my door, and it took a few tries for me to get the key into the hole. I slid into the apartment and shut the door behind me, throwing the deadbolt, and adding the extra lock up top for added protection. I set my food on the counter and walked slowly to the window, which I'd left open for some insane reason.

Peering out without getting too close, I could just see the top of the guy's head, and it was covered, so I didn't even know whether he was black, white, or something else, nor what color hair he had. All I could tell was that he was big. I mean, really big. And that terrified me.

I closed the window as slowly as I could, trying desperately to keep it from making any noise, but it kind of thumped when it shut completely. The sound wasn't very much, but it was just enough to get the guy's attention, and he looked up. Stepping back, I worked on my breathing, hoping to slow my heart and stave off any sort of panic attack that might want to show up. I fucking hated that Dylan had made me such a wimp, but he'd broken me down over and over again until I just couldn't make any decision for myself. There were times when I was fine, and really, better than I'd been, even before I met him. And then there were moments when I was just terrified of everything.

"The shop is locked," I said to myself, my voice shaking more than I'd like. "Your door is locked. No one knows how to get up here except you, and people you trust. You are safe."

Those last three words had been my mantra, something I'd said to myself repeatedly, starting when I was in the hospital right after the attack. The therapist who I first worked with had helped me come up with the best phrase for how to get my mind on the reality of what was actually happening. She'd given me lots of different words to choose from, but being safe was the biggest thing I was worried about, and I really was. There were people around me who cared for me, who knew what had happened and had helped me build my life back up to what it is now.

"I am safe," I reiterated, changing the phrasing just enough to remind myself that I was inside my own body, and I could decide what happened to me.

Feeling braver than I would have a year ago, I went back to the window and looked down at the alley, but he was gone. Whoever it had been had left in the time it took me to get my emotions under control. He'd probably seen me, but I hadn't seen him, aside from just a dude in a hoodie, which was absolutely a useless description. While I was feeling a bit braver, I was still anxious. I grabbed my phone and dialed Britta.

"Hey beautiful, what's up?" she asked when she answered the phone.

"Just needed to hear a friendly voice," I said.

"What happened?"

It was like she knew my emotions without me even telling her.

"I got spooked," I said.

"Talk it through," she said, knowing that I could figure out what was really freaking me out more than anyone could tell me.

"I went down to Genghis Khan to grab some dinner," I said, reliving the moments as I spoke. "When I was coming back up the hill, I looked down Post to see what was up at the pub. There was a dude with a black hoodie on, and he was huge. Just kind of spooked me."

My breathing had sped up, and the words came out all rushed and smashed together.

"Slow down, babe," she said. "You saw him there. Did you recognize him? Did he look familiar at all?"

"I just saw that he was big," I said. "Really big."

"Okay," she said. "Not a big surprise. Guys can be big. Was he standing outside the pub, like he was a patron there?"

"He was just a bit away from there," I said, running the scene through my mind. "He was actually facing my shop's window, like he was looking inside it for something."

"I mean, your shop is awesome," she said. "People like to look inside there."

"Yeah," I agreed. "I mean, I guess so."

"Right," she said. "Now, did you go down the alley?"

"Oh, hell no," I said. "I scooted up to First to go through the front of the building."

"Totally reasonable," she said. "What happened next?"

I told her about my struggle to unlock my door before finally getting in. How I locked it up tight, and then about how my window was open.

"Why did you leave it open when you left?"

"I honestly didn't even think about it," I said. "I opened it when I was doing some cleaning, then got hungry and headed out."

"Not like someone can get in that way," she said. "I mean, unless they can scale buildings or something."

There was humor in her voice, and I knew she was trying really hard not to chastise me about leaving my window open.

"Still shouldn't have done it," I said.

"But you're good, right?"

"Yeah," I said.

"So," she said. "That's not enough to cause this need for a pep talk, so what else?"

"I closed the window," I said. "Not really sure why. Maybe to ensure he wasn't going to be one of those people who could climb the side of the building. Maybe to make myself feel like there was something between us, not that a window is much protection. Honestly, I'm not sure why I felt the need, I just did."

"What happened after that?" she asked.

"It made a noise and he looked up," I said, my words rushed. "I stepped back, but I think he saw me."

"I mean, that's not unusual," she said. "When a noise happens, we tend to look. Why are you freaked out? Not trying to sound harsh, but this seems like a normal occurrence, so just trying to get my mind around what you're thinking."

"I think it was the black hoodie," I said.

"Ah," she said. "Yeah, probably a combination."

"That, and I've been having the dreams again," I said. "They're getting worse, too, so I think it's the combination of it all."

"All right," she said. "Is he gone now?"

"Yeah," I said, moving back to the window to make sure. "He was gone when I got my shit together to go look."

"He was probably just waiting to get into the pub," she said. "You know that, right?"

"I know," I said. "It just freaked me out."

"But you're good now, right?" she asked.

I assessed myself, looked out the window again to ensure that the dude was gone, and then did one of those self-assessments to make sure my heart was steady and not fast, and my breathing was under control. Sure enough, I was there.

"Yeah," I said, finally. "I'm good."

"Good," she said. "Anything else you need from me?"

"I don't think so," I said. "Thanks for taking my call."

"You know I always will," she said.

"I know," I replied. "But I want to make sure you know."

"Of course I know," she said. "Besides, what kind of friend would I be if I ignored you? Now, James is giving me that look, so I'm gonna go."

"Oh yeah, go," I said. "Don't let me get in the way of that."

"He understands," she said.

"Yeah, it's fine," I heard him say from somewhere near her, then she laughed.

"Go," I said. "I got this."

"See ya," she said, then disconnected the call.

I took a deep breath, looked around my home, then caught sight of my dinner sitting on the kitchen counter. All of a sudden, my stomach growled so much it hurt, and I headed over to grab the food. Once I had it, I sat on my couch and turned the television on to see if I could find something to distract me from my own imagination.

# CHAPTER FIFTEEN

*J*ohn...

Once I'd gotten into a room, which took entirely too long in my estimation, I was starving, and also going stir crazy. I knew I'd have to call my insurance agent in the morning about the apartment, as well as the cleaning company, but nothing would happen tonight. So, all in all it was a bad combination of things, and I just needed to get out and find some food before I went absolutely mad.

Unsure what was around the hotel I'd picked, I pulled up a map to see what was in the area. Somehow, without really thinking about it, I'd ended up in a hotel near Pike Place Market, which meant I was near that tea shop. I searched around to see what was in the area and found an Irish pub right next door, so decided to wander that way to grab a beer and some food before settling in for the night.

It took a couple of wrong turns before I found myself in the right alley between major streets where the pub was. It was a hopping place, with overflow coming out into the street. I stood with some of the other folks waiting to get in and realized that I was standing right in front of the shop. I looked in the window, but it was obviously closed. I wondered whether it would be open when I headed this way and was disappointed it wasn't. It was an interesting shop with all sorts of little things set on the shelves, but it appeared clean and well maintained. Might have to make a point to come back the next day to swing in and see it in full action.

As I was looking inside, I heard a thump from above me, and looked up. There she was, but just for a moment. Honestly, I was surprised I'd heard the noise over the sound of the band playing inside the pub, but I had, and it was just a jolt of excitement and confusion. She looked spooked, even in just the flash that I saw her, which I thought was odd. Maybe she was worried about something else. Whatever it was, I didn't get a chance to find out, because that was when the line moved, and I was able to step inside the pub, shoving my hood off my head.

It was an odd building in that it had two distinct sides to the bar that were sort of separated by the bar itself with just a kind of walkway between the sides. It was loud, but the band seemed to be playing in the other half of the space, which I was kind of glad about. I hadn't really wanted to come in and listen to a band, just get something to eat, drink a beer, and maybe get a chance to stop into the tea shop that had so kindly sent a pizza to me. I slid onto a bar stool and waited for the bartender to come over.

"What'll it be?" he asked, wiping down the counter in front of me, and dropping a menu on it.

"What do you suggest?" I asked.

"Depends on what you like," he replied. "We've got just about everything you could want, so what do you prefer to drink?"

"I'm good with a pale ale," I said.

"Good choice," he said and turned, grabbing a glass and sliding it under the tap, pulling the lever to fill it, being mindful of not getting too much foam in it, which I appreciated. "Getting food, too?" he asked as he set the beer down.

"Yeah," I said. "But I'm not quite sure what to get. First time here."

"We've got something for everyone," he said. "Take a look and if you have questions, I'll be back in a minute to answer them."

"Thanks," I said as he headed down the bar to attend to someone else's needs.

I looked over the menu, recognizing most of the foods, but there were a couple of things they had that weren't clear as to what they were. Instead of trying to figure out some of the terms, I decided to go with the flat iron steak, as that was pretty much a standard. I set the menu down and took a sip of the beer, enjoying the hoppy taste on my tongue and the way it felt refreshing after everything I'd been through that day.

"Looks like you've decided," the bartender said when he came back.

"Yeah," I said. "I'll take the flat iron."

"Okay," he said. "How do you want that cooked?"

"Medium rare," I said.

He asked about sides, and told me what was available, then went to the machine to put the order in so it went back to the kitchen. Sitting there and sipping my beer, it was nice to be somewhere that I wasn't recognized, at least not yet. Hopefully, I'd stay under the radar while I ate my dinner. I took another sip of my beer, and a woman slid onto the stool next to me, spinning herself so that she had her knees right next to me, then leaned forward, showing off her barely covered chest.

"Hey, big boy," she cooed, her perfume coming off her in waves. "Buy a pretty girl a drink?"

"Sorry," I said, trying to turn away from her.

"Oh, come on," she purred, really pouring on her attempt at sex appeal, which was so not something I was interested in. "Can't let me go thirsty, now, can you?"

"Ma'am," I said, emphasizing the word. "I am here for the evening to enjoy a beer and listen to some music. I am not interested in whatever it is you're selling. Now please, leave me alone."

"You know you want me," she said, barely loud enough for me to hear her.

"Hey," I said, shouting to the bartender. "Can I get that to go?"

He looked at me, then looked at the woman, and shook his head.

"Mandy," he said. "I shouldn't have to tell you this, you're not

93

allowed to work in this bar. If you want to sell your wares, you need to go to the street. We don't condone this in here, and we've told you."

"Come on, Shorty," she said, pushing her tits out like they were some sort of currency. "A girl's gotta make a living."

"Not in my bar," another man said, and I hadn't seen him before.

Whoever he was, Mandy knew him, and she scurried off the stool and out the door faster than I thought possible.

"Sorry 'bout that," he said, coming closer. "She's been told to stay out, but she just doesn't seem to take the hint."

"No problem," I said.

"If you still want to take your food to go, you can," he said. "But we'd love to have you stay a while. I'm paying for your meal…"

"No, no," I said, interrupting him.

"I'm gonna have to insist," he said. "Not the kind of welcome we want to give to a guest."

"It really isn't a problem," I said, but he kind of gave me that dad look, where he wasn't gonna take any more shit from me, so I just shut my trap.

"There we go," he said. "So, eating here or taking it home?"

"I'd like to stick around," I said. "The band's pretty good."

"That they are," he said with a smile and a wink, then walked away.

It wasn't long before the bartender was walking over with my plate, and it was a very large portion, much larger than I expected. I used the fork and knife to cut a piece off the steak, swirled it in the gravy on the plate, then stuck it in my mouth, and damn near groaned with enjoyment, it was so good. The flavor was so full, especially with the gravy, that I just closed my eyes, and let the flavors explode in my mouth. Once I'd finally finished chewing the bite and swallowed it, I opened my eyes again, and saw the bartender was watching me with a smile.

I pulled the napkin off my lap, and covered my mouth, but couldn't help but smile myself. It was probably one of the best cuts of beef I'd ever eaten, and the gravy just pushed it over the top. The bartender just nodded, then went back to making the drink he was working on. I looked at my plate, and continued eating, taking a bite of the potatoes I chose for my side, I was just as impressed as I had been with the steak. I would definitely be coming back for another meal.

By the time I finished my meal, the band was taking a break, which was a bit disappointing, but it was what it was. I gave a nod to the bartender who came over to me.

"Another beer?" he asked.

"Nah," I said. "Just heading out. Here," I said, handing him a hundred from my wallet.

"Can't take it," he said.

"Why not?" I asked.

"Mac said on the house," he said. "That means I am not at all allowed to take any money from you in any way, shape, or form. You don't want me losing my job, do you?"

He was smiling when he said it, but it was clear he was serious as a fucking heart attack. I just shook my head because it was clear that I was not going to win an argument with him.

"Next time, I'm paying double," I said and he laughed.

I headed out the door, hoping to get back to my hotel, and get some decent sleep before I had to start making calls the next morning. As I turned the corner from the alley I was in, and headed up the hill to First, Mandy was standing there, and looking like she'd been waiting for a while.

"Glad you came to your senses," she said, thrusting her tits out like they were an offering of some sort.

I tried to ignore her and walk around, but she got right in front of me, and pressed her hand to my chest. I stopped and looked at her, trying my hardest to do the don't fuck with me stare, but apparently she liked that, and sidled up against me, using her other hand to reach out and go for my dick. Instead of allowing myself to be molested, I shifted, and shoved her hand away. Unfortunately, she'd had one too many drinks or snorts or something, and she toppled off her heels onto the pavement. I didn't look back, just went on up the hill to hear her screaming at me.

"You fucking pig," she shouted. "Come back here. Come fucking back here and pay me. I swear to fucking God that you're gonna pay for this you son of a bitch."

I barely heard the last of it as I was already around the corner and heading down the street to get to my hotel. The walk didn't take long, and it wasn't too cold out, so it was a nice walk. I wasn't terribly worried about the woman figuring out where I was staying, or even seeing her again, especially since I wasn't going to be at the hotel long.

After I keyed my way into the room, I locked the door behind me, pulling out my wallet to find the business card the cop had given me at my apartment. I set it on the dresser that had the television on it. I kicked off my shoes as I pulled my sweatshirt over my head, dropping it on the end of the bed. My tee shirt came off next, then the pants, my socks coming off when I pulled my pants off.

It had been both a good and bad evening. The food was fucking amazing, but that bitch that just wouldn't leave me alone was over the top. I get she's trying to make money, but she really needs to learn to take no for an answer and not push. I'm just glad I was able to get away from her. I'm all for sex positivity, but you gotta keep your hands to yourself if you're gonna be out there selling yourself.

What I really wanted was to find the girl from the tea shop. The flash I'd gotten when she closed the window above the store wasn't nearly enough. As I walked into the bathroom, I thought about her, the fear in her eyes wasn't something I'd expected, and it was a bit of a turn on, to be honest. I wasn't into all that masochist shit, but that pain and pleasure fine line was always fun to ride, and I wouldn't mind seeing if she would be willing to ride it with me. That fine line of pushing until you know the limit, then pulling back, just a bit, in order to make the pleasure that much better.

I turned on the water in the tub, letting it heat up as I grabbed a towel from the rack, and set it on the tank of the toilet. Snagging the shampoo and soap from the counter by the sink, I took those and a washcloth into the tub with me as I tested the temperature with my foot, then pulled the plunger to activate the shower head. There was the initial burst of cold water, quickly followed by a warmer stream.

Ducking my head under the water, I let it run over me and down my back. My eyes were closed, and all I could see was the girl, the woman, that was in the window above the tea shop. Her short hair neatly combed around her face, her eyes bright, even in the dim light of the evening, wide open in fear of some sort, and her perfect lips shaped in an "O" of surprise.

With my eyes closed, I could still see them, pink and open slightly, and that was all I needed to ignite my imagination. I pictured her with me in the shower, her mouth open and willing to let me push myself into it. The only thing I knew about her was what she looked like, but only in a vague way, and that moment I'd caught her in the room above the shop.

I didn't know what she sounded like when she talked, didn't know her smell, or anything other than just those minute details. Still, my imagination wasn't something that needed every detail, just enough to get me going, which it already had.

Imagining her on her knees in front of me, her pretty blue eyes turned up, her pink mouth open, and the water from the shower running over her body, I kept stroking myself. It wasn't the same as if it were real, but I kept at it, just thinking about how it would be at some point. I was determined to at the very least meet her. Whether she would be interested in me was something that I'd have to wait to find out. For now, though, she was there, in my mind's eye, taking me into her mouth, swirling her tongue around my cock, sucking on me as I pressed into her. It was a glorious dream, one I wanted to come true.

# CHAPTER SIXTEEN

$\mathcal{S}$ kye...
My sleep was restless, tossing and turning, nightmares that chased me through the empty streets. That figure was there, bigger than Dylan, but it was him. I knew logically he was locked up, but the fact that a man was there, looking into my shop, staring up at my window, just waiting for me to be in a vulnerable position, was enough to send me over the edge. By the time my alarm was blaring, I hadn't really slept much at all.

"Why?" I cried out to the universe, herself. "Why must you torment me with the demons I thought I'd already slayed?"

She didn't answer me, just like she hadn't any of the other times I'd asked why my fate was tied to a monster. No, my journey was marked with challenges I had to overcome on my own. It was too early to be up, the sun barely above the horizon at the back of my building. I didn't see it rise but could tell by the way the sky above the sound changed in color and hue. It was written there, just not as brightly as on the eastern side.

I stretched with my arms over my head, pulling each to get my shoulders ready for the task that would be mine that morning. When I'd called Milligan Fields, they'd said they'd be here by seven or shortly after, so I knew I had to be up and out of my apartment, ready to take in the new stock, well before that.

Climbing out of my bed, I padded my way to the bathroom to get my morning constitution out of the way. Washing my hands, I looked in the mirror at my face, and could see those dark circles coming back. They'd been gone for a while now, but with the lack of good sleep, and the way I had to push myself in the shop the last few days, I was running on fumes at best. I really should take a night, and do absolutely nothing, but that wasn't in the cards for me. Instead, I splashed some water on my face, ran my hands through my hair to get it to show some sort of fashion, then went back out to get dressed.

Today was supposed to be cooler, and perhaps a little bit rainy, but I was fine with that. It just meant that I'd be able to get more done in the store. Rainy days didn't seem to draw as much of a crowd to the Market, which wasn't good for business, but for me it would be a nice reprieve from the insanity I'd been having with the shop. Maybe that would mean the inventory would last more than a day. Not that I'd complain about sales going sky high, but this ordering every day was bullshit.

I walked out my apartment door and headed down the steps to my shop, shooting a text to Mai on the way. She'd said she would be happy to come in and help with the order, so I wanted to let her know what my plan was. I opened the door, turned off the alarm, and flipped on the lights. I absolutely loved the way the shop smelled after it had been closed overnight. It was earthy and flowery, with just a hint of spice, and it was like a balm to my nerves after the night I'd had.

My phone pinged as I went toward the front, but I was sure it was Mai, so didn't bother to look. Instead of seeing my friend by the door, though, I saw the man, or at least a man, standing outside, his back to the shop window. The hood was up on his black sweatshirt, so I couldn't see anything more than his back, and he was big. I froze, my heart racing a mile a minute, trying to get me to move, to run, to get the fuck out of there and to safety. Then he turned around.

I was standing there, likely looking like a freak, my eyes wide, my phone clutched in my hands, and terror on my face. He smiled, but that's really all I could see. Those bright white teeth set in the shadow of his hood. Whatever he saw must have made him realize he was a menace, and he shoved the hood off his head, showing blond hair with just a hint of curl, one lock down his forehead to his eyebrow, the rest sort of pushed back.

It wasn't Dylan, but that didn't seem to matter to my body. I couldn't breathe, couldn't move, couldn't do anything. He raised his hand to peer in more, and I wet myself. Not that I wanted to piss in the middle of my shop, but my body just released it. I was so hyper-focused on him that I didn't see Mai until the chime above the door rang.

"Hey," she said, her voice sounding very far away. "Skye," she said again, still in that far off distance I couldn't really hear. "Skye," she nearly shouted, grabbing my arm, and I finally looked at her, blinking.

"What's the matter?" she asked, but I just started to bawl, crumpling to the floor in the puddle I'd created. "Oh, baby, it's okay," she cooed, but my eyes were still focused on the guy on the other side of the glass.

When he walked through the door, I screamed, scrambled back from my spot on the floor, and into the bathroom in the back of the store, barricading myself in.

# CHAPTER SEVENTEEN

*J*ohn…

I'd headed down to the market early, because for some fucking reason, I was up. I wanted to see if I could see the woman at the tea shop again, maybe even talk to her, but I didn't even know when the shop opened. I grabbed my hoodie before heading out because it was cold.

Instead of stopping to pick up coffee or any breakfast, I just walked straight down to the shop. When I got there, it was closed up tight, which was what I'd expected. As I was about to leave, the light came on, and I turned to see her standing in the middle of the space, just staring at me. Her eyes were wide again, and the fear was palpable, even through the windows. I pulled my hand up to kind of shade the window and my reflection, just in case she couldn't see me, and smiled.

"Who the fuck are you?" I heard a woman say from behind me.

I turned to look at her, and she was about the same age as the woman in the store, and I assumed she knew her, or maybe worked there.

"Pull your fucking hood off," she barked, shoving me. "You're gonna scare the shit out of everyone, you look like a thug."

She had a set of keys in her hand, and she opened the door and went to the woman inside. I could see she was talking but couldn't make out what she was saying. She grabbed the woman by the arm, as she crumbled to the floor, and started sobbing. I had no idea what the fuck was going on, but I didn't really even think. I opened the door to the shop and heard the woman who had come through the door before me saying something about it being okay, but then she saw me, the woman who was the owner, and screamed. It was louder than I'd ever heard, and the sheer terror in it made me realize that I might have done the wrong thing in walking in.

Scuttling backward and slipping in the wetness on the floor, she finally made traction and escaped through the back doorway and out of sight.

"What the fuck are you doing?" the woman who had yelled at me before asked. "Why are you fucking here? Who the fuck are you?"

The questions were rapid fire, without even a breath between them where I could get a word in. She was small, but the fire within her was way more than one would expect from such a small package.

"I just came by to check out the shop," I finally said when she'd stopped.

"We're not open," she barked, coming right up to me as if she could intimidate me with her small presence. "Get the fuck out."

"Is she gonna be okay?" I asked, concerned about the reaction she'd had.

"What the fuck do you care?" she shouted, raising her voice even more.

"Because I've obviously freaked her out," I said, glaring down at her. "I didn't mean to do that, but I can't help but think this is all my fault."

"Well, you're right there," she said, her voice down a little bit. "Now, will you get the fuck out of our store? I need to get her calmed down so we can get the shipment that's due any second."

As if summoned by the woman's words, a dude walked into the shop from the front door.

"Hey, Mai," he said. "Who's this? New hire?"

"Andre," she said. "This is some douche that freaked Skye out. He needs to leave but won't."

The way she said it seemed to imply that this dude was going to see me out.

"I'm just making sure she's okay," I said, my hands up in a surrender type of fashion.

"Dylan send you?" the guy asked.

"Who's that?" I asked.

"Come on," he said, clearly having more insight into the situation than I did. "Just admit that asshole sent you. It'll go easier on you."

"Nobody sent me," I said. "I honestly just came to check out the shop."

"At seven thirty in the morning on a Monday?" the woman, Mai, asked.

"Yeah," I said. "Why wouldn't I?"

"Just seems a bit too convenient," she said. "You stalking her?"

"What?" I asked. "No," I added, answering my own question, as well as hers. "I honestly wanted to come check the shop out. Also wanted to thank the owner for sending me the pizza in Houston over the weekend. She's the owner, right?"

"What the fuck are you talking about?" the guy asked.

"Hold up," Mai said. "What's your name?"

"John," I said.

"Your whole name," she pushed.

"Huffman," I said. "I'm John Huffman. Why?"

"Holy shit, it's you," she said, and went wide-eyed. "Don't go anywhere. I'll be right back."

She took off toward the back through the door the owner had gone through. I turned and looked at the dude, who looked just as confused as I felt.

"Why does your name mean something to her?" he asked after a couple of minutes.

"No clue," I replied.

"What was that about a pizza?" he asked.

"I got hit in a game," I said. "She sent a pizza to me in Houston the next day. I really wanted to check out her shop and thank her for doing that."

"Oh," he said, drawing the word out. "You're the baseball player."

"Yeah," I said.

"Don't you gotta play today?"

"I don't," I said. "Turns out the league doesn't like it when someone starts a fight, even when I wasn't the one who started it in the first place."

"Wait, so you were fired?"

"No," I said with a laugh. "Just a suspension for a few games. I'll be back with them next week when they get back to Seattle."

"Ah," he said, as if it all made sense to him.

"So," I said. "The blonde, with the short hair. She's the owner, right?"

"Skye?" he asked. "Oh, yeah. I mean, she worked here for a while, but then Miss Sylvie sold it to her. I think she's owned it for like five years or something."

I heard the chime of the door opening and turned to see a woman in her mid-forties step through the door.

"We're not open," Andre said.

"The door's unlocked," she replied. "Besides, I just need to grab something before work. I know the owner, so she'll be fine with me being in here right now."

She walked over toward the wall that had jars with stuff in them and began to fiddle with them.

"Mai," Andre shouted, and the woman looked at him.

The woman who had come in from the street came out from the back, clearly upset, but then noticed Andre pointing at the woman at the wall.

"Yeah, we're not open," she said. "You're gonna need to leave."

The woman turned around, and opened her mouth to speak, but Mai cut her off.

"Actually," she said, pulling herself up to her small height. "You've been banned from the store after the stunt you pulled the other day. Out."

Instead of doing what she was told, the woman turned fully around, holding one of the jars in her hand and threw it down on the ground, shattering it to tiny bits, the stuff inside going everywhere.

"What the actual fuck?" I asked.

"Shut up," she said, reaching for another jar.

I was on her before she even got her hand on the second jar, pinning her arms to her side. My considerable size was at my advantage at this point, because the woman wasn't nearly as small as Mai, but she was far smaller than any of the guys I'd thrown around the baseball field in my time.

"Rape!," she screamed, and I just laughed.

"Bitch, don't even," I said as I physically carried her to the door.

She was kicking and screaming, her heels hitting my shins, which just pissed me off even more. Andre was holding the door open for me, and I basically threw her out onto the street.

"If I ever catch you here again, you're gonna be sorry," I said.

"Help," she cried, and some of the folks on the street looked her way. "He just assaulted me, tried to rape me. Call the cops."

"Bitch, please," I said. "I'll call the cops right now and explain how you destroyed property in a store you've been banned from. You wanna go to jail today? 'Cause I can make that happen."

She was sobbing, but it was so obviously fake, it didn't even faze me. When she saw that I was serious, and that no one around her was taking her side, the tears dried up, she got herself on her feet, then began to storm off.

"Just wait for my review," she shouted before literally stomping down the sidewalk.

Once she was out of sight, I turned to look at Andre, who was trying desperately to keep from laughing, and finally failed. Inside the shop, I turned to see Mai was also laughing, and standing just in the doorway to the back was the owner.

"Hey," I said, looking at her. "Sorry I freaked you out."

# CHAPTER EIGHTEEN

*S*kye...

"Skye," I heard Mai call from the other side of the door. "Skye, babe, let me in."

I hadn't had a full-blown panic attack in months, but that dude was just too much for me. Nothing would have stopped me from getting out of there, except for my own fucking body, which thought it was a good idea to just piss myself, scream, then crab crawl out the store. Whoever the fuck he was, I didn't want anything to do with him.

"Come on, Skye," Mai said. "I promise it's fine."

I took a full breath and got up, my legs protesting from having been pressed against the door with such force. When I opened the door, she was smiling.

"You'll never guess who's here," she said, and I couldn't help but wonder what the fuck she was talking about. "It's that player," she added, as if it made all the sense in the world.

"Player?" I asked, and my voice sounded scratchy, even to my own ears.

"From the Cascades," she said, clearly not understanding why I wasn't getting what she was saying. "The one you sent the pizza to?"

"Wait, what?"

"Yeah," she said. "That's who that was. It's that Huffington dude."

"You mean Huffman?"

"Whatever," she said, waving her hand in front of her face. "You knew who I mean."

"I'm not understanding what you're saying," I said.

"The guy in the hoodie," she said. "The one who freaked you out? Yeah, that's him."

"Oh, God," I groaned, mortified.

"Don't worry," she said. "He's totally fine."

"What did you say to him?" I asked. "What did you do to him?"

Mai was known to be fierce, but she was so tiny that I didn't think she'd do anything that could hurt him.

"I just put him in his place," she said.

We heard a female voice from the front of the store, then heard Andre call her, so Mai headed out. I closed my eyes, trying to figure out exactly what the fuck he saw, and whether I even wanted to see him at all at this point. I needed to get changed, but the shipment was already here. I also needed to clean up the piss in the middle of the store.

That's when I heard the crash of glass hitting the tiled floor. I heard screaming, and a deep voice so full of authority that I wanted to do whatever he said, even though I didn't recognize who was speaking. The woman was screaming, the guy was talking, and I could hear Mai shouting something as well.

I stepped to the doorway that led from the back to the front just as he tossed the woman out the door. She was crying and saying he assaulted her, but he was calm, and suggested that he could call the cops if she wanted. Instead of that, though, the bitch got up, and that's when I recognized her from the other morning when we first got that rush.

"Hey," he said, and his voice was deep, but soft in a way, too. "Sorry I freaked you out."

"Thanks," I said, but it came out almost a squeak. I cleared my throat and tried again. "Thanks," I said, this time with much better results.

"Lemme help you clean up," he said, moving toward me.

Instinct made me back up, and he stopped.

"You want me to go?"

"No," I said, almost shouting the word. "No," I tried again, this time not nearly as loud. "You just don't need to clean up. We got it."

"I mean, I kinda started this whole fiasco," he said, stuffing his hands in his jeans pockets and shrugging his shoulders. "Seems fitting I should clean up the mess I made."

*The mess.* Oh, God, I peed on the floor. And he's standing right next to the puddle.

"No, no," I said, moving toward him, hoping he'd back up and away.

Instead, I stepped in the puddle and slipped. He caught me, as if it was no big deal, and held me as I got my footing again.

"You good?" he asked, and he smelled like all man.

I wanted to tell him I was fine, that I didn't need his help, but those strong arms around me, that hard chest under my hand, just made me want to not move.

"Ahem," Mai said, clearing her throat, and I stepped back and away from him, blushing all the way to my roots.

"We good to unload?" Andre asked, and I looked around the shop.

"Um, yeah," I said. "Just put everything over in that corner."

I pointed to the corner that was away from the mess that had been made, then looked at Mai.

"You got this?" I asked. "I gotta go change."

"Yeah," she said. "I got it, you go."

"Thank you," I said to the man in my shop.

"No problem," he replied.

I turned and headed back out to the hallway that led to the door, which in turn led to the stairs to my apartment. Running up the stairs, I put my hand in my pocket. My keys weren't there.

"Fuck," I muttered and headed back down the stairs.

When I got to the door to the shop, it was closed, and of course, locked. I knocked and heard someone come. Mai opened the door and handed me my keys without saying anything. I took them, smiled at her, then headed back up the stairs.

I kicked off my shoes as I went into the bathroom. Unbuttoning my jeans, I pushed them, and my panties, down, then sat on the toilet to shove them the rest of the way off, taking my socks with them. Everything was wet, and it was just so embarrassing. I wasn't even sure I wanted to go back down there, but I had a business to run, and it certainly wasn't going to do it all on its own.

Hopping in the shower after pulling my shirt and bra off, I turned the water on and quickly rinsed myself off. I didn't have time for a full shower, but I could get most of it at least somewhat cleaned up. Toweling off, I went back into my room and pulled out new clothes, getting dressed quickly. As I went to untie my shoes, I realized they were soaked, so I was gonna have to put on something else. I went to my closet and pulled out a pair of Chucks and slipped them on. Not the most comfortable, but they'd just have to do.

I tossed my clothes and shoes into the tub and would deal with them later. Right now, I had to get down and finish my job. I'd already wasted enough time, and the order was gonna be huge, so it would take a lot more time than normal to get it sorted. Locking my door, I headed back down the stairs and keyed my way back into the shop. I turned the corner from the hallway and blinked. Mai was talking with Andre as they put the rest of the boxes in the corner, and the baseball player was just finishing sweeping up the mess the woman made when she threw the jar on the floor.

"Hey," he said as I walked in. "Mai said to go ahead and just toss all of this. She said you couldn't sell it now that it'd been on the floor, and with the glass mixed in."

"Yeah," I said. "Thanks. You didn't have to do that."

"I know," he said, his voice that deep baritone that vibrates along your bones. "I didn't want you to have to deal with it, especially since it's my fault it happened."

"Totally not your fault," I said.

"We're just gonna have to agree to disagree," he said. "Now that this is cleaned up, anything else you want me to do?"

He'd asked the last as he dumped the remnants of the jar and tea from the floor into the trash can that they'd pulled out from behind the counter. I hadn't seen which one was busted, but it really didn't matter. I would have to replace both the tea and the jar at some point, but now was not the time. Looking around the small space, I noticed that the puddle I'd left in the middle of the floor had been cleaned up, and I really hoped it hadn't been him that had done it. I don't know that I'd ever live that down.

"I'm pretty sure we've got it," I said in answer to his question. "Can I make you some tea?"

"Not really my thing," he said as he leaned the broom up against the counter.

"I think I can change your mind," I said, knowing that most men didn't drink tea because they'd never been given a good cup. "Do you trust me?"

"You do know how to find a good pizza," he said with a smile, and those bright teeth were there, just as they had been under the hood earlier.

I shuddered as I took in a breath, then moved toward my office to heat water in my electric kettle. It wasn't the absolute best way to do it, but it worked in a pinch. Once it was set to warm, I went back to the store.

"Anything else you need, Skye?" Andre asked.

"As long as you got everything in the order here, I think we're good," I replied.

"I've got the invoice," Mai said. "It's all here."

"Great," I replied. "Thanks, man."

"No worries," he replied. "Hey, nice to meet you, dude."

"Thanks," the player said. "Good to meet you, too."

Mai turned and grabbed the hand truck to move some of the stock to the storeroom in the back, and brushed past us, giving me the whole eyebrow wiggle once she was behind the man.

"We haven't officially been introduced," he said. "I'm John."

"Nice to meet you," I said, taking the hand he'd held out to me. "I'm Skye, owner and operator of Darling Teas."

"It is my utmost pleasure to finally meet you," he said, that voice rumbling straight through our joined hands, up my arm, and down through my body, causing a throb in intimate points I wasn't ready to acknowledge.

"Just my imagination," I mumbled, but he must have caught what I said, because he asked, "What?"

"Sorry," I said. "I tend to talk to myself on occasion."

"I get it," he said. "So, how long have you owned this shop?"

"It'll be seven years this summer," I said, smiling at the memory of my first full day as the owner.

"Were you twelve?" I blinked at him, confused by the question. "Because you don't look old enough to have owned it that long, that's all."

He must have confused my look as criticism or something because he was quick to add the extra sentence.

"Oh, no," I said. "Although, I've worked here since I was just older than that. I've never actually worked anywhere else, except my grand-parents' stalls."

"Your grandparents have shops here, too?" he asked. "Must be like a family business kind of thing, huh?"

"You could say that," I said. "My grandparents have been here since they first got married, working at my Grampy's parent's flower stall. It's been passed down through the generations. My uncle owns it now."

"Oh yeah?" he asked.

"The whole Market is basically one big family," I said. "We all watch out for each other. Even folks here on Post Alley are sort of extended family. Miss Sylvie was like a great-aunt to me, and when she decided to hang up her hat, she offered the shop to me. It really was just the best thing I could do."

"Kinda like a team," he said. "We all watch out for our teammates, having their backs."

"Yeah," I said, nodding at his understanding. "Speaking of which, why are you here?"

"I live here," he said.

"I meant, here in Seattle," I explained. "Aren't you guys back East somewhere?"

"Not me," he said, but didn't expand.

"Do you mind if I ask why?"

"I was a stupid fucker," he said, then added, "Sorry 'bout that. I was stupid and ended up with a suspension."

"From when you got hit?"

"Yup," he said, popping the last letter.

"But that wasn't your fault," I complained.

"Preaching to the choir, darlin'," he said.

"Skye?" Mai asked, having come back from the storage room.

"Yeah," I said. "What's up?"

"Just making sure I was good to come out," she said, her smile full of mischief.

"Of course you can," I said. "Oh, hey, you guys meet officially?"

"After she cussed me out," he said. "Told me I was an asshole and was going to scare the shit out of people with me looking like a thug."

I laughed. I couldn't help it.

"Mai," I said. "You shouldn't be talking like that. What would your mother say?"

"She'd ask me why I didn't knock him on his ass," she said, hand on her hip.

"Not gonna lie, that's exactly what she'd say," I said.

"Your water's hot," she said, throwing a thumb over her shoulder.

"Oh, right," I said, heading that direction. "Gonna make him a cuppa, see if I can get him to like it."

"You doing the good stuff?" she asked.

"Of course," I replied, ducking through the doorway.

"Mai," I shouted, looking back into the shop. "You want some?"

"Not today," she said. "I already had coffee."

"Suit yourself," I said, then continued into the office.

I pulled down a mug, grabbed a tea ball, and scooped some of the

Jump Start blend I had made up. It wasn't always enough for me, but most folks found it worked well to get them going in the morning. Some even swore by it more than coffee, which in Seattle could be construed as fighting words.

Normally I would brew a whole pot, but I wasn't in need of this today, so I just did enough for one cup. Placing the ball into the pot, I poured the water over it, then put the lid on for it to steep. Taking the mug and pot with me, I headed back into the shop.

# CHAPTER NINETEEN

*J*ohn...
When she'd gone fully through the doorway, I turned to the other woman.

"I don't drink tea," I said to her. "I don't want to upset her or make her think I don't appreciate her work, but I'm afraid I will."

"Trust me," she said. "You'll like this. Do you drink coffee?"

"Does a bear shit in the woods?"

"Then you'll like this," she said. "Try it without cream or sugar first, just so you get the full taste. Then, if you need to, you can add the other things, but you probably won't."

"You're sure?"

I wasn't normally so sensitive to how I came across to someone else, as it was usually their issue. But this was different. This was something that seemed important to me, like I really needed to be considerate.

"This shit'll make you swear off coffee altogether," she said, and I looked at her, wide-eyed. "Don't you dare say that in front of any coffee shop, but it's true. I like the taste of coffee, but this is seriously like coffee on steroids or something. It's like she's infused it with some sort of magic or something."

"What magic are you spouting off about now?" Skye asked as she came out from the back, a steaming mug on a small tray, a couple of other cups on it as well.

"Your good shit," Mai said. "You put some sort of magic into it, I swear."

"Not magic," she responded. "Just science."

"Beg to differ," Mai said. "It's gotta have something special, 'cause that shit will keep you awake for days if you drink more than a cup of it."

"Shut up," Skye replied. "You're gonna scare him."

I watched as the women bantered back and forth about the supposed magical powers of tea, but I could smell it, and it was something I couldn't describe. There was a floral scent of some sort, but it wasn't super strong, and I couldn't tell anything other than that. Then there was the smell of the earth, like the rich greens and woods back home. Added in there was tobacco, which just confused me, because I never thought of that having a smell, but it was like a good cigar before you lit it. There were other scents in there as well, but those were the strongest ones I could identify.

"It's still steeping," she said, turning to me. "Give it about five minutes, and it should be ready for you to try. Please don't be scared to say you hate it. It can be an acquired taste, but I swear I love it, and it's perfect if you're not in the mood for coffee."

"I'll keep an open mind," I said.

"Seriously," she said, looking me straight on. "If you hate it, I won't be upset. I just want you to try it."

"I promise I'll be honest," I said, lying through my teeth. There was no way I would tell her it was awful, even if it made me want to gag.

"This isn't a traditional English tea," she continued. "It comes from South America, and it was something that I added to the store after Miss Sylvie passed away. She was very much a purist when it came to tea and is probably haunting me as we speak because I dared to bring in anything that wasn't from England originally."

"Bullshit," Mai said. "She would have loved it, and all the other ones you've brought in. She was all about exploring the unknown. Why do you think she started the ghost tours?"

Skye looked at the other woman, clearly taking what she said into consideration, and then nodded.

"You know what?" she asked. "You're right," she said, responding to her own question. "She really did embrace all things new and exciting, and she would probably love the fact that I figured out a way to compete with the coffee companies in the area."

"There you go," Mai said with a smile. "Now, do you want me to start filling up the jars or what?"

"First," Skye said. "Which one broke? I need to see if I have a replacement jar in the back."

"You don't," Mai said. "I already looked."

"Shit," Skye said. "Well, I guess we're just gonna have to improvise for a bit."

"I could go grab something," I said. "If you tell me what you need and where to get it."

Skye looked at me as if she'd forgotten I was there, confusion on her face.

"Seriously," I said. "I have nothing to do today, so put me to work."

"Umm," she hummed, insecurity on her face. "I mean..."

She stopped, and it was clear she wasn't sure what to make of my offer.

"How about this," I said. "I take a picture of the jars that are there, you tell me where you got them—"

"I bought them online," she interrupted.

"Somewhere around here has to have something that'll work," I said.

She looked at me, and I could see the wheels turning inside her mind, trying to figure something out, but what it was, I wasn't sure. Instead of pushing, I decided to wait her out, let her come to her own conclusions on what she wanted. It wasn't my store, wasn't any skin off my back if something didn't work right, so I had to let her make that decision.

"There's that store at the mall at South Center," Mai said. "I'm sure they have something like this."

Skye turned to look at her, then back at me.

"You good with that?" she asked.

"Sure," I said. "Let me take a picture so I know what to get."

"Yeah, sure," she said.

I walked over to the jars that were still there and pulled one out of the little row they were in, holding it in one hand, and took a picture. This would help me know the size, too.

"How many do you want me to get?" I asked.

"Oh, just the one," she said. "I'll do an order for some more online today so I have some extras."

"If you're sure," I said.

"I am," she replied. "Here, let me give you some money for it."

"I got it," I said. "Consider it my reimbursement for the one that was broken on my account."

"It's not your fault," she argued.

"Like I said," I returned. "We're gonna have to agree to disagree on that one."

"Skye," Mai said, and we both looked over to her. "He's gotta have some go juice before we send him out into the big, bad world."

"Oh, shit," she said. "I forgot about that."

I had forgotten as well, but honestly wasn't sure I wanted to try it.

"Just take a sip," she said, obviously reading my expression. "If you hate it, it's totally fine. But give it a shot. Please?"

Her face was full of hope and a promise of things that might come after, and that was the only reason I took the drink. It had cooled down some, what with the time that had passed as we discussed the broken jar, and its replacement. The smell that came from the mug she'd handed me was strong, but it was better than when she first came in. The flavors must have mixed together or something. I took a tentative sip, unsure what to expect, and was surprised with how smooth it was.

"Well?" she asked after I'd had a moment to taste it.

"It's actually pretty good," I said. "Not at all what I expected."

The smile lit up her face, and I'd have lied completely just to see that. But it was the god's honest truth. I took another sip, letting it sit in my mouth for a moment, and it was even better the second time.

"Told ya," Mai said, her smirk one full of mischief rather than the pride that was on Skye's face.

"Wish I had a go-cup to take it with me," I said.

"Oh, I got you," Skye said, and turned to go into her office. She came back with one of those travel mugs that you see all over the Market and took the mug from me, pouring its contents into the other one. "Just bring it back," she said, handing it over to me after she'd put the top on it. "It's one of my favorite ones."

"I will protect it with my life," I said.

"It's not that special," Skye replied with a laugh.

"I'll be back soon," I said and turned to head out the door.

"Thank you," she said as she followed me to the door.

"Absolutely," I replied.

I wasn't sure how I was gonna get to or from the mall, but I'd figure it out on my own. Not having my car was a serious drag, but I'd make it happen. I had to.

# CHAPTER TWENTY

*S* kye...
"Oh my God," I said after he'd left and I'd locked the door back up.

"He's fucking hot," Mai said.

"Tell me about it," I replied. "And he's super nice, and really just a kind guy. I hope it isn't just a front or something, but it doesn't seem to be."

"I don't think it is," she said. "He was really upset when you were gone. Like, he felt really bad that he'd freaked you out, and even worse when that bitch came in and threw the jar."

"Yeah," I said. "What the hell happened there?"

"Bitch walked in like she owned the place," Mai said. "Said she knew the owner, walked over to the jar that had the most in it, and then got pissed when we told her to leave, so threw it on the ground. Dude straight up threw her ass out. It was pretty epic."

"That's nuts," I said. "I just don't understand some people."

"Girl, same," she said.

"Let's get shit sorted," I said. "We can fill the hole when he gets back, but in the meantime, we do have other work to do."

"You got it, boss," she said.

We figured out what was needing to be filled, what we had for extras like the tea balls, cups, teapots, and such, and where we could fit in the new product that Milligan Fields had given us to try out. It was an all-out stocking insanity until we finally had to actually open the shop. Like that first day, there was a line up the block, but thankfully, they were all nice folks. I did keep an eye out for the bitch, but she didn't show her face again, thankfully.

By the time my stomach started growling, the crowd had slowed down a bit, and I wondered whether I'd have time to sneak out and grab something for lunch. Just as I was pondering where I wanted to go, he walked in, a big ass bag on each arm.

"Got a few," he said as he came to the counter. "I know you said you only wanted one, but I figured this way you'd have extra, just in case."

He set the bags on the floor next to the counter and I looked in. There were six jars, three in each bag, and damn near identical to the ones we had on the shelves. The seals were white instead of black, and they didn't have the stickers on the front that I could put the name of the tea on, but all of that was totally fine. He'd come through, and with flying colors, too.

"Those are perfect," I said. "Thank you so much. How much do I owe you?"

"Nothing," he said. "It's my pleasure to replace the one that was broken, and to give you some extras for next time."

"I feel bad that you paid for them," I said.

"Trust me," he said. "It's not that big of a deal."

"Well, thank you, again," I said. "Can I buy you lunch as a way of repayment?"

"No," he said, and it was so serious. "But I'll get you lunch, just because."

"You don't have to—"

"It's not an issue," he said. "Please, let me take you to lunch. I'd like to actually get to know you rather than just messaging through that social media app."

I blinked at him, confused as to what he was saying.

"Go," Mai said. "Get something next door. I'll text if it gets crazy."

I glared at her, but she just gave me that shit-eating grin she got when she knew she was pushing me into something I wanted but wasn't willing to do on my own.

"Thanks," he said to her, as if it were a done deal. "Shall we?"

He stuck his elbow out, as if it were a hundred or more years ago, and I needed someone to escort me everywhere I wanted to go.

"Sure," I said, not taking his arm on purpose.

He smiled, but didn't protest, which was honestly good. If he'd made a big deal about it, I'd have stayed put, given him cash from the drawer, and kicked his ass out. I had learned a thing or two in the couple of years since I'd kicked Dylan to the curb, and the biggest one was that I was my own person, and only I could decide if I wanted to do something or not. At least therapy from the state had helped with that.

We stepped into the Irish pub next door, him holding the door open for me, and it was dark, which was normal, but after being outside, even for just the couple of minutes it took us to get there, it made it hard to see.

"Welcome in," the bartender said. "Sit wherever you want."

John held out his hand, indicating that I should choose where we should sit, which was a nice change from what I'd been used to. I walked over to a table that was close enough to the door that I could get out if I needed but tucked far enough back as to not have the breeze from the door should it open. I sat with my back against the wall, leaving the chair across from me open. The tables were small here, which would be nice if you were on a date. This wasn't a date, though. This was just him feeling sorry for me and taking pity on me.

"What'cha thinking?" he asked, pulling me from my mind.

"Just that I haven't eaten here in a while," I said. "Used to come more often, but work is taking up more time lately."

"I was here last night," he said. "They have really good food."

"So that was you," I said, the words coming out in a rush.

"Yeah," he said casually. "I saw you up above your shop. Is that where you live?"

*Fuck.* I didn't want him to know where I lived.

"It's one of the storage spaces," I lied.

"Looks more like an apartment," he said. "At least from what I could see from the street. Granted, it was kind of an odd angle to look up into the place, but still."

He said it without even looking at me, as if it didn't really even matter, but the fact that he saw me, in my apartment, with my window open, was really freaking me out.

"Hey," he said, looking at me. "You okay?"

I nodded, but too fast. I could feel my chest tightening up, my heart pounding in my ears, my vision closing in around me.

"Breathe," he said, his hand on my arm on the table. "Breathe with me."

He was showing me, slowly taking a breath in, and then letting it out slowly, over and over, again and again, until I was mimicking him with my own breathing.

"There you go," he said with a smile. "I'm safe, I promise."

"I don't know you," I said, then clamped my hand over my mouth.

"I know," he said. "But I want you to know I'm safe. I won't hurt you. I promise."

I wanted to believe him, and the earnestness I saw in his eyes was begging me to, but I just couldn't risk it. I'd trusted Dylan and he'd broken me. When I finally gotten free of him, he just broke me further. Now that I'd built myself back up, though, and was actually feeling like I had made great progress, and that maybe I'd start looking to date at some point.

"Not asking you to marry me," he said, and I cut my eyes to him, only to see a smirk along his lips.

I laughed. I couldn't help it. And honestly, it felt good. Like, really good.

"Probably should know a little about each other before we get there," I said, just as the waiter came to the table.

"You guys know what you want?" he asked. "Or do you want menus?"

"I'm gonna have the same thing I had last night," he said. "But I'm not sure about my beautiful date."

I blushed. I honestly couldn't remember anyone ever saying I was beautiful. Certainly not Dylan. Maybe Grammy when I was little, but in the last several years, nah. That wasn't something anyone called me.

"I'm having Bangers and Mash," I said. "It's been a minute, and it sounds good."

"Oh," John said. "What's that?"

"Sausage and potatoes," I said. "Super good."

"That actually sounds good," he said. "Make it two."

"You want soup?" the waiter asked.

"Not for me," I said.

"No thanks," John said.

"Drinks?"

"Water for me," I said.

"Same," John said.

The waiter walked away to put our orders in, and I turned to look at my lunch companion. He was smiling at me, just a hint of it on his lips, but it was there. I shifted in my seat, uncomfortable under his scrutiny. I didn't like feeling like I was in the zoo, a specimen to be examined. Dylan would look at me like I was the prize he won for a shooting game of some sort, but this somehow felt different. No, John wasn't looking at me like he wanted to control me, or like he wanted to punish me. This had a much different feel. Like he wanted to figure out what made me tick, what got me going or something. Like he was fascinated with me.

"Would you stop looking at me like that?" I hissed, trying desperately to not draw any more attention to myself.

"I like looking at you," he said, as if that explained everything.

"Well, I don't like it," I said, leaning forward, trying to put some sort of power behind my words, when in all reality, I had absolutely no power whatsoever.

His smile got a bit bigger and he asked, "Why not?"

"I just don't, okay?"

"Okay," he said, but didn't stop looking at me.

I let out a frustrated breath, blowing my bangs up and off my forehead.

"You look better with short hair," he said, and it was just so out of left field I didn't even know what to say.

The waiter came back with our waters and set them on the table between us, then walked away. I took a sip of my water, looking into the cubes of ice as they clanged around in the glass.

"You looked sad when your hair was long," he said, and it was quieter than the previous statement, which made me look up at him.

"What?" I asked, confused at what he was saying.

"On the website," he said. "There are pictures of you with long hair. But you don't look like you're very happy in them. It's when you cut your hair that you really look like you got your spark back."

I was again confused by what he was saying. Nothing made sense, and I wasn't sure whether I wanted to understand him.

# CHAPTER TWENTY-ONE

*J*ohn...

"On the website," I said. "There are pictures of you with long hair. But you don't look like you're very happy in them. It's when you cut your hair that you really look like you got your spark back."

I had no idea why I'd said it, but it was true. Did I want to know all her secrets? Absolutely. Did I have any right? None whatsoever. She was taken by surprise with my question, for sure, and I wasn't sure she was gonna answer it. But then she did.

"I was in a bad place," she said, and it was so soft I would've missed it if I weren't paying attention.

"I'm sorry," I said.

Not much else you could say to something like that, but it was what it was.

"Not your fault," she said.

"Still sorry it happened to you," I replied. "I know I didn't do anything whenever it was, but that doesn't mean I can't feel bad it happened."

She blinked, like what I said made no sense, which, honestly, I wasn't sure it did. Still, I didn't want her hurt, which is what it sounded like happened.

"Thanks," she said, finally, after mulling my words over.

The waiter brought over our food right then, and she was right in that it was sausage and potatoes, but it was the biggest hunk of sausage I'd ever seen, and it smelled amazing.

"I'll be back with some water," he said after setting the plates down, then pulling a couple of bundles out of his pocket. "Anything else you guys want?"

"Actually," I said. "Mind if I get a beer?"

I directed the question to her, and she looked at me like I was crazy.

"You can have whatever you want," she said.

"Want one, too?" I asked.

"No," she said, almost before I finished my question.

"If you'd rather I didn't, I'm good with that," I said. "Didn't want to bring up any bad memories."

Again, she blinked at me as if what I said made no sense, then she smiled, and my God, it was the most beautiful thing I'd seen.

"You go ahead," she said. "They've got great beer."

"A pale ale, please," I said to the waiter, who went to fill my request. "I know it's not something I should say to any woman, but you really are beautiful when you smile."

Even though it was dark, she blushed, and it just enhanced her beauty. I couldn't help but smile at her. If I could make her smile more, I'd do whatever it took to do so.

"Thanks," she said, again quietly. "Now eat, or I'm gonna feel uncomfortable eating by myself."

The waiter brought my beer, and then refilled her water, which she'd been sipping throughout our conversation. Mine had remained untouched, mostly because I couldn't think of doing anything other than stare at her. Instead of making it awkward or making some sort of crass joke about her eating a sausage, and offering her my own for later, I opted to try to be a gentleman. I wasn't one, that's for fucking sure, but I could play one on occasion.

Cutting into the sausage, I stuck the bite in my mouth, and damn near died. I thought the steak the night before was good, but this was out of this world. With as much traveling as I've done with the team, I'd had amazing food everywhere, but this was absolutely top-notch. Like, I would come here every chance I got, and would suggest it to all the guys looking for good food.

"You okay over there?" she asked, and when I opened my eyes and looked at her, she had this smirk that told me she knew exactly what was going on in my head.

Once I'd swallowed, I replied, "Trying to figure out how to be able to eat this every day and not end up looking like the Goodyear Blimp."

"Yeah," she said. "They do good food here."

"For sure," I said, then took a drink of my beer. "You sure you don't want one?"

"Water's good for me," she said, and there was that hint of fear, but it didn't seem quite as devastating now.

"Suit yourself," I said. "You decide you want one later, just order it. I'm good for it."

"Thanks," she said, but ducked her head and continued to eat her food.

We sat in silence, which wasn't as awkward as I thought it might be, as we ate. I, of course, finished mine, but she kind of picked at hers. Eating some, but not much. I wondered if there was some trauma to go along with eating and drinking, or if she was just nervous.

"You want a box?" the waiter asked when he came back to refill her water.

"Please," she said, her tone quiet.

"Dessert?" he asked.

I looked at her, but she wouldn't look up.

"Give us a minute?"

"Sure," he said. "I'll be back with the box in a minute and you can let me know then."

Once he was gone, I reached my hand out and took hers, but she quickly pulled it away, tucking it into her lap. I left my hand open on the table, as an offering.

"Up to you on dessert," I said. "I could eat, but don't need to."

She alternated looking at my hand and up at my face, like she was trying to decide whether it was a snare sitting in front of her, or an offering of kindness, which for me, it was the latter, but I could see her wheels turning, and assumed she thought it was the former.

"I won't hurt you," I said, low so only she could hear me.

Shuddering, she raised her eyes to me, and they were glossed over, like she was looking at me, but seeing something completely different.

"I'm not him," I said, making a guess at the issues she'd had. "I won't ever hurt you. You're in charge, what you say goes, and I'm just along for the ride. You say fuck off, and off I'll fuck."

Her eyes were wide, clearly not understanding how I was guessing her secrets. Honestly, though, it was just from understanding guys, because we were absolutely horrible, for the most part. Sure, we all had our good sides, but as a gender, we fucking sucked. All I had to do was look at Hennings. Before he met Fi, he was the worst. I swear he fucked anything that would let him. I wasn't like that. Never had been.

No, if I was gonna be with a woman, there better be some emotion behind it, and I could see all the emotion in Skye. She was someone I could see being with for the long haul. Like the way Jonathan and Lucy were with each other, that's what I wanted. Something that would stand the test of time, through thick and thin, forever and ever, Amen.

"Why do I believe you?" she asked.

"'Cause I'm telling the truth," I said. "I don't believe in lying, even for convenience. It's fucked up, and not the way to be a decent human being."

She looked back down at my hand, then up at my face again. I tried like everything to put into my face the truth of what I said. There were times I was a fucking animal, but it usually happened between the chalk lines on the field, and only when someone was fucking with me or my boys.

"We decide on dessert?" the waiter asked, shattering the fragile moment we were building.

"No," Skye said.

"Just the check," I said, pulling my hand back to my lap.

He set the box he'd brought for her food down on the table and cleared my plate before heading back to the bar to get our tab. By the time he was back, she'd pushed her food into the paper receptacle and I'd pulled out my wallet.

"I'll be your cashier," he said. "Any time you're ready."

I glanced at the bill, and seeing as it was under fifty bucks, I just put a hundred on the bill and told him to keep the change.

"That's a big tip," she said, sliding off the bench against the wall.

"It's just money," I replied. "I have plenty."

I stood with her, letting her go past me toward the front door. I pushed it open when we got there, guiding her out with a hand at the small of her back. It was an intimate gesture, one I didn't usually do, and normally wouldn't push on someone, but it felt right in the moment. Like, she needed that comfort, and to know I was as good as my word, that I wouldn't hurt her.

# CHAPTER TWENTY-TWO

*S*kye...

His hand was warm at my back, and I wanted to believe his words, wanted to trust what I saw in his eyes, but he was a man, and every man I'd ever met had some ulterior motive. Dylan was the worst, by far, but even before him, guys were after one thing, and that was what I could do for them. Whether it was what my business offered them or what my body did, it was all the same. I was only a commodity to be traded for pennies on the dollar. Hell, even my dad had wanted to use me to further his own business. Thankfully, Grampy and Grammy were on to his bullshit and helped me do what I wanted.

It was nice to think he'd be true to his word, that he wouldn't hurt me. But I couldn't trust that. Not now, and probably not ever. No, he had something to gain by being with me. I just had to figure out whether it would be worth it if I wanted to test those waters.

I'd be lying if I said I wasn't attracted to him, physically. I mean, that blond hair with that little curl that came down on his brow, looked soft, and I desperately wanted to see if it was. His chest, even covered by the hoodie he was wearing, was broad and seemed to be everything a woman could want. I'd seen him on the television, and baseball pants didn't lie, so he had an ass that would be great to grab, to hold on to as I pulled him into me.

God, I was getting wet just thinking about it, and that wasn't like me. I didn't fantasize like this. I just did what felt good, but it had been a while, like entirely too long, and I was sure that my little toy was going to get a workout tonight, so long as I could hold out until then.

"Hey," Mai said as we walked back into the shop. "You guys are back soon."

"We ate," I said. "And I've even got leftovers."

"For me?" she asked.

"Did you want something?" he asked, his hand still on my back. "'Cause I can run over and grab something for you if you want."

"Aw, that's sweet," she said. "But, no, I don't really need anything. Pop came by with some lunch for me, and it's been dead here, so I had plenty of time to eat it."

"If you're sure," he said, and the heat from his body was radiating into me.

He was close, like too close, but I didn't want to move away. What I wanted to do was push back into it, into him, and feel his whole body against me. I could smell his cologne around me, as if it were wrapping me up. I cleared my throat and went to step away, but he stayed with me, like he didn't want to let me go or something.

"You probably have to go to the stadium," I said, trying desperately to get some distance between us.

"Actually, no," he said. "Suspension starts today, so I'm here until the team is back with nothing to do, and nowhere to go."

I'd gotten the space, making my move to stand behind the counter, setting my leftovers on the top. I tried to calm my body, make it stop the fantasies I was seeing. Him pulling the hoodie off, him sliding his hands up my sides, pressing me against the wall, his whole body against me. I licked my lips, pulling the bottom one into my mouth, and his eyes widened and he shifted his stance. At least I wasn't alone in my attraction. I couldn't help but smirk, seeing him uncomfortable.

"You two wanna go?" Mai asked, and we both turned to look at her. "I mean, the sexual tension is thick."

"Mai," I said, slapping her arm.

John shifted, then looked at the floor. Guess we weren't hiding it from anyone, least of all ourselves. Just then, the door opened and a customer walked in.

"Welcome in," I said, going around the counter and past John to get to her. "How can I help you today?"

"Are you the owner?" she asked.

"I am," I said. "What can I do for you?"

"I wanted to do a piece on your shop," she said, holding out a business card. "I saw your post, and the way it blew up, and I wondered if you'd mind talking to me about that, and about what you were looking for with that post."

"Fuck," I heard John whisper behind me.

"I really wasn't looking for anything," I said honestly. "I saw someone get hurt and thought I'd do something nice for him."

He was right behind me, and I could feel him trying desperately to become small, to hide from this woman to keep her off his scent.

"It seems to have done something good for you, too," she said, pushing for more information.

"I mean," I said, then stopped. This was something that might help my business, and I'd be stupid to turn this away. "Honestly, I had no idea it was gonna blow up the way it did. I just wanted to do something nice, especially when the whole city he was in seemed to be against him. All it cost me was the price of a pizza and delivery. It isn't that expensive to be kind to people."

"Well, your story is surely something different," she said. "I've heard of guerrilla marketing, but this takes it to a whole new level."

"Yeah," I said. "Not what it was meant to be, but glad it seems to have boosted my sales. I'm just happy he was appreciative of the gesture."

"Have you spoken to him?" she asked.

I wanted to grab him and shove him in her face, but I understood the need for anonymity, so I just said, "We've chatted a bit in the app. He sent me thanks, and I wished him well in the next game."

"Too bad it didn't turn into something more," she said.

"I'm just glad he appreciated the gesture," I said. "That's all I was looking for."

"Do you mind if I take a couple of shots of you in the shop?" she asked.

"Maybe a little later," I said. "I'm not really camera ready. I'd feel very awkward having my picture taken today. Thanks for the offer, though."

"Can I take a few shots of your product?" she asked. "Maybe one of the front of the store? I'll make sure no one is in them."

"I mean, I guess," I said. "But I appreciate you not taking pictures of me, or my employees."

"I'll keep it to inanimate objects only," she said.

"Thanks," I said, then turned and pushed John through the doorway that led to the office, following behind him. "Mai, you good?" I asked before ducking through the doorway myself.

"I got it," she said, and the smile told me everything I needed to know. She knew I was trying to keep John from being caught, and that I was trying to not make this into the actual story.

I kept pushing him until he was in front of the door to my office, and he twisted the knob to let himself in.

"I'm so sorry," I said once I was in the space and the door was closed.

"Not your doing," he said. "But I appreciate your sensitivity to my not needing to be in the media's eye right now."

"I can't even imagine," I said.

"It's not always fun," he replied. "Sometimes you can use it to your advantage, but then other times it's just annoying."

The small space was taken up by my desk on one wall, the safe on the other, and a small sofa next to the door. It was almost too small but had always been plenty big enough. Of course, I'd never had anyone else in there with me, and John was an imposing man of enormous size, and it was close and intimate, and almost too much. Almost.

"How long do you think we'll have to stay in here?" he asked, and it was almost like he wanted to get out.

"Mai will let us know when she's gone," I said. "Unless she wants to torture me and leave me in here until we're closed."

He licked his lip, and a storm rolled through his eyes. I tried not to think about how close we were, how close he was to me, and how much I wanted to reduce the space and get right next to him. Yeah, it had been way too long since I'd had any kind of good contact.

# CHAPTER TWENTY-THREE

*J*ohn...

I wanted to step closer, to press her against the door at her back, but I knew she was scared, and I didn't want to push too fast. Her eyes were wide, her pupils dilated, and she was breathing heavy and shallow.

"How long do you think we'll have to stay in here?" I asked.

"Mai will let us know when she's gone," she said. "Unless she wants to torture me and leave me in here until we're closed."

"Why would she do that?" I asked.

"She thinks I need to get back out in the dating pool," she said, and blushed, turning her face away from me.

"Hey," I said, reaching out. She jumped, so I stopped. "Talk to me."

"You're a stranger," she said, her eyes still turned to the floor.

"I feel like we've gotten to know each other pretty well the last few days," I countered. "The long talks we've had through messages, the things we've shared. I think we know each other better than you think."

She didn't move, but she'd slowed her breathing some. I tried again, reaching out again and this time she didn't flinch. I touched her chin, tilting her head up to look me in the eyes.

"I know it's hard to trust," I said. "Especially when you've been hurt. And by my guess, you've been hurt pretty badly. I'll wait, let you drive this bus, but I want you to know that I'm a safe person. You can come to me and tell me anything, and whatever it is, I'll take it all in stride and do what I can to make it better."

"Why do I believe you?" she asked, and it was pushed out on a breath.

"I don't know," I said. "But you can. It's hard to push past the broken pieces. Trust me. My friends have some broken ladies, and I've watched how they learned to trust again. I feel like I've learned a few things from them, and hopefully I'll be able to help you get over that fear. If you'll let me."

Taking a deep breath, she closed her eyes, and I was afraid I'd lost her. But then, she opened her eyes and nodded. Her smile was tentative, but the fact that she hadn't said no, that she was willing to give this a chance, was more than I could have hoped for. I couldn't help but smile, which was a rare thing.

"You should smile more often," she said, her smile growing with each word.

I laughed and she jumped, but then relaxed again. There was a knock at the door, and she jumped one more time, then turned. I couldn't help myself, I had to take a peek at her ass, because the little moments I got to see it, I knew I wanted more.

"She's gone," Mai said through the space in the door.

"Thanks," Skye replied.

She was almost up against me, and I wanted to move that tiny bit forward, but didn't want to freak her out.

"You good if I head out?"

"Sure," she said. "You coming back tomorrow?"

"Yeah," the woman on the other side of the door said.

I couldn't see the other woman, but the way Skye was shaking her head, I was sure that she was asking something so low I couldn't hear.

"See you then," Skye said, and tried to pull the door further into the room.

When she bumped into me, she froze, like she was worried I'd be pissed or something. Instead of saying anything, I just put my hand on her hip, sliding her to the side so the door had more room to move. The way her breath caught when I touched her made me suck my own in.

"Sorry," she said, turning and moving out of the room.

"Not a problem," I said. "I didn't mind at all."

Even though she was facing away from me, I knew she was blushing. It ran all the way around her neck and down to her shirt collar. Her ears were pink as well, barely covered by her short hair. As she stepped out of the room, out of my space, I felt her absence, and it was something I hadn't expected. Decker had talked about how he fell hard and fast for Kylie, but I didn't believe in it. Now, though, he'd be laughing his fucking head off at me.

"You have plans for the rest of the day?" she asked as we made it to the shop area.

My guess was she was trying to clear her mind, but I could have been wrong.

"Not a damn thing," I said. "I figured I'd turn the game on at some point, but other than that. I've got nothing going on."

"Oh," she said, and I wasn't sure whether that was a happy word or not.

"Wanna go somewhere?" I asked.

"I don't usually do the night life," she said. "Not in a long time, anyway."

"Want to try?"

"I don't know," she said, and I could tell she was struggling.

"Tell you what," I said. "Why don't we find a restaurant that's close, but not overly crowded? Maybe something that has the game on. We have dinner once you close up and see how things go. Sound good?"

"That sounds nice," she said.

"Great," I replied. "Do I have time to run to my hotel first? Or are you closing soon?"

"I've got another hour or so," she said. "I'm not really gonna be hungry, though. I mean, we just ate."

"So we have dessert," I suggested. "Something light, just have some time to get to know each other better."

"Okay," she said. "That actually sounds good."

"Great," I said. "How about I swing by and pick you up in an hour? Or should I give you a little time to get things closed up, too?"

"Maybe an hour and a half?" she asked.

"Sure," I said. "Want me to meet you in front of your shop?"

"Umm…" she hemmed.

"Do you want to meet at the restaurant?"

"No, no," she said. "Here's fine. I gotta change, though, so maybe we should make it two hours instead. Is that okay with you?"

"Sure thing," I said. "Remember, you're driving this bus. I'm just along for the ride."

She kept asking my permission for every decision we were making, and I knew it had to be past trauma, which just made me want to punch whoever it was that hurt her.

"Okay," she said.

"See you then," I said.

"See ya," she replied, her smile looking genuine, if still a bit hesitant.

Yeah, fuck that fucker all the way to hell.

I left the shop and headed back to my hotel. She'd seemed freaked out by the hoodie, so I decided to change out of that, and into something closer to what I'd wear going to and from a game, rather than the jeans, tee shirt, and hoodie I had on. The other thing I was going to need to do was release the sexual tension within my own body. I didn't want to be pushing that on our first date. I mean, would I? Sure. But that wasn't what this was about. Hopefully we'd get there, but for now it was about getting to know her and letting her know that not every man out there was trash.

# CHAPTER TWENTY-FOUR

*S*kye…
  I waited about fifteen minutes before I decided to go ahead and close up early. Sales had dropped, which was actually fine. I didn't have to put in an emergency order, and I didn't have to think about getting up early to meet the delivery driver. Taking that extra time, I headed up the back steps to my apartment, deciding to take a real shower to get myself cleaned up.

When I walked into the bathroom, I saw my wet clothes in the tub and the morning came flooding back to me. How had he turned my day around so much that he went from freaking me out so much that I pissed myself to now going to dessert with him? That wasn't a normal progression of steps, at least where my mind went. And yet, here I was, getting dressed up to go out with him.

Throwing a towel on the ground, I pulled the clothes and shoes out of the tub and set them on the towel. I'd worry about them another day. Stripping down, I stepped into the shower and turned it on, giving my hair a quick wash, then soaping up my body and letting the water rinse the suds off. Drying off, I ran a comb through my hair to let it dry as I went to get dressed.

Mai would've told me to put something sexy on, but I wasn't

feeling quite that confident. John was nice, and he seemed like a decent guy, but a lot of guys come off that way until you really get to know them. Even then, it could take years for them to show their true colors.

I didn't want that on my mind tonight, though. No, I wanted to give him the benefit of the doubt until he showed me he was a monster under that pretty package. After putting on some panties and a bra, I pulled out some leggings and slid into them, then went to my closet to find a nice sweater dress to put over top. Once I had those on, I pulled my high boots over some fuzzy socks, then grabbed a light sweater to go over the short sleeves of the sweater dress to ward off the chill that was likely to come once the sun fully set.

Back in the bathroom, I fluffed my hair, trying to give it the body it didn't naturally have. The fact that it was short, and undercut, was the only reason it didn't stick to my head like some sad hair helmet. Pulling out my makeup bag from under the sink, I looked at the sad state of what was left in there and opted to just put some mascara on and add a little lip gloss. He'd seen me all day without makeup, so if he balked at the fact that I didn't have a full face on, that was on him.

I went back into my bedroom and stood in front of the full mirror I had in there, turning this way and that to see how I looked from as many angles as I could. It was a stall tactic, I knew, but it was what I wanted to do. Lunch today was the first time I'd done anything with a guy that even resembled a date since I broke up with Dylan, and here I was, doing it again the same night.

"Quit freaking out," I told myself, chastising myself.

Finally, when I felt I'd stalled about as much as I could, I grabbed my phone from the charger on my nightstand, headed to the door to slide my purse over my head and arm, letting it drop across my chest, and picked up my keys.

"Just do this," I said before taking a deep breath and opening my front door.

I hesitated as I got to the bottom of the stairs. Did I go through the hallway that took me to First, or go out the front of the store. I said I'd meet him in front of the store, so that was the way I'd go—in the back door, shut off the alarm, unlock the gate at the front, back to turn the alarm on, move the gate, unlock, and open the front door, gate back and locked, and door shut. Now I just had to lock the door.

Sticking the key to the lock, it didn't want to go in. I shifted it, but it still wouldn't go in. Then someone wrapped my hand in theirs. It was big, warm, and calloused. I froze, but he used it to help me guide the key into the hole. He wasn't touching me anywhere except my hand, but I could feel the heat radiating off him at my side. I had to close my eyes and take a deep breath before I locked the door and pulled my key away. He let go as soon as it was locked.

"Thanks," I muttered.

"Happy to help," he replied, and it was low and for my ears only.

I swallowed hard, then turned to face him, and wow, that was not what I was expecting. He had changed from the hoodie and jeans to a button-down shirt with a sports jacket over slacks. It was like he went from a jock to a business casual look, which was not in my wheelhouse, but something I saw all the time. And he made it look good. Button-down shirt that matched the green flecks in his eyes, with a dark blue jacket. His slacks were black, and he was wearing dress shoes instead of the sneakers he had on earlier. I was glad I'd opted for a little bit dressier outfit so we matched up better.

"Where do you want to go?" I asked.

"I was hoping you could help with that," he said.

"What were you thinking, food wise?"

"Honestly," he said. "I'm good with whatever. I don't have any food restrictions or allergies or anything like that. Someplace that has good desserts and where we can talk, so not something that's playing loud music."

"I have just the place," I said, knowing we'd be fine for dessert only.

"Lead the way," he said, holding his hand out to indicate I should go ahead of him.

We took the few steps up Post Alley and across from my shop and walked into The Pink Door. It had a dim interior, with candles at the tables, and was one of my favorite places to go when I got dressed up. When I was in high school, all us girls would dress up and come here, just to pretend we were adults. We'd order virgin drinks and pretend we were all grown up. It was the best place to be, and I loved it.

"Hey, Skye," Rachel said as we walked in.

She gave me a bit of a flutter with her lashes, then looked at John and smiled wide.

"Hey, Rachel," I said, trying very hard to not make a big deal about the fact that I was there with a guy. "Can we get somewhere near the back and away from the door?"

"Lemme look," she said, running her hand over the map they had on the podium by the door. "Yeah, I think I got something. Come on."

She picked up a couple of menus, along with what I knew was the wine list, and led us over through the scattered tables to something close to the back wall. There weren't a ton of people in the place, what with it being a Monday night, but there were a few folks sitting around. I had been a bit worried about walking in with John, but either no one recognized him, or they just didn't notice. Either option was fine with me.

"Here we go," she said, setting the menus on the table.

"Thanks," I said, and went to sit, but John pulled the chair out for me and helped me in. Once I was down, he pushed me into the table, then took the seat across from me. "Thank you," I said.

"Absolutely," he said. "What's good here?"

"Gotta admit," I began. "I haven't been here in a while, but I'll tell you what looks the same."

"Okay," he said, pulling the menu from the stack to open it.

I did the same and was just beginning to see what was new and what I'd had before when the waiter came by with some water.

"Would you like something else to drink?" he asked.

"I haven't gotten that far," John said. "Skye?"

His question made me look up.

"Umm..." I hummed, then opted for the safe route. "I'll stick with water."

"Let's go with water for both," John said.

"Great," he said. "Would you like a starter? Something to tide you over while you decide what you want for dinner?"

I looked at John, who was looking at me, expectantly. I had no idea what he wanted to do, and kind of panicked. Like, no way was I going to make that decision. He must have seen the look on my face because he answered for the both of us.

"Let's hold off," he said smoothly. "We're still trying to decide."

"Sure thing," the waiter said. "I'll be back in a few to check and see if you're ready."

"Thanks," John said and I watched the waiter walk away.

"Thank you," I said.

"Not a problem," he replied. "Order whatever you want. I'm paying."

"You bought lunch," I complained.

"And I'm buying dinner, too," he said, his voice was firm, and offered no room for argument.

I kind of liked him taking charge like that, not pushing me to do things, but also not allowing me to argue with him when it wasn't something that needed discussing. It was completely different from the way Dylan had been. No, he was just a bully who wanted what he wanted and didn't give a fuck about what anyone else did. Everything I did with him was what he wanted to do, and none of it was what I wanted, especially toward the end. When I'd finally had enough, he still had one more thing he wanted to do to fuck me over, and it nearly cost me my life.

When John touched my hand on the table, I jumped, but thankfully didn't scream.

"Sorry," he said. "You looked like you were lost in a nightmare."

"Not a bad description," I replied.

"You good?" he asked.

I took a deep breath, then nodded, trying a smile on that didn't seem to fall flat, thankfully, because he returned it.

"You really should smile more often," I said. "It lights up your whole face."

His smile broadened and he squeezed my hand in his, just enough to let me know he was there, but not in a way that hurt, which I appreciated more than he would likely ever know.

"You said you'd tell me what was good," he said, breaking the silence that had settled around us.

"Oh, yeah," I said, looking back at the menu. "Anything grabbing your eye?"

"The ribeye and the lamb chops," he said, and I looked at him.

"Go with the lamb," I said. "They know how to do it right."

"Perfect," he said. "What about you?"

"Since you mentioned it, I'm doing the lamb, too," I said, setting the menu on the table.

As if we'd summoned him, the waiter stepped up to the table.

"Looks like you've decided," he said.

"Ladies first," John said, looking at me.

"I'm going with the lamb," I said.

"Wonderful choice," he said, then turned to John.

"Same as the lady," he said, looking to me with a smile.

"Great," the waiter said. "Let me just put that order in. Did you decide on something to drink? Or are we sticking with water?"

"Just water," John said, not taking his eyes off me.

"I'll be back with it once it's ready," he said, then walked away.

John hadn't let go of my hand, but had switched the positioning, as he'd slid his fingers underneath mine, his thumb stroking the back of my hand. It was soothing, which I hadn't expected. My experience with men was minimal at best, and nonexistent in the last two years. Just this little bit of touch, the kind words, the way he was looking at me, I had to press my thighs together to try to get some relief from the pressure building there.

Whether I telegraphed my emotions, or he noticed the shift of my body in my chair, his smile increased. Like, it was nice before, but suddenly, he ramped it up, eyes sparkling in the candlelight, a knowing look in them.

"What?" I asked, trying to get my mind off what was going through it.

"Just looking at the most beautiful thing in the room," he said, and the fact he said it without cracking a smile that wasn't genuine, that had no notes of teasing in it, made me just that much more turned on.

I knew I was blushing, could feel the heat rising from my throat up my cheeks, and all the way to my forehead. Damn my fair skin showing everything. His hand hadn't stopped its movement, still stroking circles with his thumb on the back of it.

We both jumped when the waiter moved in front of me to set my plate down, then do the same with John's. Of course, that meant we'd been sitting there, staring at each other for quite a while, which I wasn't at all gonna complain about.

"Enjoy," the waiter said, then walked away.

As much as I didn't want to let go of him, the smell from the plate in front of me was calling to the baser instinct within me, and I had to. It seemed he had the same feeling, as it took a while for us to separate our hands. I wanted to wait for him to start, but he looked me in the eye, then looked down at my plate, obviously wanting me to begin first.

# CHAPTER TWENTY-FIVE

*J*ohn...

"Enjoy," the waiter said, then walked away.

I hadn't taken my eyes off her since we'd put in our order, and I didn't want to stop looking at her, but the food was calling to my stomach. Instead of taking the first bite myself, I looked down at her plate, then back up at her, trying to tell her without saying the actual words, that she should start first.

She followed my unspoken instructions and let go of my hand, then pulled her silverware from inside the napkin they were wrapped in, placing the cloth on her lap. Her eyes didn't leave mine until she looked down to cut a piece off the lamb. It was tiny, the piece she cut, and I wasn't sure she'd even get the flavor from such a small sample size. She brought the fork to her mouth and looked at me as she slid it between her lips, her tongue coming out to taste it before it fully entered her mouth, and that small thing caused my dick to twitch.

Closing her eyes, she chewed the morsel, and I found myself waiting anxiously as she did so, wondering what she thought of it. Not that it was a big deal. It wasn't like I'd made it, so if she didn't, it wasn't anything to do with me, but still, I wanted her to enjoy the food the way I was enjoying watching her eat it. The tiniest moan escaped her lips and her eyes shot open. I couldn't help but smile at the sound and took that to mean it was as good as it smelled.

"Would you eat?" she said under her breath. "I feel really weird having you watch me eat."

"I'm rather enjoying watching," I said, and her eyes widened. "But if it makes you uncomfortable, I'll stop."

"That's not..." she stopped, cutting herself off.

She again closed her eyes, but this time it wasn't to enjoy her food. No, this time it looked like she was trying to control something within her, and I didn't want her to have to censor herself around me.

"What?" I asked, with a bit more force than I likely needed.

Instead of answering, she clamped her lips together, and had this fearful reaction I wasn't prepared for. Whoever had been with her before had fucked her up royally, and that just pissed me off even more, but I needed to cool my temper or I'd scare her off before anything even started.

"I'm sorry," I said.

"For what?" she asked, and she sounded angry rather than scared, which was better.

"I shouldn't have pushed you," I said. "I want you to know that you can talk to me, tell me anything, even if it's something I'm doing that's pissing you off. You shouldn't have to be anyone but yourself around me."

She stared at me, and I could see the wheels turning in her head. I could tell she was trying to figure out if what I was saying was real, or if I was lying to get something from her. I waited patiently, watching her think about whatever was running through her mind. Finally, she broke the silence.

"I had a boyfriend who was controlling," she said. "He would tell me what to think, how to act, and what I was and wasn't allowed to do."

"I'm sorry you had to experience that," I said. "You can tell me when I'm being pushy, though. I kind of have this overbearing person-ality, or so I've been told, and tend to get ahead of myself and assume everyone is on the same page when they aren't."

"I can see the dominance in you," she said, but she didn't sound like that was a bad thing. "I'm just gonna need a little more grace than you're probably used to. If you wanna just tell me to fuck off, I'm good with that."

"Yeah, no," I said. "I don't want you going anywhere if I can help it. But, like I've said before, you're driving this bus, so what you say goes. You tell me to fuck off, and off I'll fuck. You tell me to slow down, then I turn into a turtle and go as slow as possible. You want to move things faster, I'm all in."

Her smile started small, but it grew with every word I'd said, which just encouraged me to keep on talking. By the time I got to the end, the waiter had come back over, interrupting our conversation.

"How's it taste?" he asked.

"Great," Skye said.

I just nodded, not wanting to actually talk to him, but much more interested in the woman across from me.

"Just let me know if there's anything else I can get you guys," he said, and there was something in the way he said it that made me look at him.

He wasn't talking to me, just Skye, and the way he was looking at her made me pissed. Like, did he not realize we were on a date, and that she wasn't in here trolling for someone. I was much larger than him, and could probably knock him out with one punch, but I didn't want to do that in front of her. No, she made me want to be better, and we'd only met that morning. Fuck, I was so fucked it wasn't even fucking funny.

"Hey," she said, and I turned to look at her. "Don't worry about him. He's been hitting on me for years."

"I don't like it," I said, and couldn't keep the growl out of my voice.

"Possessive much?"

She said it with a smile, but there was an edge to it.

"Sorry," I said, knowing that what I was doing was total caveman vibes, and not the way to get on her good side.

"Eat," she said, and just that one word helped me to see I was in the wrong and needed to redirect my attention.

I nodded, then pulled my fork and knife out of the napkin, placing the cloth on my own lap, much as she did, then cut off a big hunk of the lamb. Placing the bite into my mouth, she watched as I took it from the fork and began to chew, and oh, damn, the flavors were all mixing together just the way they should. I didn't know when the last time was that I had such a good meal, other than the one I'd had earlier that day, and the night before. Apparently, I hadn't eaten near the Market in entirely too long and needed to remedy that real quick. Having someone to come down and see was more than enough incentive for me to make this a regular thing.

Once I'd finished my bite, she picked up her silverware as well, and continued to eat her food, both of us enjoying each other's company without having to fill the space with words. The waiter came back a couple more times to check on Skye, but not me, until he finally dropped the bill off, placing it in front of me without even looking my direction. It was all I could do to not snap at him, but that wasn't what Skye needed, so I bit my tongue and held myself in check.

# CHAPTER TWENTY-SIX

S kye...
   Tony was about as subtle as a bull in a tea shop, with him only looking at me, only addressing me, and basically ignoring John the whole time. It was comical if not annoying, and I was glad when he brought the check over. John pulled out his wallet and placed a black credit card in the folder right away, without even looking at the bill. Tony took it without even addressing us, just watching me as he left.

"How long has he been after you?" John asked.

"Probably since I first came in here and he was working," I said. "It's usually just my friends and I, so I think this might be the first time he's seen me with a guy. My ex never wanted to go out to places like this, so we didn't."

"Well, I'm glad you let me bring you here," he said, his smile both brilliant and mischievous. "Might have to do it a few more times for him to realize you're not just here for his entertainment, though."

"Are you asking me on another date?" I asked.

"I'll take you out every night if I can," he said. "I'm here all week without a job, so I'm available all day, all night, anytime you want me."

The way he said it, and the underlying indication that he meant more than just as a friend or something, had me squeezing my thighs together again. I swear he could see the reaction he was getting in my face, because he smiled again, that devilish smirk that just made me even hotter.

Had I really been that starved for interaction, for companionship, for kindness? I must have been, because he was saying all the right things, and honestly, I just wanted to take him back to my place and have my way with him. But I couldn't do that. Not yet. It was too soon. Would I enjoy myself? Absolutely. Except I'd probably be thinking about what Dylan would say, which just fucked me up even more.

God, I did want John. He was sexy, powerful, had a great job, and was dominant without being possessive. Like, he indicated what he'd like, and was happy when I chose it. If it were Dylan, he'd have told me to fucking do it because he said so, no argument. It wasn't that I wanted to compare the two, because from what I'd experienced so far, they were nothing alike.

"I took the liberty of adding a tip," Tony said when he brought the receipt, and John's card back.

"Pretty bold of you," John said, glaring daggers at him.

"I just assumed…"

"Yeah," John said, cutting the waiter off. "You don't get to assume anything. I am the customer, and I decide if your service was sufficient to warrant a tip or not. The food was excellent, but your service was the bare minimum when it came to me. All you were doing was catering to Skye, which I can understand. She's beautiful. But you excluded me in your service, which means it was subpar at best."

"But…"

"No," John said, and it brooked no argument. "You don't get to decide what I tip, or if I tip."

He wasn't loud, he didn't draw the attention of other patrons, but he was firm in his statements. When Tony didn't say anything, John opened the little black folio, pulled his card out, as well as the receipts, and read them over, verifying what we had ordered was all that was charged, and then changing the tip amount that Tony had handwritten to about half of what that was, if not a little less. He signed the receipt, made a note on the one that was for the customer to keep, and then put his card, and the receipt into his wallet.

"If I see more than what I have authorized on my card, you will be hearing from an attorney for fraud allegations," he said when he handed the folder back to Tony. "Next time, don't let me down."

The last was said in a somewhat fatherly tone, as if he were chastising a child. I held my laughter, covering my mouth with my napkin to keep from letting Tony see how amused I was with the whole situation.

"Shall we?" John asked, getting up from his seat and holding a hand down to me.

I set my napkin down, looking at John's hand, and more importantly *not* at Tony. I stood, and John placed his hand at the small of my back, guiding me toward the door and out into the cool spring air. As soon as the door closed, I burst out laughing.

"Oh my God," I said between breaths. "I have never heard anyone be reprimanded in such a nice way, while still being told to go fuck themselves."

"Was I wrong?" he asked seriously.

"Absolutely not," I said while still giggling.

"Good," he replied. "Now, shall I escort you back to your home?"

I turned to look at him, confused.

"I know you live above your shop," he said. "It's not a secret, and I'm not going to stalk you or break in or anything. I just want to make sure you get home safely."

"How did you…" I didn't finish it because he was looking at me as if the question was stupid, but not that I was. I took a deep breath and said, "Thank you."

"Absolutely," he replied. "Like I said, you're driving this bus, so what you say goes. But," he added, looking me in the eye. "I will *not* allow you to be hurt. I won't push you, but I would like to know who broke your heart and made you think you weren't valuable. You're beautiful, smart, generous, and kind. And I've only known you for a day. Whoever was telling you that you were not worth the world was wrong, and an idiot. Got it?"

I nodded. I mean, how could I argue with that? He was right of fucking course. Dylan wasn't worth anything, and he was the one who told me that I wasn't good enough. John was right, I was worth more.

He could tell that I'd thought over what he said, because once I'd realized he was right, he smiled, and continued with me down the alley. It was hopping more now, but not nearly as full as it would be come Friday night. Mondays were pretty boring around here, which was actually nice.

Once we got to the shop, he stopped and I turned to look at him.

"Would you mind if I kissed you?" he asked.

I'd never been asked if it was okay for someone to kiss me. They'd always just assumed it was fine and done it without asking, so this threw me for a loop.

"You are perfectly welcome to say no…"

"Yes," I said, cutting him off. "I'd like that."

He licked his lips, and I mirrored the motion, licking my own. I wanted to kiss him. Like, more than anything else, I wanted to kiss him. It'd been too long since I'd had that touch, that feeling of someone else's lips on me, and I wanted it so much it ached within me.

Stepping closer to me, but not touching me, his head began to move down, slowly, as if he were expecting me to stop him at any moment, and I loved that he thought that highly of me, that he thought I might not want to do it, and he would stop if that was the case. Raising my hands, I placed them on either side of his face, cradling it in my palms, then pushed up on my toes to get closer.

His lips hit mine, soft at first, but I pushed to get more contact, shifting my body next to his, hoping he would take the hint that he could wrap his own arms around me. Thankfully, he did, but not in the way I hoped. No, he placed his hands on my hips, holding me there, as his mouth moved against mine. He pulled back entirely too soon, and I blinked, looking up into his eyes that were shadows in the darkness of the alley.

"I didn't want to push," he said, his voice husky with desire that mirrored my own.

"I don't mind," I said, pressing my body against his.

"You're sure?"

"I want this," I said, trying to put all the emotions I had running through me into my voice.

He hesitated for a moment, then slid his hands around my back, pulling me closer than even I had made us, his mouth coming back down, pressing his lips against my own. Instead of a gentle, tame kiss, this one was full of wild abandon, and a passion I hadn't felt in entirely too long, if ever, and such a kindness that it was inexplicable.

I parted my lips, and he took it as the invitation it was, sliding his tongue between them, past my teeth, and alongside my own. Heat pooled in my belly and lower, and it was all I could do to keep from wrapping my legs around him, telling him to take me to my bed, and fuck me until I forgot everything. His hands rubbed against my back, one closer to my waist, the other running up and into my hair as he held me where I was to take more control.

After moments or eons, he released me and pulled back, adding a peck against my lips a couple of times before finally separating enough that we could look in each other's eyes.

"That was amazing," I said, pulling my hand from the side of his face to my lips as if I could hold the feeling there for eternity.

"It was absolutely my pleasure," he said.

"What do you have planned for tomorrow?" I asked, feeling emboldened by my new power.

"Like I said," he replied. "I'm yours for the asking. Whatever you want to do with me."

Oh, did I want to take him up on everything that implied, but I needed to slow down. Needed to get my head right before jumping in with both feet, even though it pained me to do so. I wanted nothing more than to take him upstairs and do all the things I wanted to do to and with him, but I had to play this smart. I had to think with my head and not my heart, not my libido that was starved for attention.

"That sounds…" I hesitated, unsure exactly what to say.

"I'll send you my phone number in the messages that we've been using," he offered. "Feel free to text me, or use the messages, and let me know what you want. The only thing I have to do is deal with the mess at my apartment and figure out how to get out of the lease, because, well, reasons. I was supposed to do that today, but I got a little distracted, which I'm thrilled by, believe me."

"Okay," I said, unsure what was going on, and now concerned about it more than I wanted to be. "So, I'll let you know, okay?"

"Absolutely," he said. "Now, go ahead and get into your store and head up to your apartment. I want to make sure you're safely inside before I head back to my hotel."

"Thank you for a lovely night," I said.

"It was lovely because of you," he replied, and damn if that didn't just get my fires going again. "One more kiss?"

The way he asked, as if he was never going to see me again, made my heart do something I hadn't expected when it fluttered in my chest. I leaned forward, raising up to let him place his lips against mine. It was chaste, sweet, and simply just a kiss. When we separated, he placed his hand on my face, and I turned into it, his thumb stroking against my cheekbone in a soft caress.

"You better get inside," he said.

I nodded, then turned and opened the gate, keying myself into the business, locking the gate behind me as the alarm did its countdown. I only had a minute to get to it and shut it off, so I had to be quick. I shut it off at the back of the store, then came back up to lock the front door, and he was still there.

"Wanted to make sure you got the alarm off and could lock the door," he said as an explanation.

"Thanks," I said through the gate. "See you tomorrow?"

"Any time," he said with a smile.

"Okay," I said, not really wanting the night to end. "I should go."

"Me, too," he said, but it appeared neither of us was interested in that notion.

I took a deep breath, then closed the door, locking it before one last wave and walking back to the back. I looked out one last time before I went through the doorway and he was still there, still watching, so I waved. Yeah, this was complicated, and it hadn't really even started yet. I just had to figure out whether it was going to be worth it.

# CHAPTER TWENTY-SEVEN

*J*ohn...

I watched her walk across the shop to the back, then she turned and waved, and I waited until she was through, and could hear the chirp of the alarm before I turned and headed back to my hotel. This was going to be a long walk, but at least it was cool enough, and my pants were loose enough that I didn't think I'd end up with anyone noticing the chub I had going on. In just one day she'd swept me off my feet, tumbled me into a head-over-heels passionate feeling for her, and I wasn't at all sorry about it.

While it only took me about five minutes to get to my hotel, it took entirely too long, especially when all I wanted to do was get in, undress, get myself into the shower and think about what it would be like to have those lips on the rest of my body. She was soft in all the right places, and firm in so many more, particularly her internal strength. Whoever had fucked her up was awful, but at least she was away from them. Hopefully, they weren't anywhere they could come back into her life and cause more havoc.

Walking through the lobby of the hotel, I ignored all the stares that came my way and powered over to the elevator, punching the arrow to go up. Waiting, I turned a bit to look out and saw that several women were watching me and whispering behind their hands. They looked to be closer to my mom's age than mine, which wasn't really anything new. Hell, the event that happened early last season had women with gray hair falling all over themselves around us.

The ding of the elevator shocked me just a bit, but then I stepped aside to let those on it out before stepping in myself. The door was nearly closed, when an arm stuck in and bumped the sensor to open the doors again. One of the women from the lobby stepped in and I scooted over, giving her plenty of space to decide where she was going.

"What floor are you on?" she asked me.

"I'll get there," I said. "Go ahead and push your floor."

She looked at me, then pressed the button for the penthouse, which was well above what I was willing to pay for. After she'd done that, I pressed the button for the third floor and waited as the elevator began its trip up.

"You can come up to mine if you want," she said, and there was just the slightest hint of a slur in her words.

"No thank you, ma'am," I said, making sure I had plenty of room between her and me.

"No need to call me ma'am," she said. "You can call me Joy. I'd be happy to give you as much joy as you can stand, too."

"I'm already attached," I said, just as the bell rang for the floor I was on. "Excuse me," I said, slipping past her, and she took a moment before moving out of my way.

When I was just about out, she grabbed my ass, and I reached back and slapped her hand away, walking briskly down the hall toward my room. Before I keyed my way in, I turned to make sure she wasn't following me, which thankfully she wasn't. I opened the door, stepped in, and closed it, flipping the little lock at the top of the door.

Breathing a sigh of relief, I flipped the light on in the bathroom, then headed toward the bed to turn the lamp beside it on, before kicking off my shoes. Draping my jacket on the back of the chair at the desk, I undid my belt and slid my slacks off. I sat on the edge of the bed to finish the job, then pulled my socks off as well. I undid my shirt and set it on my bed before standing to drop my boxers.

Now naked, I walked to the bathroom to turn the water on for a shower. I'd taken one earlier, but it was mostly just to relieve the pressure from the day, and the anticipation of the dinner to come. Now, I wanted to spend some time actually fantasizing about those lips, that body, and just how wonderful it would be to explore all of it in a slow, tantalizing fashion.

The benefit of most modern hotels was that the hot water would last for a long time before it even thought about cooling if it ever did. I wanted it to be hot, steaming, to nearly scalding when I was in there now. I was definitely not interested in a cold shower in the least. No, it needed to be as hot as her, as steamy as she made me, and with enough force to keep me where I was instead of heading back down to stand outside her building.

I took a towel and set it on the back of the toilet, stepping into the water that was coming from the showerhead, ducking under the spray to get some of that heat onto my back and shoulders. Closing my eyes, I could still see her. That smile, those lips parted in surprise on occasion, and the way her deep blue eyes danced when I told that waiter exactly where he went wrong. Then I could see the way they were hooded, passionate as I leaned in to kiss her, and God, that did so many things to me.

Grabbing the soap, I slicked it on, sliding my hand down onto my cock, sliding it up and down the hard shaft, thinking about what she would feel like if she were here. I imagined her kneeling in front of me, her pink tongue going out just before she took me into her mouth. The way she would slide me between her lips, taking me all the way to the back of her throat, sliding me back out to let her tongue slip around the head before taking me all the way back again.

Just the thought of it was more than I could take, and I came hard and fast, hitting the shower wall with the burst. If she was anything like my imagination, I'd be in real trouble trying to hold out. I finished the shower, cleaning myself as well as wiping down the wall with a cloth, before shutting the tap off, and pulling the curtain out of the way.

Taking up the towel, I dried my hair, which had gotten a bit too long, but wasn't overly so. Then, after finishing drying myself off, I headed back to the bed, shutting the light in the bathroom off on the way. As I sat on the edge of the bed, I looked and saw that there was a message in the chat we'd been using.

*Didn't get your number. Here's mine.*

She gave me her number, and like a dumbass, I hadn't given her mine, so I remedied that quickly by shooting my own number back to her.

*Sorry. I got distracted.*

I sent it, then looked at what I wrote and figured I'd need to explain more, but then thought about what my explanation would be, which was the fact that I was imagining myself fucking her mouth, which didn't exactly sound like something I should tell her, so I left it. If she asked, I'd be honest.

*Hope she was good.*

*Fuck*, I thought. How to explain without being crass was the real problem.

*She was imaginary.*

I decided to settle on the truth, vaguely at least. Maybe I'd get away with this without telling her the absolute truth. Then again, maybe she'd like it.

*I see.*

Those two words were all that was there, but then the little bubble showed she was typing something else, and I prepared to be blasted.

*Might be seeing someone imaginary myself soon.*

At least I knew I made an impression on her. The question now became whether I pushed or let it go. I could offer to fulfill her fantasies in real time, live and in person, which I was not at all opposed to doing. But if I pushed too hard too fast, she might just shut it down.

*I'm always available for an in-person session.*

There we go, honest but not pushy. Maybe she'd bite, maybe she wouldn't. Either way was fine with me, I just had to wait to see what she chose. The little dots came back up indicating she was typing again, so I held the phone and watched as they showed up, then went away, then showed up again. She was going back and forth on something, obviously, but what it was, I had to wait to see.

# CHAPTER TWENTY-EIGHT

*S*kye...
*I'm always available for an in-person session.*
Not what I expected to get from him. We'd been much more flirta-
tious over messages, which was nice. Whether he actually felt the same
way was hard to say, although if dinner was any indication, he was
definitely into me.

I started to type a response, but then stopped. Did I want to go all in
on the first date? Probably not the best idea. Then again, a quick fuck
would be nice, since I haven't had one in entirely too long. I typed an
answer, asking him to come back, or to tell me where he was so I could
go there, then deleted it. Why was this so hard?

Instead, I typed that we should hold off for now, but even that
sounded awful, like I was friend zoning him already. I didn't want him
to think I was pushing him off, but I didn't want to seem so needy,
either.

Three or four times I typed a response, only to delete it again.
Instead, I called Britta. She'd know what to do. She was always good
with interpersonal relationships. Hell, she was the first one to tell me to
dump Dylan, and I hadn't listened to her then. Now, though, I would
take her words to heart and follow them.

"Hey, chick," she said when she answered.

"I have a problem," I replied.

"Oh no, what's wrong?"

"It's what's right that's kinda the problem," I said.

"Spill," she said, and I heard James in the background asking who it was. She whispered my name, but then was full on in paying attention.

"I met him," I said.

"Who?" she asked.

"The player," I said. "The guy who I sent a pizza to. He showed up at my store this morning. I had a full on, out of body, piss myself panic attack in the middle of my shop."

"What?"

"Yeah," I said. "He was wearing a black hoodie and looking in the window when I came in to open up and get the delivery. Thankfully, Mai was there and able to get in from the front and calm me down. I had to go up and take a shower, but of fucking course, I forgot my keys, so had to come back down and get them before making the trek back up the stairs. When I came back down, he was sweeping up, because apparently that bitch from the other day came in and threw one of my jars."

"Holy shit," she said, surprise clear in her voice.

"Oh yeah, it was a whole shit show," I said. "Then, he asked if he could buy me a new jar, since I didn't have a spare and wouldn't take no for an answer. Instead of just getting one, though, he got six. Paid for them himself and wouldn't let me pay him back. Then, he took me to lunch next door, and paid for that. He basically spent most of the day with me. We even went over to The Pink Door for dinner."

"Please tell me Tony waited on you," she said. "And please tell me your guy put him in his place."

"Yes, and yes," I said with a laugh. "It was really great. When he walked me back to the shop, he told me he knew I lived above it, but that he wasn't going to be stalking me or breaking in or anything, just that he wanted to make sure I got home safe."

"Stalkers usually tell you they're not stalkers," she said.

"I know," I said. "But he actually was very nice. We kissed good-night, and my God is he good at that. Like, melt your panties good."

"And you're calling me now because?"

"We've been messaging, and I gave him my number, and he gave me his, but we've just been using the app," I said. "I sent him my number because he said he was gonna, but then it was like half an hour or more and he didn't, so I was afraid he'd fucked off."

"Okay, and…"

She left the word hanging, the question unasked, but clearly there.

"Well," I said, then paused.

"Well, what?"

"He said he was distracted," I said.

"Fuck," she said. "Why are all the sexy guys fucking assholes? Not you, James."

I laughed, because while James wasn't my kind of sexy, they were absolutely couples goals if there ever was such a thing.

"Yeah, I thought that, too," I agreed. "So, I told him I hoped she was good, and he said she was imaginary. Like, I think he was thinking about me. I told him I was probably going to be with someone imaginary myself, which, maybe I will, but yeah."

"What did he say?"

"He said he's available in person if I want," I said. "I want, but then again, I don't. You know?"

"Yeah," she said. "But you do need to get out there."

"I know," I said. "Except, I just met him. Like, this morning is when I met him. I can't go fucking him tonight."

"Why not?"

"Why not?" I asked, my voice raising. "Because I just fucking met him. It's not right. That's not how civilized people do things."

My voice was getting higher and higher with each word, and I was having trouble breathing, too.

"Hey," Britta barked, and I stopped. Like, just full on stopped. "Okay, now that I have your attention. Go use that toy you bought, think about the man you met, and see how it goes. Maybe you'll fuck him tomorrow night."

"Oh my God," I said. "You're horrible."

"No," she countered. "I'm practical. You needed someone to give you permission, so I just did. Now get to work, girl. The night's getting away from you. Meanwhile, I'm gonna see if I can get some action, too."

"Geez," I said. "I don't want to hear that."

"Then you better get off the phone," she said with a laugh.

"Bye," I said, disconnecting the call before she could say anything else.

She was right, though. I did need to do something because I couldn't stop thinking about him. I grabbed the toy, which was thankfully fully charged, and headed to the bathroom. If I was gonna do this, I was gonna get the most out of it.

# CHAPTER TWENTY-NINE

*J*ohn...
I waited and waited, but no answer came. Either I'd fucked up and scared her off completely, or she was contemplating my offer. I wasn't sure which option scared me more. Instead of continuing to think about it, I grabbed my laptop and got it started. Might as well work until I had to sleep.

Somehow, I must have slept because my phone was ringing and it woke me up.

"What?" I asked when I answered.

"Did I wake you up?" Hennings asked.

"Yeah," I said. "What the fuck do you want?"

"Fi wanted to know if you wanted to come to dinner tomorrow," he said.

"And you had to call me in the middle of the fucking night to ask?"

"Dude," he said. "It's like not even ten."

"It's the middle of the fucking night in Houston," I barked. "Call me in the morning."

I disconnected the call, not even bothering to wait for an answer. I fucking hated getting woken up in the middle of the night. Especially for shit that wasn't important. If it had been Skye, I'd have been fine, but it wasn't.

Unlocking my phone, I opened up the messaging app to see if she'd responded, but she hadn't, which made me more than a little upset. Not at her, but at myself. Maybe I'd pushed too hard, but fuck, I wanted her. That little taste of her in front of her shop was nowhere near enough of her. Honestly, I didn't know if I'd ever get enough.

Since I was awake anyway, I headed to the bathroom to piss and wash up. Looking at myself in the mirror, I wondered again whether I'd fucked it up. Wouldn't be the first time, and probably not the last, either. I was just pissed that it had to come at her expense. Never intended to hurt her, but apparently I'd fucked up my chance.

"You're a fucking moron," I told my reflection.

Almost as soon as the words were out, my phone rang.

"It better fucking not be Hennings," I growled as I went to grab it. The number was just that, a number without a name. But it had the Seattle area code, so I took a chance, hoping it was her. "Hello?"

"Um, hi," she said, and wasn't that just music to my ears.

"Hey," I said.

"I didn't wake you up, did I?"

"Nah," I said. "Hennings already did that."

"I should let you…"

"I'm already awake," I said. "And I don't mind talking to you in the least."

"Oh," she said, and it was soft.

I plopped down on my bed, sliding my laptop further away so I didn't fuck it up, and waited. She'd called me, so I just hoped it wasn't to tell me to fuck off.

"So, um," she said, hesitantly. "About tomorrow," she finally said after a long pause.

"I'm all yours," I said.

"Yeah," she said. "Would you mind if you came a little later in the day than you did today? I don't want to push you away, but…"

"No problem," I said, and thank fuck she wasn't telling me not to come at all.

"It's just that I kind of need the morning to get myself ready to people," she added. "I'm kind of an introvert, so working all day is hard."

"I get it," I said. "I don't want to cause you any trouble at all."

"You're not trouble," she said. "I don't want you to think that."

"It's fine," I said. "I should probably make some calls in the morning anyway. Try to get my apartment situation figured out."

"Oh yeah," she said, as if I reminded her. "What's going on with that? If you don't mind my asking."

"It's no problem, but probably not something you want to hear," I said. "I mean, it's kinda morbid and gross. To be honest, I don't even want to think about it."

"You don't have to tell me," she said, but sounded disappointed.

"I don't mind," I said. "I just wanted you to be aware that it's not exactly a pleasant thing to think about, and I would hate for you to have nightmares because of it."

"Oh, now I gotta know," she said, her mood obviously perking up.

"So, I've lived there since the season started," I began. "I've never bought a house anywhere because I didn't know if I'd be traded or not. Instead of trying to deal with buying and selling a place, I decided to just rent. Anyway, I got home yesterday and when I opened my door, the smell was awful. Like, I knew something died, I just didn't know if it was in my apartment or what."

"Ew, gross," she said.

"You don't know the half of it," I said. "Called the landlord and he said to call maintenance, who told me they couldn't get anything done about it for a few hours. I called the cops, and they were more than happy to know that something like this was going on, and they took one look at the light above my coffee table and told me there was likely a dead body upstairs."

"Oh no," she said. "Was it someone you knew?"

"Nope," I said. "No clue who any of my neighbors really are. I have such a fucked-up schedule that I rarely see anyone."

"So, what happened?" she asked, clearly interested.

"I'm not really sure," I said. "All I know is I have to have someone come in and clean it up, and it's probably gonna cost me a shit ton of money, too. Honestly, I'm thinking about just leaving pretty much everything that's there with the apartment and getting all new stuff, because I'm not sure that smell's ever gonna come out."

"Wait, you're just gonna leave your stuff?" she asked. "Won't that be kind of expensive?"

"I mean, yeah," I replied. "But it's not really worth trying to fix it. I'll ask the cleanup people what they think, but it wouldn't be the end of the world. Most of that stuff I can replace. I'll get what's sentimental, but it's just stuff."

"Wow," she said. "I've just never heard of someone just tossing everything and starting over. Well, at least not to this extent. Like, throwing away some stuff, sure, but your whole ass apartment? That seems extreme."

"You don't understand that smell," I said. "Just thinking about it is turning my stomach."

"We should probably stop talking about it, then," she said.

"Yeah," I replied. "I'm sure there are much more interesting things to talk about. Like you."

"Um, no," she said. "I'd rather not."

"Okay," I said, letting it go, even though I wanted to know everything about her. "How about we talk about the shop?"

"Now that I can talk about for days," she said.

She told me about the origins of the store, and how her grandfather helped to get them established in the family that is the Pike Place Market. The fact that her family was so prominent in the Market was something I didn't know, but it made sense that people around her would protect her the way that Mai did. Everything she said was full of hope and delight, each new topic was more enthusiastically discussed, and I could just hear that her eyes were lighting up with every word.

"Sorry," she said after she'd been talking for a while. "I tend to go off on tangents when I get started."

"Don't stop," I said. "I'm enjoying learning about you through what fuels your passion. I can totally get behind someone being passionate about their work. I play a game for a living, so there's no way I'd bash someone who clearly loves what they do."

"I never thought about it that way," she said.

I could hear that she wanted to tell me more, but she seemed afraid for some reason.

"Anyone who told you that you shouldn't talk about yourself, or that you shouldn't be passionate about what you do was wrong," I said, hoping she'd take it to heart. "You obviously have a lot of love for the store, and the Market and its people. I would hate for you to think that what you love isn't important because it is."

"Thanks," she said.

It was quiet for a while, with us just in our own heads. I was tired, but somehow rejuvenated by talking to her.

"You give any thought about my offer?" I asked.

"Your offer?" she asked in response.

"In-person, mutual enjoyment," I said, beating around the bush a bit, but wanting her to come to her own conclusions.

"Oh," she said, drawing the word out.

I waited for more, but she didn't come out with it right away.

"You can totally tell me no," I said, giving her the out if she wanted to take it.

"It's not that," she said, and I could hear hesitation in her voice.

"So, you're saying there's a chance," I replied, using that line from the movie from forever ago.

She laughed, and it was a beautiful sound. I wanted to hear her laugh like that more often, and I hoped she'd give me the chance.

"Maybe," she finally said once her laughter had subsided. "It's just, I've got some baggage."

"No worries," I said. "I'm strong. I'll happily help you carry it."

"Not like luggage," she said.

"I know," I replied.

It must have dawned on her that I was serious about being willing to help her carry whatever the fuck had her so messed up.

"I have an ex," she said.

"We all do," I replied.

"Is yours in jail?"

"Oh," I said, not expecting that.

"Yeah," she said. "Mine tried to kill me, so I'm kinda gun-shy about relationships right now."

"Totally understandable," I said. "Am I pushing too hard or trying to get you to move too fast? I'll slow down to whatever speed you wanna go. You're driving this bus."

"It's not that," she said, then paused. I didn't think she was gonna say anything else, and just when I was about to tell her to think things over, she said, "I really want you. Like, *really* want you."

The way she emphasized the second really was clear that she was more than interested. I was afraid to jump on it, but I didn't want her to think I wasn't as into her as she seemed to be into me.

"I like you, too," I said. "Pretty sure I showed that when I kissed you. But, if it's not clear, let me just tell you outright. I am *very* interested in getting to know you better, and finding out all the things you love so I can shower you with those things. You deserve to have everything your heart desires."

"I haven't scared you away?"

"Baby, I fight every day," I said. "Sometimes more than I should. You being in my life would absolutely be the balm I would need to get me through everything bad that happens to me. From the shitty hitting situation to the crappy fielding I've been doing to arguing with players from other teams. All of that would be worth it if I knew I had your voice to soothe my soul."

She was quiet, and I was sure I'd just fucked everything up. It was too much too soon, and I was going overboard with the love bombing in words, but she needed to know she was worth it.

"You okay?" I asked when she'd been quiet for too long.

"Yeah," she said and sniffed. "Just trying to figure out if you're for real or not."

"I'm for real," I assured her. "I don't play around, don't do things I don't want to do, and everything I do want to do, I go all in."

"Okay," she said, and I could hear the emotion in her voice.

"If I'm pushing too hard, let me know," I said. "I know you've got issues with trust, and I get it. Don't let me push you into something you're not ready for. Tell me you need time, that you want me to slow down, that I'm being an asshole. I don't care. You are in control. You will always be in control."

A sob came out, and all I wanted to do was crawl through the phone and hold her.

"You want me to come over?" I offered.

"Mmhmm," she managed to get out.

"Give me about ten minutes," I said. "I gotta get dressed, and it'll be about a five-minute walk to your front door."

"Okay," she said with another sob.

"Wanna stay on the line?"

"Yeah," she said.

"You got it," I replied. "Gonna put you on speaker while I get dressed, then I'm out the door. You don't have to say anything if you don't want to."

"Thank you," she said.

"My absolute pleasure," I replied, pressing the button to put her on speaker.

I don't know that I'd ever dressed as fast in my life, but I was out the door in two minutes, and running down the stairs to get out of the hotel faster. By the time I was at her door, I'd heard her unlock her apartment, and the alarm chirp when she went into her shop. I purposefully didn't wear the hoodie but threw my jacket over the tee shirt and jeans I'd pulled on. It was far from fashionable, but I didn't give a fuck. I just needed to get to her.

# CHAPTER THIRTY

*S*kye...

"Thank you," I said.

"My absolute pleasure," he replied, and I heard the tone difference when he put me on speaker phone.

There was the rustling of cloth, and it was obvious he was getting dressed. I hadn't changed, and was still wearing my sweater and leggings, but I'd pulled off my boots. Instead of putting them on, I slipped into a pair of flats next to my bed and headed down the stairs. It sounded like he was going to be here faster than he said, and I didn't want him to stand outside forever.

I turned off the alarm as I walked into the shop, and flipped the light on in the back hallway, going through the doorway just as he showed up. Unlocking the door, I pulled it open, and worked the lock on the gate, having trouble getting the key into it again. His hand on mine as I fumbled made me look up.

"I got it," he said, and I handed him the keys.

Without any trouble, he slid the key into the lock and turned it to pop it open, sliding the gate out of the way so he could pull me into his arms. Without even thinking about it, I wrapped my own around his neck, and let go of the sob I'd been holding.

"Come on," he urged, pushing me back into the shop. "Let me lock these up, and we can go up to your place."

I nodded against his shoulder, and pulled back, giving him space to return the gate to its place, locking it, then shutting and locking the door.

"Okay, baby," he said. "Let's head up to somewhere you can really relax."

I took his hand and led him to the back of the store, hitting the button on the security system to re-arm it, then flipping the light off, and opening the door to the back stairway. We walked up the stairs, him behind me, but holding my hand. I'd never let anyone into my space except for the girls, and it was a bit odd to be bringing a near stranger up the stairs to my sanctuary, but it also felt right. Turning the doorknob, I opened the door and stepped into my apartment.

"You don't lock the door?" he asked, concern in his voice.

"I do," I said. "But I was just going downstairs, and no one really has access to this place."

"As long as you stay safe," he said, and I turned to look up at him.

The concern on his face was almost too much. How could a man I'd barely met be so worried about me when the dick I'd been dating for years had no fucks to give?

"I must be dreaming," I mumbled, not intending for it to be said out loud.

"Probably more like a nightmare," he said, but that wasn't the case, and I shook my head, saying, "No."

"You sure you're good with this?" he asked, and it was so kind it hurt.

"More than," I said, pulling him to me.

I wrapped my arms around his neck and went up on my toes to offer my lips to him, hoping against hope that he'd be willing to at least kiss me. Thank fuck he obliged because I didn't think I could take rejection from him. He pulled me closer to him, his hands going around me, one down on my waist and the other up to the back of my head. While he was strong, he wasn't using it to punish me, and that made the kiss that much sweeter.

Parting my lips, he slid his tongue into my mouth, and I moaned with pleasure. It was weird that just a kiss from him seemed to chase all the darkness away. He was the light I'd been looking for, and he'd found me in the most unusual way. Never in a million years did I think that a stupid post on social media could bring me someone who actually gave a fuck about me.

He pulled back and looked down at me, eyes hooded, but dark with emotion.

"I don't wanna push," he said. "But I also don't wanna stop, so you're gonna have to be the adult in this situation and pump the brakes if we get too far."

"Please don't stop," I begged.

"Keys?" he asked, pulling the hand that was at my back away, my keychain dangling from his strong finger.

I took them, and moved to hook them on the wall, turning the dead-bolt on my door as I was there. When I turned around, he was watching me, and the heat that was coming from him was palpable. I might combust being with him, but gods did I wanna go out that way. It was then that I realized how truly big he was. I mean, I wasn't short by any stretch of the imagination, but he actually towered over me. It was intimidating, and yet I felt safe at the same time.

"What'cha thinking?" he asked.

"Probably shouldn't say," I said, embarrassed by my own thoughts.

"Hey," he said, moving closer. "You can tell me anything."

"I'm just thinking how I wanna climb you like a tree," I said, feeling the rush of heat climb up my neck and into my cheeks.

"Climb away," he said, holding his arms out.

I closed my eyes, took a deep breath, and felt him close the space between us. He put a hand on either side of my waist, and they were warm and soothing. When I opened my eyes, he had a look of both lust and concern, which was an odd combination, but my God did it just make me want him more.

My arms went up and around his neck, pulling his face toward me. I went on my toes, and his arms went around my waist, doing to my body what I'd done to his lips. I was pressed against him, chest to hip, but his face was still too far away for me to actually kiss him. He slid his hands down, cupping my ass, and lifted me fully, pressing me between his body and the door, and my God, did it make things heat up.

Crashing my lips against him, I wrapped my legs around his waist, wanting to be closer than I already was. His hands didn't stray from my ass, as his cock pressed into me, and I was sure he would feel my desire for him through my pants, but I didn't even care. I wanted him, no, needed him. He was what I would use to banish all thoughts of anyone else from my brain and my body.

He came up for air, pulling his lips from mine, pressing his forehead against my own, eyes closed for a moment as he focused. When he opened his eyes, he stared into my soul, and all I wanted to do was fall. Not literally, but figuratively, right into him. I wanted him more than I wanted my next breath. More than anything I'd ever wanted before in my life.

"You okay?" he asked, and that just turned the heat up again.

"More than," I said. "Except I think we're overdressed."

He chuckled and pulled back, my legs unlocking from around him, and I slid down to the floor. He took his jacket off and turned to see where to put it.

"Sorry," I said. "Don't really have a coat rack. You can put it on one of the stools at the bar, or on the back of the couch."

Tossing it to the couch, he turned back to me, heat still radiating off him.

"Your turn," he said with a smirk, and I kicked off my shoes.

"Next?" I asked, enjoying the playfulness in him.

"Oh, that's how we're gonna play?"

"I never lost at strip poker," I said, sticking my hand on my hip, defiance in my face.

He kicked his own shoes off, then reached over his head, pulling his shirt off easily, and tossing it on the back of the couch where his coat had landed. Watching the muscles ripple under his skin was way more erotic than it probably should have been, but maybe it was because it'd just been *that* long since I'd had a man.

On his shoulder there was a tattoo of a flower in full bloom with lines coming off the edge to go across his shoulder blade. There was writing on top of the artistic lines, but I couldn't quite read it from where I stood. Stepping closer, I slid my hand across the images, reading the words that were there. As if he were sent by the gods themselves, his tattoo read, "With Pain Comes Strength" and I hadn't seen anything that fit me more in my entire life.

I could feel his eyes on my skin. He was watching me, but it wasn't in a creepy way at all. No, it was as if he was fascinated by me and what I was doing.

"What does this mean to you?" I asked because I knew what it would mean if it were something I'd chosen.

"Had a friend," he began, and I could see him swallow.

"You don't have to share," I said.

"It's okay," he said. "I want to."

He paused, but only for a moment, then continued.

"My good friend, Cameron," he said. "He got cancer in our senior year. Initially he thought it was just some sort of bug, but he kept getting sicker by the day. Finally, the rest of the team convinced him to tell his parents and have them take him to the doctor. He'd waited too long, though, and it ended up killing him. The whole team was fucking wrecked by it because it all happened so fucking fast. His funeral was brutal. I don't think I've ever cried that hard in my entire life."

His face had gone from stoic to sad in almost a moment.

"We were all a mess," he continued. "I don't think I'll ever forget him, and as soon as I turned eighteen, I got this tattoo. It was my first, and I wanted to honor him."

"That's beautiful," I said. "Absolutely horrible, but so kind that you permanently made a place in your life for his memory."

"He was the best player we had," he said, and I could tell it was hard for him to talk about it. I was almost ready to tell him he could stop when he added, "Thank you for asking. No one's ever asked before."

"I'm sorry it was painful," I said. "But thank you for sharing."

His hand came up and cupped my face, his thumb sliding along my jawline. I pressed my face into the touch, reveling in the kindness this man held within him. He had come out in the middle of the night, when I was falling apart, and simply offered himself to me. No questions, no judgment, just kindness, and it was almost too much.

I wrapped my arms around his waist, pressing my ear against his chest to hear his heart beating beneath the skin, muscle, and bones that held it. The hand that was on my face slid to the side of my head, holding me against him, as the other went to my back. It was a quiet moment, one built of tragedy, but he was warm, and I was in need, and as much as I didn't want to mess with that memory, I wanted to chase the sadness away.

Pressing my lips to his chest, I kissed him, feeling the intake of air as I did. The way I was pressed against him, I could feel his dick start to stir, and I was sad I'd caused it to soften. Turning my face in his hand to look up at him, I wondered what I would see. Instead of the sadness that had been there moments before, there was a fire in his eyes. The green more prominent, the flecks of gold shimmering, and I wondered if I had a mirrored reflection in my own eyes.

He slid his hand from the side of my face down my back, smoothing the sweater that was entirely too warm on the way. There was a smirk on his lips, one that held passion and pleasure.

"I believe it's your turn," he said before gathering the sweater in his hands and pulling it up and over my head.

My arms went up automatically as he pulled the garment from my body. I was still wearing my leggings, as well as my bra and a tank top, so I wasn't completely bare like he was, which was equal parts amusing and sad. I wanted to feel his skin against my own. Wanted to press my body to his and let his heat, his passion, his power, infuse me with it all. Not waiting for him, I did as he had with his tee shirt, and reached back to pull my tank top off, dropping it on top of the growing pile of clothes on my living room floor.

"Wow," he said, the word blown out on an exhale of air. "You are breathtaking."

I wanted to hide myself, but his words, and the honesty I saw in his eyes, told me he was telling the truth, that to him I truly was breathtaking. No one had ever said that to me. Not a single person had been this open with me, and I couldn't help but want him that much more.

"Your turn," I said, but it was breathy and full of all the desire I had building inside me.

"I don't think you're playing fair," he said. "You have more clothes left, which means I'm gonna end up naked before you."

"And that's a bad thing?"

As if it were a challenge, he slowly unbuckled his belt, easing it through the loops on his jeans, the sound of it slipping through the material sent shivers up my spine as he set it on top of his shirt and jacket. Then, he lifted an eyebrow at me. Challenge accepted. I slid my feet back, slowly pulling off my socks, kicking them to the side. Like it was a game, he mirrored my movements, removing his own socks. Instead of doing what he probably wanted, I slid my leggings down, stepping out of them when they reached the floor.

I was in my bra and panties while he was still dressed from the waist down, and it didn't seem quite even, but also, man was it turning me on. His hands went to the fly of his jeans and he eased the button out of the hole, unzipping them ever so slowly, and I couldn't help my tongue slipping out to lick my lips.

"You keep that up, we're not gonna make it," he said, and my eyes snapped up. "I may just drop everything and snatch you up. Kiss those plump lips of yours and slide my tongue in that pretty little mouth. Hold you so tight you'll have to cling to me as I take you to whatever flat surface I can find and let my lips devour every inch of you."

It was like he'd lit me on fire, and I was consumed by passion, wanting him to do everything he'd just said and more. I didn't wait for him to continue, but reached behind me and undid the hook on my bra, letting it flutter to the ground. To watch his face fill with desire, and for me, was almost too much. Never had anyone looked at me the way he did. It was like he wanted to eat me up, and I would willingly sacrifice myself to that.

# CHAPTER THIRTY-ONE

*J*ohn...

Her bra fell to the floor and I nearly died right then and there. While her breasts weren't big, they were generous enough, and her dusky pink nipples called out to me. I'd been teasing her with my words, but she'd called my bluff, and I wasn't about to lose this prize.

Stalking to her, closing the space in just a couple of steps, I snatched her up in my arms, pressing her chest to mine, lifting her up off her feet, and capturing her mouth with mine. She parted her lips in surprise, and I used it to dive into her mouth with my tongue, tasting every dark corner of her mouth, sliding my hand down from her naked back to the globe of her ass, lifting her leg with pressure to wrap around my hip. I'd seen enough of her apartment to know there was a bar between the little kitchen and the rest of the living area, so I headed that way.

When I set her on the edge, the cold marble hitting her warm body causing a gasp that I swallowed. She was so full of passion, so responsive to my touch, that I wasn't sure I'd last long if we got to that point, but God, I wanted to feel her under me. I wanted to watch her arch her back and moan my name as she fell completely apart.

Pulling back, I used one hand to sort of lay her down, not quite pulling her back, but guiding her in the direction I wanted her. She was breathtaking, and I couldn't take my eyes off her. I wasn't sure where to start, but I wanted to taste every inch of her.

"You're beautiful," I said, looking up to watch the heat rush up her face.

I was pleased to see that the blush ran down and over her breasts as well, and I leaned over her, kissing her collarbone just where it met her neck. She took a shuddering breath, letting it out in a sigh that told me she'd been touch starved for entirely too long. I aimed to make up for as much as I could, starting right then.

My lips caressed along that collar bone, sliding toward her shoulder, then moving back toward her throat. I hit the pulse point on her neck, then moved lower, taking my time to taste each place I pressed my lips. Her legs were wrapped around my waist, pulling me toward her as I moved down her body. I was pretty much at my limit of how low I could go without unhooking them, so instead moved back up to her lips, taking everything she was giving, and returning it as best I could.

"I want to taste you," I said, and she sucked in, looking me in the eye, hers hooded in passion. "Can't do that with you wrapped around me like you are. If you're good with me staying up here, I will, but if you want me to…"

I didn't even finish when she unhooked her feet, spreading herself open, pulling my mouth back to hers with a hand on either side of my face. I took what she was offering, giving as much as I could back, my tongue again delving into her mouth to run along the side of hers. Kissing along her jawline toward her ear, I nibbled on the lobe, sucking it into my mouth as she sucked in a breath.

"You are delicious," I purred in her ear, sliding behind it to press a fresh kiss behind it. "So good," I continued, giving love bites down her neck and toward her chest wall. "I want you to come apart while I hold you together," I said, hoping my words were doing as much as my mouth was.

"God, yes," she said in a rush of air. "I want that so much."

I hummed as my mouth moved further down, loving the feel of her hands in my hair as she guided me along her body. It wasn't that she was pushing me, just encouraging me with gentle direction. I was more than willing to let her put me where she wanted me, because she knew her body better than I did, so I definitely took her lead.

As I moved my head to the top of her breasts, she arched her back, pushing harder on my head to lead me to her nipple, which I took into my mouth, and the moan that escaped her made it clear I was on the right track. Sucking her into my mouth, I let my teeth take hold of the tight nub that had risen from my attention, pulling it, and stretching her skin with enough force to cause the friction I wanted without making it painful.

"Yes," she hissed through her teeth, pulling herself flat against the counter to increase that stretch.

I'd kept my hands on either side of her on the counter, but decided to get them involved in this ministration I was giving her, sliding one down her side to her hip, pressing against it, my fingers digging into her soft skin as she pressed against both my mouth, and my hand. Shifting my hips, I moved my hand toward her stomach and then lower to the edge of her panties, and she moaned again, shifting herself so that my hand went right to the apex of her thighs, to the heat that was radiating from her core.

Pulling my mouth from her breast, I looked up at her. She'd moved her hands to her sides, each one gripping the counter on either side of her, holding on as I moved against her body. Her eyes were closed, and she was just enjoying the attention I was giving her, which I was totally down for. My initial intentions had been to taste her first, but my God did I want to see her fly, watch her burst into a million pieces while I held those in my hand and carefully put her back together.

My hand on her slid down, feeling her excitement in the wetness on the outside of her panties, and it fucking thrilled me that I'd caused it. Pressing my palm against her, I moved it back and forth, causing friction that I hoped was enjoyable, and judging by the way she pressed her hips into my hand, it was doing the job.

"That's it, baby," I said. "Let go and let me love you."

She stilled, her eyes going wide as she looked down her body at me. Sliding away from my hand, she sat up more, and I worried about what I'd done wrong.

"What is it?" I asked, confused.

Her arms went across her chest, hiding herself from me, and I was sad. Not because I couldn't see her, but because she felt the need to hide.

"What did I do?" I asked, worried I'd broken this before it even began.

"You can't love me," she said, her voice hoarse with emotion as tears welled in her beautiful blue eyes.

"Why not?" I asked.

"I'm unlovable," she said.

"Oh, no," I said. "You are definitely lovable. Let me prove it to you. Please?"

It was begging, but I didn't care. I wanted her, wanted to show her how wrong she was about being unworthy of love. Taking my hand and placing it along her cheek, I caressed her jaw with my thumb, watching her eyes as they held fast on the tears, not letting them fall. Her lower lip was trembling, and I was sure it was over, at least for right that moment, so I put the other hand behind her, and pulled her to the edge of the counter, pressing her head to my chest, wrapping her up in my arms to let her get herself settled.

The first sob broke so quickly I didn't realize what it was until the wetness hit my chest. It wasn't loud, but it was powerful, her whole body shaking with it. I held her firm against me, stroking her hair, and just let her get it all out. Nothing else mattered in the moment, just her comfort and safety, and I would be fucked if I'd let her feel like any of this was her fault, or that it was something she caused.

She let it all out, crying against my chest, her tears running in rivers down my torso. After a time, she tried to push away, but I made a shushing noise, holding her fast against me. She was still shaking, and I didn't want her to pull away until I was sure she'd gotten herself back in control. Until then, I would hold her together.

When she finally stilled in my arms, I let her head go, allowing her to pull away from me some. The look she gave me, from below me as she sat on the counter, was a combination of awe, gratitude, and something I wasn't sure I could name.

"Thank you," she whispered.

"Absolutely," I replied. "I got you, however you need me."

She nodded, and I could tell she didn't trust her voice. As much as I wanted to continue from where we left off, I didn't think she was up for it, so I kissed the top of her head.

"You wanna go to bed?" I asked. "You look like you could sleep."

"You don't mind?"

"Not at all," I said. "Here, let me help you down."

I stepped back, putting some space between us, and picked her up, letting her slide down my body until her feet were on the ground. I waited a beat, making sure she was solid, before I stepped back, and turned around to pick up her clothes off the floor. When I turned back, she had her arms across her chest, once again hiding herself from my view. Untangling the articles of clothing, I found her tank top and held it out to her. Turning around, she pulled it over her head, then looked back over her shoulder at me.

"You want me to go?"

"Oh, God, no," she said, and I was so thankful she said that.

I was gonna have a hard enough time sleeping as it was, but to not be able to hold her while I did it wasn't something I wanted to even think about. She reached her hand out behind her, offering it to me, and I grabbed it, allowing her to lead me through her place to the bedroom. Once we were in there, she went to the side of her bed, turning on the small lamp that was on the nightstand, casting a warm glow around the space.

"Bathroom is there," she said, not looking at me.

"Thanks," I said, setting her clothes on the bench at the end of her bed. "Which side do you want me on?"

"Umm," she hummed, clearly having a hard time making decisions.

"I can be between you and the door to protect you from intruders," I offered. "Or I can be on the other side so you have an escape route."

The look she gave me was one of gratitude, and I wondered who had cornered her, kept her captive, and mistreated such a glorious creature in a way that made her afraid of love. Finally, after she went through every calculation she probably had in her head, she looked back at me again.

"Can I be on the side with the door?" she asked.

"Certainly," I said. "It's your bed. You get to decide how this goes."

"Okay," she said, and she sounded fragile. "I'm gonna use the bathroom really quick, then you can have it."

"Take your time," I said. "You want me to keep my pants on?"

She stopped mid-step on her way to the small room of hers.

"You don't have to," she said, but I cut in and asked again, "Do you want me to?"

I could see her actually thinking about what I was offering, and thankfully she didn't take long to decide. Instead, she shook her head, her eyes going down to my open fly before the blush returned to her skin, and she turned and walked into the bathroom. This was going to be a glorious torture, but I was all in.

# CHAPTER THIRTY-TWO

*S*kye...

I left him in my bedroom, and closed the door to the bathroom, turning my back against it, and slid to the floor. I cried again, this time alone, and didn't even have to think about being quiet. No, Dylan broke that part of me. Every time he'd make me cry, he'd laugh at me, bitch at me, and smack me around, saying, "I'll give you something to cry about, bitch." It didn't take long for me to learn to not make any noise when I cried.

So I let it all out, even more than I already had. Fuck, I hadn't cried this much in years, but the fact that he'd been so kind, so considerate of my feelings and what was going on with me, it just released the dam of all the unspent emotions I'd kept bottled up inside me.

How long I cried, I didn't know, but when he knocked on the door lightly, I jumped.

"You okay?" he asked through the closed door.

"Yeah," I said, and could hear the roughness in my voice. "Give me a second."

I got up as quietly as I could, turned on the cold water in the sink, and scooped some up, pressing the cool liquid to my eyes to reduce the puffiness I was sure was in them. I didn't bother to look in the mirror because I knew it would be bad. Not the first time I'd gone to bed with red eyes. Hopefully, though, I wouldn't be subjected to the whims of the man that was going to be beside me.

Taking a deep breath, I let it out in a rush, grabbed the hand towel from the rack next to the sink, and dried my face off. I hadn't turned the light on in the bathroom, so the only way I knew where things were was from the small nightlight and memory.

Finally ready to face the music, so to speak, I opened the door, and he was just there. Standing in his jeans still, looking big, powerful, and terrifying, except for his face. It was full of concern and care, something I wasn't used to.

"Are you okay?" he asked, reaching a hand out to me.

I flinched automatically, and he froze, arm out still, but not moving toward me.

"Sorry," I said, looking to the ground.

He brought his hand closer, in the slowest of movements, like I was a frightened rabbit in the sights of a wolf. Instead of grabbing me, holding me against my will, making me do what he wanted, he placed his fingers under my chin, barely touching me.

"Will you look at me?" he asked, his voice pitched low, but gentle.

Doing as he said, I turned my eyes up to him, trying to do it without making him mad. No, he wasn't gonna get mad. He'd been kind to me and had shown that he wasn't like my ex. Emboldened by that truth, I lifted my head, his fingers coming with me as if he were helping me when I couldn't do it on my own. His smile was sad, but it was still there. I tried to mirror it but was sure it paled in comparison.

"Need a hug?"

It caught me off guard. So much so that a laugh bubbled out, which I quickly squashed, smacking my hands over my mouth, my eyes growing wide.

"Don't hide that laugh," he said. It was firm, but kind. "Let that laugh out. You deserve it. Nothing wrong with laughing, even if it ends up being at my expense."

I nodded, unsure exactly what he was expecting. He opened his arms, waiting for me to decide. As much as I wanted to shut the door between us, I moved to his arms, wrapping my own around his waist. One of his hands went to the back of my head, the other smoothed down my back, pressing me against him. Another shuddering breath left me, and I relaxed a bit into him.

"There you go," he said, his chin on the top of my head. "Just let me hold you."

Feeling him running his hand up and down my back, the other massaging my head against his chest, was exactly what I needed to settle me down. His heart was beating a steady rhythm against my ear, and it just soothed me that much more. I closed my eyes, and just took it all in, letting myself experience this moment.

"Come on, baby," he said, stepping away from me. "Let's get you settled into bed. Once you're there, I'll use the bathroom, then join you. I want to hold you through the night. Make sure you feel safe."

Nodding, I went with him as he walked over to my bed, the covers already pulled back where I could climb in. I scooted a bit back, turning to my side, and slipping my feet under the covers he was holding up. He set them down over me when I was finally flat, my head on the pillow.

"Be right back," he said, then turned and walked to the bathroom.

It didn't take long before he opened the door, and was walking back across the room. The way it was set up, he had to kind of crawl over my cedar chest, and up onto the bed. Instead of bitching about it, though, he just did it. No complaints, no grumbling, nothing. Just up and over the box at the foot of the bed, then up along the wall. He'd left his jeans on, which I thought was odd.

"You can take those off," I said.

"I don't have any underwear on," he replied. "Wanted you to have the freedom to not see my dick if you didn't want to."

I laughed, and this time, I didn't cover it up. What surprised me was he joined in, laughing at himself.

"Please get comfortable," I said. "I'll turn away since you're shy."

Turning my back to him, I felt the bed shift, and heard the rustle of fabric, along with his grunting, as he took the jeans off. He leaned across me to drop them on the floor, then I felt the covers pull up, and again the grunting as he got underneath.

"There we go," he said, shifting in my bed.

I'd never worried about having a big bed because I'd never shared it with anyone that was very big. A few times we'd have a girls' night here, but most of those ended with everyone just crashing on the floor or couch. But with John, it felt entirely too small.

"You got enough room?" he asked. "Because I can roll onto my side if you need more."

I looked back over my shoulder to see him already somewhat on his side. He had his elbow on the pillow, his hand under the side of his face, and he was just looking at me, his lips turned up in a small smile.

"You're the one who's gonna need the room," I said. "I don't usually take up much space."

"If you're sure," he said, and the smile didn't change, just there, like a Cheshire cat.

"Why are you being so nice to me?" I asked, shifting myself so I was facing him.

"Why wouldn't I be?" he countered.

"I'm nothing special," I said, knowing it was true.

"Bullshit," he said, and the indignance behind that one word shocked me. "I don't mean to be mean, but you are very special. Whoever it was that got into that beautiful mind of yours and lied to you is a monster who should never be around people again."

"Well," I said. "He is locked up, so he's not really around many people."

"Good," he said.

"Seriously, though," I said. "Why are you being so nice?"

"You seem like you haven't had anyone be nice to you in a very long time," he said, and the seriousness was something I could more than just hear. I could feel it, taste it. "Someone as beautiful as you should be cherished."

"Pfft," I sputtered.

"Seriously," he said. "I want to spoil you with everything your heart desires. I want to make you cry out in delight as I bring you to climax after climax. Feel you find that place in the stars where you can explode into a million pieces. To hold you when you cry. When you're scared, I want to be your protector. Those are the things you deserve."

Everything he was saying were things I'd been looking for, what every woman was looking for. Not someone to control them, but to love them, care for them, and want what was best for them. How had I missed the warning signs when I first met Dylan? He only looked for what he could get out of the relationship. He'd used me, abused me, and nearly killed me. Now, there was a man in my bed telling me that all he wanted was to give me everything.

"What's going through that beautiful mind of yours?" he asked when I'd obviously been quiet for too long.

"How you're saying all the right things," I replied. "And I want to believe you. I really do. But my track record's far from stellar when it comes to picking guys."

"Then it's a good thing I picked you," he said, his smile getting bigger. "You sent me pizza, but I found more than just someone who owned a tea shop. I found a woman who had everything going for her. You're smart, beautiful, and stronger than anyone I've ever met."

"You must be around a bunch of idiots," I said.

"You're not wrong," he replied, and I laughed. "But I'm also around some fucking geniuses. Trust me when I tell you, you are all that and a bag of chips."

"A bag of chips?" I asked.

"Yeah," he said. "What? You've never heard that expression?"

"Not in like a decade," I said. "You been living in a cave?"

"Might as well be," he said. "Because I'm obviously well out of the loop on what's hip slang nowadays."

"Oh my God," I said, rolling my eyes. "You're as bad as my dad."

"You can call me daddy if you want," he said, and I burst into a fit of giggles.

"Please tell me that isn't a kink of yours," I said through laughter.

"Only if it turns you on," he said, and the seriousness was back. "I'd let you call me whatever you wanted if it meant you were happy."

"You're serious, aren't you?" I asked.

"As a fucking heart attack," he said.

We lay there, facing each other in the dim light of my bedside lamp, and I wasn't even sure what to make of him. Everything he was saying was what I'd always longed to hear. The difference here, though, was that he seemed to be willing to put his money where his mouth was, so to speak. And I believed him.

"You should sleep," he said.

"Yeah," I replied, rolling back over so I could shut the lamp off.

We were plunged into darkness, and I waited for him to force himself on me. It was just a matter of time. But it didn't happen. He didn't even move. Shifting in the bed, I scooted back a bit and heard him suck in his breath, and I froze.

"You want to cuddle?" he asked in hushed tones.

I nodded my head, but then realized he couldn't see me, so said, "Please."

His hand smoothed along my waist, and I felt the bed dip as he moved closer. When his body came into contact with my back, I stopped breathing, but he angled his body so that his dick wasn't at my ass. I wasn't sure how he did it, but it wasn't there.

"Breathe," he said in my ear, and the warm air rushing along my skin made me shiver and suck in a breath. "That's it," he cooed. "Just relax. I'm not gonna hurt you. I'll keep you safe."

The words were soothing, a caress on my soul, and I faded quickly into the darkness that was sleep.

I TENSED AS I REALIZED I WAS DRAPED ACROSS A VERY LARGE MAN. His breathing was deep and steady, so he wasn't awake, but I was still terrified. As carefully as I could, I shifted, sliding my leg off from his, pulling my arm off his chest, and as quietly as possible, slid out of bed.

It was clear that we were in my apartment, but my brain wasn't coming up with why there was a man in my bed.

Once I was in the bathroom, I took care of my morning ritual, and washing my hands my memory came back. I sighed with relief as it all came flooding back. John had stayed, and he'd been as good as his word in simply holding me. What was odd was that I didn't remember dreaming. No running from monsters or shadowed figures. None of the terror that I'd been dealing with off and on for the last several years. That, and I felt about as well rested as I'd been in entirely too long.

When I opened the door after shutting off the light, I looked back at my bed. He hadn't moved, still lying on his back, one arm across my side, the other up over his head. I stared for a bit, wondering whether I could get used to this type of situation. He just seemed too good to be true, and everyone knew how those things went. Nope, gonna have to push this away. Nothing good ever came into my life, so why would I expect this to be any different?

Except he'd been good to me. Cleaned up the shop when I fell apart. Bought new jars when one broke, through no fault of his, and took blame for it when he didn't have to. Then, he'd taken me to lunch, given me my space, took me to dinner, and came over when I asked. None of that was something a person who was looking to use someone would do. Except I had this sick feeling that he was going to pull the rug out from under me. Use his power, his physical and financial strength, his popularity, and his fame, and take all of that to punish me.

It was all too much for me to deal with at that moment, so I grabbed my clothes from the end of the bed, slipping into my leggings and pulling my sweater over my head, not bothering with a bra. Walking from the bedroom, I shut the door quietly, going to the floor behind the couch where my socks had been left. I pulled them on, then found my boots. Grabbing my phone from the counter, I pushed the power button to see that it was nearly dead.

"Fuck," I said, going to the door and grabbing my keys.

Unlocking the door, I stepped outside, turning the deadbolt with my key once I'd closed it. I took the stairs down to my store, knowing there was a charger in my office. I opened the back door, flipped on the light in the back hall, and turned the alarm off. I took the few steps to my office and turned the light on in there as well, looking on my desk and finding the cord that was plugged into the wall. Sliding my hand down the length of the cord, I got to the end and plugged it into my phone, hearing the chime that indicated it was charging.

I felt bad about just leaving him up there, but I didn't know what else to do. Wondering whether I should text him or not, I kind of just sat in my office looking at my phone. I closed my eyes and thought back over the day before and everything that happened, starting with my initial freak out at seeing him outside my window even a night earlier.

Had it really only been a couple of days? Not even, actually, but boy had the last thirty-six or so hours been filled with so many changes. Honestly, it had been less than a week since I first made that post on social media, and everything had changed in a dramatic way. My phone pinged indicating a notification, and I opened my eyes to see what it was.

*You okay?*

I hadn't thought he was awake, but he was now.

*Yeah, I didn't want to wake you.*

He'd seemed to be sound asleep when I'd left, but something woke him up.

*You in the shop?*

Fuck. I guess I couldn't really hide from him any longer.

*Yeah. I'll be up in a minute.*

I didn't want to have this conversation yet, but I guess it was gonna be thrust upon me. I unplugged my phone and grabbed my keys, turning the light off in my office before heading across the hall to the back door. I reset the alarm, went out the door, and back up the stairs. On the way, I sent a text to Mai, asking if she'd mind opening that morning.

*I got you. Take your time.*

I was really thankful she'd been sent to my shop a few days earlier. My uncle seemed to know more than I did at that point that my business was going to boom before the night was even over. I stuck my keys into the door, unlocking the dead bolt and stepped inside.

"Hey," he said, leaning on the back of the couch in his jeans.

He'd pulled his shirt on, but hadn't had time to button it up, yet, which just made me want to close the gap and run my hands over those hard abs that were peeking out.

"Hi," I said, pulling my eyes away from his body, and up to his eyes.

There was a smile on his lips, and it seemed he was pleased he caught me looking.

"How did you sleep?" he asked, as if normal conversation was something we did all the time.

"Good," I said, not wanting to admit to him, or myself, that it had been the best night of sleep I'd had in months, hell, years.

"I don't think you moved all night," he said, just sitting there looking like every girl's dream guy. "Did you want some breakfast?"

The change of subject threw me, and I took a minute to get my brain onto the new thing.

"I mean," I said, trying to buy myself some time. "I don't normally eat breakfast."

"Most important meal of the day," he said. "Besides, how can you not eat with all these amazing options all around you."

"Just never been that big of a deal for me," I said. "I usually just get some tea or coffee, depending on the day and how I've slept."

"How about I go find something for us," he suggested. "Just let me know if you have anything you absolutely don't want."

"You don't have to do that," I said.

"I feel bad about fucking things up last night," he said, and he'd stood up and moved toward me.

I hadn't realized he'd moved until he was placing his hands on my shoulders. I stared up into his eyes, which were bright in the sun coming in off the reflection on the building across the alley from my own. The green was darker, but the gold flecks stood out. I could get lost in those eyes, and I wasn't sure I'd find my way out.

"You didn't fuck it up," I said. "That was all me."

"Nope," he said, sliding his hands down my arms to grasp my hands. "I said something that freaked you out. Shouldn't have done it, but I won't in the future. That is, if there is a future."

"I'm not pushing you away," I said.

"Good," he said, and his smile was brilliant. "I'd like to try to finish what we started last night, if you don't mind."

"Sorry about that," I said. "I know you were probably uncomfortable."

"That's not what I'm talking about," he said. "I want to see you fly."

He'd pulled our hands up between us and put his lips to my knuckle, kissing it softly. I swallowed hard, trying to figure out how to breathe with him this close to me. Instead of pulling back, he leaned in and I automatically rose up on my toes to meet him halfway, his lips caressing my own in a soft butterfly of a kiss, which caused the same kind of fluttering in my stomach. When he pulled back, I felt the loss of the connection deeply, wanting him to deepen the kiss more. His chuckle made me open my eyes and look up at him.

"I don't think we have enough time for me to do everything I want to do with you right now," he said. "Otherwise, I'd be down for starting it up right now."

All I could do was nod, not trusting my voice. He pressed his lips to my forehead, lingering there for longer than was likely proper, but we'd gone far past proper already.

"Breakfast," he said when he pulled back.

"There's a coffee shop across first," I said. "They have really good coffee as well as great pastries. Nothing protein wise, but definitely enough to take care of a sweet tooth, if you've a mind for that type of thing."

"That would be a good start," he said. "But I'm gonna need something much larger to get me through the morning."

"Let's go there first," I said. "Then I can go to work and you can find something more."

"Sounds good," he said. "How long do you have?"

"Mai's opening the store for me," I said. "So, I have a little bit of time. But," I added when he wrapped his arm around my waist, "I do need to get there sooner rather than later."

"Damn," he said, but it was done with a smile. "Let me finish getting dressed and we can go."

"Okay," I said. "I need to grab a bra, too."

"Not on my account," he said.

"I think you're biased," I said, stepping away from him.

He let me go and moved to finish putting his own clothes on. I went to the bedroom, pulling my sweater off over my head, and grabbed my bra from off my cedar chest and walked into the bathroom. When I closed the door and turned around, I caught sight of myself in the mirror over my sink. I'd seen myself in this mirror a million times over the years and had watched as my hair grew and my light faded. Now, though, it was as if someone had turned me back on, flipped a switch in me, and reignited the fire within. The way my eyes glowed were something I didn't think I'd ever see again, and it was startling.

Moving closer, I reached out, as if I could touch that other person, the one looking back at me. But all I saw was her, mirroring my own movements, doing as I was, and it was almost surreal, like I'd been dropped through the looking glass and into another reality. The girl on the other side was happy, and it showed in everything about her. Her eyes were bright, her smile was there without even trying, and she just glowed. My God, how I had missed that woman.

"Hey, babe," he said after a knock on the bathroom door. "You okay?"

"Oh, yeah," I said, turning around and opening the door.

"Did you wanna put that on?" he asked, pointing to the bra hanging from my hand. "Or were you gonna take my advice and go without?"

Looking down, I realized I'd not done what I'd gone in to do. Instead of closing the door, I just reached back and pulled the tank top off, handing it to him as he watched in stunned silence. I got myself into the contraption that was my bra, took the tank back from him, and put it on. His mouth was open wide, just looking at me in stunned silence.

"Need to grab my sweater," I said, trying to get him to move.

"Sorry," he said, shifting to the side.

"What?" I asked as he kept staring. "Not like you didn't see them last night."

"You're not the same," he said. "Did someone put a clone of you out here or something?"

He was peeking into the bathroom as if looking for another person, with a very confused look on his face.

"I think I'm finally back to who I was supposed to be," I said as an explanation, because that's the only thing I could think of.

# CHAPTER THIRTY-THREE

*J*ohn...
    She'd changed in front of me, not even batting an eye. It was like she was someone completely different all of a sudden, and it did kind of make me a little nervous. I mean, she had that flipped switch thing the night before, but it was obviously because of what I'd said. Now, though, she was just kind of... different.

"I think I'm finally back to who I was supposed to be," she said.

"I gotta admit," I said. "This is not something I was expecting. It's like you've flipped some switch or something."

"Yeah," she said, pulling her sweater over her head. "I'm not sure why, but I feel more like myself today. Maybe it's because of the good night's sleep or something."

She was so nonchalant I didn't even understand it.

"You ready?" she asked as she headed toward the living area of the apartment.

"Uh, yeah," I said, following her out.

She opened the door and stepped through, holding her keys in her hand, her purse having been slung across her chest. I followed her out, and she closed the door behind us, locking the deadbolt before stuffing her keys into her bag before zipping it up. Walking down the stairs, she turned to the right instead of the left toward the store, and it was a hallway that was just kind of there. Nothing really interesting about it, other than it was small, cramped almost, especially with my frame. My shoulders were nearly touching the walls as we walked along it.

The door at the end opened up onto First Avenue, and the busy sidewalk that was there. I stepped out behind her and she shut the door with a firm push, pulling on the handle to make sure it was locked.

"What?" she asked, looking up at me.

"I just didn't know this existed," I said.

"Back door kind of thing," she said. "Not how I usually go up to my place. But, in off hours, especially if I'm heading out without opening the shop, I come through that hallway."

"Okay," I said, not having a reason to doubt her.

"That's the coffee shop," she said. "We can get coffee and pastries, eat that, then I can send you to somewhere that has real food."

"Okay," I said again, still just kind of living in the moment.

It wasn't late by any stretch of the imagination, but it wasn't early, either. It was kind of that in between time, where some offices were open, but most were still waiting on staff to show up. We walked along the street up to the light and waited for the signal to change so we could make our way across. She'd slid her hand into mine when we'd stepped out of the building, and I had to admit it gave me a little bit of a thrill when she did it.

As we walked into the shop after crossing the street, I smelled that classic coffee scent that filled most coffee shops in Seattle. It was as if the entire town knew how to brew coffee, and I was totally fine with that.

"Hey, Skye," the person behind the counter said as we walked in.

"Hi, Reagan," Skye replied.

"Your usual?" Reagan asked.

"Yeah," she said, then turned to me. "What do you want?" she asked.

"Oh, um," I said, having not quite gotten back to the normalcy that was life. "How about a mocha?"

"Sure thing," Reagan said. "Figure out your pastries, and I'll have these ready for you."

"We skip the line?" I asked under my breath, seeing some of those standing and waiting, looking at us with less than hospitable faces.

"Market family perk," Skye said, squeezing through a couple of people to head over to the case that held their food items.

I looked in the case, and she'd been right in that it was pretty much all just pastries, and nothing that looked the least bit interesting.

"Well?" she asked, looking at me.

"I'm gonna pass," I said. "Too many carbs."

It was only slightly a lie. Eating too many carbs wouldn't be good for me, but I could totally brush off one of these little things. Honestly, it was more that I didn't want to put her, or the coffee shop, out on my account.

"That's a lie," she said under her breath. "But I'm gonna let it pass, seeing as how you're super sexy right now."

I was taken aback by what she said, and kind of just looked at her. She squeezed my hand with hers and looked up at me with this bright pink on her cheeks.

"I guess you are all kinds of new," I said. "Glad you decided to share this new you with me, not that I needed a new you in the first place."

"Skye," Reagan called from the other end of the shop.

"Come on," she said, pulling me back through the line, and over to the counter where both of our drinks were set.

"You guys want anything else?" Reagan asked.

"Nah," Skye replied. "We're on the hunt for protein."

"Have fun," the barista said, and gave Skye a wink that I was sure meant all sorts of things I wasn't privy to.

We walked out onto the cool streets, and turned to head back the way we'd come, but instead of crossing First Avenue, she crossed the other street, Pine, and then turned to head up the hill a bit. The hotel on the corner looked nice, and just about when I thought we were going to keep going, she turned into the door under a striped awning.

Stepping inside, the place was pretty busy, and I wasn't sure we were gonna get a spot to sit, but she kind of just pulled me along, and over to the end of the counter where there were some stools bolted into the floor. She sat down on the one at the end and indicated I should sit on the one beside her.

"Hey, Skye," the man behind the counter said. "Haven't seen you in here in forever."

"For sure," she replied. "This is John. He's visiting, and I wanted to show him the best breakfast in town."

"Aw, sugar," he said. "You say the nicest things. No one has better tea than you, and I'll shout that from the rooftops. Good to meet you, John. Name's Gus. Gus Stone. Been working this counter going on thirty years. Known this little muffin since she was born and her grand-daddy brought her in for her first cup of cocoa. My how you have grown, girl."

"Good to meet you," I said, taking the hand he'd offered.

"Well, now," he said. "I reckon you both would love something that'll stick to your ribs, get you through that cold morning out there. How about some steak and eggs? Sound good?"

"Gus," she said. "Can you give us a menu? I mean, Grampy always had steak and eggs, but it's not my thing."

"Oh, of course," he said, pulling two laminated menus from behind the counter. "You just give a holler when you decide. I got folks down the way I gotta get to."

"Thanks," Skye said, taking the offered items. Once the man had moved down the counter, she handed one to me and smiled, saying, "He loved my grandfather, and misses him terribly. I think he's just feeling nostalgic. Don't mind the push he has; he thinks everyone should order that."

I laughed because I couldn't help it. Looking over the menu, I saw that they had a really wide selection of options. I decided to go with an omelet, and when Gus came back by, he asked for our order.

"Denver omelet, please," I said.

"What kinda toast you want with that?"

"Oh," I said, not realizing it came with sides. "You got sourdough?"

"Sure do," he said. "You want regular hashbrowns or country potatoes?"

"Hashbrowns, please," I said.

"You got it," he said, not writing anything down. "How about you, sugar?"

"That actually sounds good," she said. "I'll have the same."

"Hashbrowns and sourdough?"

"Yup," she said.

"Coming right up," he replied, then turned to the little kiosk thing behind him. He swiped the little card he had attached to his apron, used his boney fingers to punch away on the screen, then turned back to us. "All up to them folks in the back, now. Shouldn't take long."

He swiped the menus off the counter and tucked them back into wherever he'd pulled them from, then headed back down the counter to check on the other patrons.

We sipped our coffee, which I felt a bit odd about having in a restaurant, but Skye seemed fine with it, and when I looked around, most everyone had a cup from one of the multiple coffee shops around the area. Apparently, coffee was an acceptable food to take into a restaurant, at least this one. True to his word, Gus was back in hardly any time with our food, setting it down in front of us.

"You want ketchup, Tabasco, or anything else?" he asked.

"Ketchup," Skye said, then looked at me.

"That seems like it should do the trick," I added.

"Sure enough," Gus said, turning and taking a few steps down the counter, pulling a bottom from the back, and walking it back to us, setting it between us. "Water?" he asked.

"If you don't mind," I said.

"Ain't no bother," he replied, moving efficiently around his space to get a couple of glasses, scoop some ice into them, then fill them from one of those fountain type things on the counter. "You need anything else, you just give a holler," he said after he'd set them down.

"Thanks, Gus," Skye said.

"Yes," I added. "Thank you very much."

"Sure thing," he said, knocking on the counter a couple times before heading down to the other end.

Picking up the ketchup bottle, I shook it, then squeezed some onto my hashbrowns before handing it over to Skye.

"Thanks," she said, taking it and doing likewise.

I sat watching her, baffled at the complete change in her. She was somewhat shy and much more reserved when we first met, and all through the night, but now, in the light of day, with the sun peeking through the clouds of a cool April morning in Seattle. Now, she was a powerhouse, a woman of determination, and someone that would put most anyone to shame with her self-confidence.

"What?" she asked around a bite of her omelet.

"Sorry," I said. "I'm still trying to figure out what happened overnight."

"Eat," she said. "It's gonna get cold."

Knowing how gross eggs were when they were cold, I obliged, using my fork to cut off a hunk of the omelet, and stuffed it into my mouth. It was hot, but not so hot that it was uncomfortable, but the flavors were out of this world. The spice of the peppers and onions, mixed with the smooth taste of the cheese, was the perfect combination. I must have moaned or something because she smiled.

"That good?" she asked.

"Mmhmm," I hummed around the bite. "You gonna eat?" I asked once I'd swallowed.

"Just wanted to make sure you liked it," she said, then dug into her own plate.

The bustle of the restaurant around us settled to a din of background noise as we ate. She finished her entire plate, which I was glad for, as I didn't want her to feel like she had to not eat when around me. I also cleaned my plate, taking the last of the toast and swiping it across my plate to pick up the remnants of food that was left behind by my fork.

"Well?" Gus asked as he cleared our plates.

"I consider that one of the best meals I've had," I said. "And I've eaten all over the states, so that's saying something."

"Good to hear," he said, then looked at Skye.

"The best, as always," she said, and Gus smiled.

"Be back with a check," he said, and Skye swung her purse around to pull out her wallet.

"I'm buying," I said.

"Nope," she replied, looking me dead in the eye. "You've paid for damn near everything in the last few days. You need to let me treat today."

Hands up in surrender, I said, "All right. I know when to not argue."

"You sure about that?" she asked, but there was a smile, so I was sure she was teasing.

"Here we go," Gus said as he held the check out to me.

"I'm paying," Skye said, and Gus gave me a look.

"She insisted," I said. "I offered, but she's kind of stubborn."

"Oh, don't I know that," he said with a smile, handing her the check. "When she was just a wee one, she would come in here, hands on her hips, acting like she owned the place."

"When I was seven, I was convinced that Grampy and Grammy owned the entirety of the Market," she said. "They just never corrected me."

"Truth be told," Gus said, as if it were a big secret. "I think they would have been able to buy the whole place, lock, stock, and barrel, if they'd asked. Everyone loved those two."

"Yeah," Skye said. "Still miss them."

"You and me both, sugar," Gus said. "Be right back."

He walked the short distance to the cash register at the end of the counter, punched a few buttons, scanned the bottom of the receipt, then plugged her card into the reader.

"You gonna call those guys?" she asked, and I turned back to her, confused for a moment. "The cleanup guys," she added.

"Oh, yeah," I said. "I do need to get that sorted. I've got the hotel for a couple more nights at least if I need it, but if I can get into my place, that would be good. I just have to see what they say when they come."

"You could stay with me," she said. "If you want to, that is."

Her confidence was there, but I could see it wavering. I didn't want to disappoint her, but I also wasn't sure what the actual plan would be until I talked to the guys.

"Mind if I bring my shit over?" I asked. "At least until I figure out the next few days?"

"Not a problem," she said. "If you wanna call from my place to set something up, you can do that, too. I just don't want strangers in my apartment."

"Of course not," I said. "If I need to meet up with them, I'll set it up for my place. That's where they're gonna be working. Besides, I need to figure out exactly what happened."

"That's right," she said, her eyes growing big. "I'm definitely gonna need to know what happened. I'm nosy, so I will for sure be waiting to hear all the gory details."

"There you go, sugar," Gus said, placing the receipt for her to sign, along with her card and a pen, on the counter.

"Thanks, Gus," she said, picking up the pen to sign the receipt.

I pulled my wallet out and shifted through the cash I had in there to find a hundred and handed it to Gus.

"Oh, no, sir," he said, not wanting to take the money. "I can't rightfully take that kind of cash."

"You've been amazing," I said. "And I want you to have it. Share it with the cooks as well, as their meal was for sure one of the best I've had."

"I still don't feel right taking that kind of cash," he said.

"I'm just gonna leave it here on the counter," I said as I stood up, Skye having already signed the receipt and pocketed her card. "What happens to it after I leave is none of my business."

I dropped the bill on the counter, slid my hand around Skye's back, and guided us out of the restaurant, each with the last of our coffee in our hands.

"That was really nice," she said once we were out of the shop.

"What good is having a lot of money if you can't share it?" I asked.

"I wouldn't know," she said, looking away.

"Hey," I said, stopping and pulling her up to me. "I didn't grow up rich, and I sure as fuck don't deserve all the shit I've been given. But, if I can help out a fellow man, give someone a good time, and share the wealth with those who work hard and aren't paid nearly as much as they should be, then shouldn't I do that?"

"When you put it that way, it makes sense," she said. "I just never thought about it like that. I always thought that celebrities were money hungry and kept all their wealth to themselves. That's how they stayed so rich."

"Not everyone is like me," I said. "But one of the things I learned early on was to always think about how I would feel if I were the person I was interacting with. Most of the time, folks who work do it because they have to. Some do what they love, like you and me. The rest of them do it because it's what puts a roof over their heads and food on the table. If my playing a game gives me such amazing gifts, I feel like it's kind of my obligation to better the world around me."

"You're a remarkable man," she said, and the light that was shining from her eyes was nearly blinding. "Now, kiss me and walk me back to my shop so I can get to work."

"As you wish," I said, leaning down as she raised up on her toes, kissing her gently.

Her arms reached up and wrapped around my neck as she deepened the kiss, opening her mouth to allow my tongue to slide inside. I knew it wasn't going to last long, but it was much shorter than I'd have liked. Of course, what I'd have liked was to take her back to her place, undress her, and kiss every inch of her skin from the top of her head, with its short, blond hair, down her long neck, along her creamy skin covering her shoulders, and further down, finding those pretty pink nipples, her toned stomach, and finally finding joy at the apex of her thighs.

"You look deep in thought," she said as we parted.

"Just wondering how I'm going to survive not being near you for the next few hours," I replied.

"The same way you have for the last however many years," she said.

"Well," I replied, turning to her as we moved down the street. "All those years were wasted because I didn't know you then, and if I could have, I'd have met you as soon as I could so I could spend more time with you."

"You're kind of a sap," she said.

"Yeah, well, I guess it just took the right person to bring out my sensitive side," I said.

"What's with that?" she asked. "Every time I see you on the field, you're scowling or arguing or yelling at someone."

"That's what happens between the lines," I said. "In there, it's life or death, even though it's only a game. I take my work seriously. Don't get me wrong, I do try to have fun. But it's work, and if I'm going to keep doing what I'm doing, I have to do it well."

"Makes sense," she said.

We'd made it back to her shop, her bringing us around to the front instead of going in through the back doors. The gate was open, but the door was still locked, which told me that Mai must have been there already and working to get things going.

"Should I leave you here?" I asked.

"Unless you want to come in now," she offered.

"I do have shit I gotta get done," I said. "But if that weren't the case, I'd stay with you forever."

"Wow," Mai said as she stood in the open door. "Them's some mighty big words, boy. You got anything to back them up with?"

"Just my heart," I said, not looking away from Skye at all. "See you later?"

"Okay," she said. "You can bring your stuff here if you want. Or whatever works for you."

"We'll see how the day plays out," I said. "So many things I gotta get done. Hopefully they'll be done sooner rather than later."

"I'm not going anywhere," she said, looking up at me.

"I'll see you soon," I said, then leaned down as she rose up.

It was like we had this connection that we just knew what the other was going to do well before it happened. I could definitely get used to this. The kiss was sweet and short and all things I didn't want, but that I knew were right.

"I'll call you or text you when I know something," I said.

"Okay," she replied with a smile.

I squeezed her one last time, then headed off in the direction of my hotel. I really needed to get my car from the stadium, but I also needed to figure out what the fuck was going to happen with my apartment, and that was something that needed to happen sooner rather than later.

# CHAPTER THIRTY-FOUR

*S*kye...

"I'll call you or text you when I know something," he said.

"Okay," I replied with a smile that was likely more sad than happy.

He hugged me tight, then walked away from me. I sighed, then turned to Mai who was just standing there staring at me.

"What?" I asked, sharper than was necessary.

"I'm not judging," she said. "Whoever you wanna fuck is fine with me."

"Oh. My. God," I said, punctuating each word. "I just met him."

"Doesn't matter," she replied, watching him walk up the alley. "That fine ass would happily find a spot in my bed if he didn't have eyes only for you."

"What do you mean?" I asked.

"That I'd fuck him if he gave me a chance," she replied, as if it were obvious.

"No," I replied. "I meant the other thing."

"Oh, only having eyes for you?" she asked. I nodded and she said, "It's so obvious he's head over heels, fall down drunk on the thought of you. You can see it in the way he touches you, the way he stares at you. It's like he's afraid you're gonna disappear or something."

"You think?" I asked.

"Girl, you must be blind," she said, backing into the shop. "Now," she said once we were both in with the door locked behind us. "Tell me everything, and I mean absolutely every single solitary morsel of detail from your night."

"You're serious," I said after I'd stared at her for entirely too long.

"As a heart attack," she said. "Gimme all you got."

I blew a breath up that fluttered my bangs that were starting to get a little too long for my liking and shook my head.

"Nothing happened," I said.

"I call bullshit," she said, hands on her hips, not moving an inch, which meant I was blocked from going further into the shop.

"We have work to do," I said, trying to push past her.

She moved, finally, and stepped out of my way, but kept her hands on her hips, that glint in her eye that said she wasn't done with me.

"The way he kissed you," she said, looking over her shoulder at the alley outside. "Yeah, he's got that, been there, done that, kind of vibe going, so I know something happened."

"He kissed me good night, then went back to his hotel," I said, hoping that a version of the truth would suffice.

"And…" she said, letting the word hang in the air between us.

I'd made my way to the back hallway and turned the corner to go into my office, hoping that by stalling, I'd get her off my trail, and not have to spill every secret. I hung my purse up on the rack and grabbed the tray for the cash box from the safe. When I walked back into the shop, she had the spot open for me to drop it in and was working on ensuring that all the jars were full, and everything looked showroom ready.

"Well?" she asked, spearing me with her dark eyes.

"You're not gonna let this go, are you?"

"Nope," she said. "I don't have a boyfriend, don't even have any prospects, so I need to live vicariously through you."

"You only don't have a boyfriend because you're picky," I said, not that I could talk. We were both very particular with whom we shared our lives.

"Because I don't wanna end up with a dick," she said. "Except one that is planning to be inserted into me, that is. Those I want. All the time."

I laughed. I couldn't help it. Just thinking about it was more than just a little bit funny.

"They make toys," I said.

"Like you would know," she replied. "You haven't used one in entirely too long, of that, I'm sure. I thought you were gonna use it last night, but I'm guessing you got more than just some good vibrations from your B.O.B."

Closing my eyes, I shook my head, feeling the defeat of a battle I was never going to win surrounding me.

"Fine," I said. "He came back over later. I called him because I kind of felt like I wanted to talk, but then I was kinda freaking out, so he offered to come back over."

"You're gonna have to do better than that," she said, arms crossed over her chest, her toe tapping.

"Okay," I said, pulling the stool that we had behind the counter over and sitting down. "He came over, and I had a hard time opening the lock on the gate, so he took the keys and did it. Simply taking charge, but not in a way that said he was pissed that I couldn't do something so simple. No, it was like he saw my struggle and wanted to help me out. Just that little bit of kindness was overwhelming, and I kinda just fell apart. God, that's all I seemed to do around him was be a hot mess."

"He doesn't seem put off by it," she said. "Which, honestly, is kinda nice."

"Yeah," I said. "And he just let me be who I am, without trying to push me to do anything I didn't want to do."

"Speaking of which," she said. "What else happened?"

"Fuck," I said. "I was hoping you'd forget about that."

"Girl, you know me," she said. "When it comes to sex talk, I am all about it, and won't stop till I get it all."

"Yeah," I said. "That's a nice way of saying you're nosy as fuck."

"You know it," she said with a laugh. "Now, spill."

"Well," I said, getting up from the stool. "It's time for the shop to open, so I guess it'll have to wait."

"Except we don't have a line," she said. "And you can open the door, but we both know you're gonna end up telling me, so you might as well start."

I unlocked the door and pulled the cord on the little sign that read *Open*, so that folks walking down the street would know. Pushing on the door to make sure it was actually unlocked, I thought about just stepping outside to put some space between Mai and myself, but it was too cold, so I just let it close and turned to see her smiling at the counter.

"Fine," I said with a sigh. "I cried and he held me. Then we went upstairs. We played a little game of strip poker without cards. More of a tit for tat kind of game. He complained that I wasn't playing fair because I had more clothes on, but I ended up with less on than him, eventually. Boy can talk me out of my clothes faster than anything, which was both a delight and kinda freaked me out. Like, I wanted to take them off, and all he had to do was sit there and smile."

"He does seem to have a nice smile," she said.

"You don't know the half of it," I said.

"So, you're naked," she said.

I opened my mouth to continue, but the door opened and someone walked in.

"Welcome in," Mai said with a smile.

With those words, our day began, and just got busier as it went along. While it wasn't nearly as busy as the last few days had been, it was still a steady stream of people stopping in to get their favorite tea, or to try something new. Neither one of us really had any time to do much more than make the quick run to the restroom if needed, and take a sip of water, but it was a good kind of busy. Steady, but not over-whelmingly so, and before we knew it, we were seeing the crowd trickle down and thin out until it just stopped. I looked at the clock on our point-of-sale device and realized that we were past our regular closing time, so I took the keys and locked the door, pulling the cord to shut the open sign off.

"Well, that was fun," she said as I turned around.

"Both better and worse than the last couple of days," I said. "At least we got a little bit of down time to restock today."

"It'll be interesting to see whether our sales are close to what we've been getting," Mai replied. "Although, nothing is gonna distract me from our conversation we started at the beginning of the day."

"Shit," I said. "I was hoping you'd forget."

"Forget about that fine man with that fine ass walking away from you after he kissed you so sweet it was nauseating?" she asked. "Not likely. Now, spill. We got time, and we aren't gonna get distracted. Unless we get dickstracted, as in, he comes back to the shop."

"You're terrible," I said. "You know that, right?"

"But you love me," she said.

"Fine," I said, not at all happy about having to relive my night with someone who wasn't actually there. "Where did I leave off?"

"He unlocked the gate for you," she said. "You cried, he held you, and it's really boring so far, so I expect spice soon."

"God, why did I start this?" I asked but didn't expect an answer.

"Just tell me," she said. "You'll feel better after you do."

I glared at her, but knew she was right, so I began at the beginning, with him coming into my shop after he helped me unlock the gate.

# CHAPTER THIRTY-FIVE

*J*ohn...

"Clean Scene Biohazard and Waste Removal," a woman said as she answered the phone. "How can we help you?"

"Yeah," I began. "I have a job I need to get a bid on."

"What's the city?" she asked.

"Seattle," I replied.

"Home or apartment?"

"Apartment," I said.

"Was it the actual location of the crime?" she asked. "Or were you an adjacent space?"

"It was the apartment above mine," I said. "I don't know exactly what happened, but I was given your card by one of the responding police officers."

"I see," she said, and I could hear her typing things into her computer. "What's the address?"

I rattled it off to her, then asked, "Do I need to be there to let folks in?"

"Has the scene been released?" she asked.

"I have no idea," I replied. "I've been at a hotel the last couple of nights."

"We'll have to confirm with the police department that the scene has been released," she said. "Also, do you have renters' insurance? If you do, we can bill them directly and you would just be responsible for the deductible."

"Didn't even think of that," I said. "I do have that. Should I call them? Or will you call them? I've never had to deal with this before."

"Most folks who call us are new at this," she said. "I'll be happy to walk you through the process. Do you have the information for your renters' insurance with you?"

"I think I do," I said. "Can you hang on while I turn my laptop on and go hunting?"

"Sure," she said. "In the meantime, I'm going to place you on hold, and check on the status of the scene. Do you have the apartment number of where it actually took place?"

"I assume it's the one above mine," I said. "So, same apartment number, just a four at the beginning instead of a three."

"Great," she said. "I'll put you on hold while I get this information. You can look up your insurance information, and I'll get the ball rolling once I have that as well. Before I do, can I get your name and a good phone number, just in case the call is disconnected?"

"Sure," I said. "My name's John Huffman."

I rattled off my phone number and she said, "Thanks. I'm going to place you on hold now."

"Okay," I said, then heard the classic music that came on when you were placed on hold.

Grabbing my laptop, I plugged it into the outlet on the desk in the hotel room, opening the top to get it moving. I put my phone on speaker so I had two hands to work with. Once it was up and running, I logged on and went to my browser to get the insurance information she'd asked for. There was so much to this that I hadn't even thought about, so it was nice that the woman I was talking to knew what to do. After I logged into my insurance site, I pulled up the rental insurance I had with them and jotted down the number on the notepad that was on the hotel's desk. I also made a note of the name and phone number for my actual agent back in Colorado, just in case they needed that as well.

"Mr. Huffman?" she asked when she came back on the line.

"I'm here," I said.

"Great," she said. "Looks like the scene has been released, so we're good to go there. Did you find your insurance information?"

"I did," I said. "What do you need?"

"Let's start with the carrier," she said. "Then I'll get the policy number and ask a few more questions specific to that."

I gave her the carrier, then the insurance policy number. She asked me about deductibles and what specific kind of coverage I had, but I wasn't able to answer those questions, so gave her my agent's name and number.

"Do you want me to call him to get all that information?" I asked.

"No need," she said. "I'll just call corporate to get a copy of the policy. Are you available to meet with a crew today?"

"Sure," I said. "I'm off work currently, so any day this week will be fine."

"Perfect," she said. "Let me check my crew status and I'll be right back."

Again, I heard the music, but it was only for a moment before she was back on the line.

"We have a crew that is at the site now," she said. "Family of the deceased called us as well, so if you're close, I can have them meet you once they've finished."

"I'll have to get a car back to the apartment," I said. "I'm a bit away from there right now. What time would work to meet them?"

"They'll be there all day," she said. "If you can get there by, say, four, it should be good. Can you make that happen?"

"Definitely," I said. "Should I meet them in the lobby or what?"

"Whatever works for you," she said. "Can you get into your apartment?"

"I don't know that I want to," I said. "The smell was pretty bad when I was there a couple days ago, so my guess is it isn't any better."

"I understand," she said. "Well, can they reach you at this number?"

"Yeah," I said. "That's my cell, so it goes with me everywhere."

"Great," she said. "I'll have them give you a call when they're finished for the day and let you know where they want to meet you."

"Sounds good," I said.

"Perfect," she said. "While you're getting those things situated, I'll work on the insurance front and make sure we get you covered for this cleaning."

"Should I contact my agent?" I asked.

"You don't have to," she said. "But you can if you feel like it. I usually work with the corporate portion of the company, and you're likely to have a personal agent, so they may be able to walk you through what to expect on your end."

"Great," I said. "Thanks again."

"No problem," she said. "I understand the stress this is likely causing you. Make sure you mention to your agent that you have stayed in a hotel while you couldn't access your apartment. You may be able to use what you've paid toward your deductible, or at least a portion of it."

"Never thought about that," I said.

"There are a lot of things folks don't think about," she said. "Unless you've dealt with it a lot, you won't know what to look for or ask. It's why we're trained to ask these types of questions. We work with a lot of crime victims, so we try to ask all the questions so the family doesn't have to worry about those kinds of things."

"Well, you've been very helpful," I said. "I really appreciate everything you've done for me today. I'll look forward to talking to your techs later today."

"All right," she said. "And if you don't hear from them by about a quarter to five, give me a call back, and I'll reach out to them. I don't want you to be waiting too long if you don't have to."

"I appreciate that," I said. "You really do think of everything."

"It's what we do," she said. "I appreciate your patience as we worked through all this. Are there any other questions I can answer for you?"

"Not that I can think of," I said. "I assume they'll give me a time frame for cleanup once I talk to them, right?"

"They should be able to give you a ballpark time frame," she said. "But it will be a best guess kind of thing, not a guarantee."

"Oh, yeah," I said. "I completely understand that. Just wanted to see if I'd know, or at least have an idea."

"For sure," she said. "Any other questions?"

"I don't think so," I said. "Thanks so much."

"Sure thing," she said. "And thanks for trusting Clean Scene Biohazard and Waste Removal."

I disconnected the call and realized that there was a whole lot more I was going to have to do. Instead of giving Skye a play-by-play of what was going on, I decided to start making the rest of my calls. One thing I wanted to do was get my car, and the sooner I could do that, the better. So, I pulled up my list of numbers in my phone to find the number for the stadium, and who we needed to call in off hours or when the team was out of town, making the call.

"Cascades Stadium," the woman who answered the phone said. "How can I direct your call?"

"Yeah, I need to pick up my car from the parking inside the stadium," I said. "I'm in Seattle on a suspension, so will need to pick it up as soon as possible."

"Sure thing," she said. "Can I get your name?"

"John Huffman," I said.

"Thanks, Mr. Huffman," she said. "Let me just take a look and see what I can do for you. Would you mind holding for just a moment?"

"No problem," I said, figuring I'd have to do that.

I looked around my hotel room as I waited on hold, trying to decide whether I should gather everything up or leave it here, and figure it all out in the morning.

"Mr. Huffman?" the woman said as she came back on the line.

"I'm here," I said.

"Great," she said. "Looks like you can come in any time before five tonight. Just make sure you bring your team identification with you so we can let you in."

"I will," I said. "Where should I plan to come in?"

"Come through the press entrance," she said. "Show them your card and they'll direct you through the doors to the tunnels. You know how to get to the parking lot from there, right?"

"Oh yeah," I said. "Done that walk enough times to know it pretty well."

"Great," she said. "We close that door right at five, so make sure you're in before then so you can get your car out before we lock the building up."

"I'll probably be there pretty soon," I said. "I have a few things to do before but will be heading out fairly soon."

"We'll see you when you get here," she said.

"Thanks," I said, then disconnected the call.

The first two calls were easy, which was nice, so I decided to go ahead and make the last call on my list, which was to my insurance agent. Hopefully, they'd have good news for me.

"Colorado Insurance Company," the man who answered the phone said. "How can I help you?"

"I've had an incident at my apartment," I said. "I already have a company that is going to come out, and give me an estimate on cleaning the place, but wanted to see if my hotel for the last couple of nights, as well as the next one, would be covered by this as well."

"Let's take a look," he said. "Can I get your name?"

"John Huffman," I said, then gave him my policy number, since I was sure he was going to be asking for it.

"If you wouldn't mind, I'm going to place you on hold so I can check your policy," he said.

"Totally fine," I said, knowing it was coming anyway.

It didn't take long before he came back on the line.

"Looks like you have a one-thousand-dollar deductible," he said. "What type of incident happened?"

"Someone died," I said. "Not in my apartment, but the one above. There's just damage to my apartment."

"Have you contacted the apartment company?" he asked.

"They didn't even want to send someone out to look at what was happening," I said.

"Their insurance should cover the damage to the building itself," he said. "If you want, I can work to try to get them to cover the damage to your property, too. It will likely take a few days to get everything ironed out, but we should definitely be able to do something about your housing situation at the very least."

"Can I move?" I asked. "I mean, my lease is until the end of October, but I don't really want to stay there."

"Again, that's something that you'll have to discuss with your apartment complex," he said. "Oftentimes, they're understanding about these sorts of things. If you have any other issues, we can try to assist in making that happen."

"Great," I said. "I gave the company that's going to be cleaning up the insurance information and the policy number, and they said they were going to be getting that side of things handled. Should I have them contacting the apartment building as well?"

"It would be a good idea," he said. "Most larger complexes have their own insurance that covers these types of situations. There's always those who don't, or don't think they need to, which is why you have renters' insurance. It will cover what theirs doesn't and give us the chance to work on getting it covered."

"I didn't realize this was gonna be such a big thing," I said. "Like, how does this even happen to me?"

"I can't tell you that," he said. "But I can tell you that we'll do everything we can to make it as simple and painless as possible."

"Thanks," I said. "It's already been too much, and I'm just getting started."

"Well, let me be the first to tell you how sorry I am that this has happened to you," he said. "And, like I said, I'll do my best to help mitigate the complications involved. Let me just make sure I have all the contact information for you should we need additional information."

He asked for my address, phone number, email, and the name and number of the company that I'd asked to do the cleanup. Once that was done, he thanked me for my call and disconnected it.

It looked like this was gonna turn into a whole thing that may take all day, and I didn't want to leave Skye in the dark if I could help it. I sent a text, letting her know things were more complicated than I thought, and I may not be available the rest of the day. She didn't respond, but I guessed it was because it was busy for her, so I didn't take it personally. I figured I'd hear from her when she had the chance.

# CHAPTER THIRTY-SIX

*S*kye...

"Let me get this straight," Mai said when I'd finished. "You had him in your apartment, he only had his jeans on, you were naked except your panties, and you didn't have sex?"

"I mean," I said with a shrug.

"Girl," she said, hand on her hip. "How the fuck did you let him go? Like, there's no way I'd not let him fuck me any which way he wanted."

"I can't really help my trauma responses," I said, embarrassed that it had fucked everything up the night before.

"I know, babe," she said, then gave me a hug. "You gonna try again tonight?"

"I dunno," I said. "I suppose I should check my phone and see what's up. I completely forgot that I plugged it in this morning."

Walking to the office, I grabbed my phone and tapped the screen to see that I did have several notifications. Swiping the screen, I unlocked the phone and went for the texts that were there. A few from my parents, and one from my uncle, all checking in to see how things were going with the store. I quickly replied to them, letting everyone know that I had plenty of help with Mai, and that supplies were lasting more than just part of the day. Then I found what I was looking for. A text from John.

*This is turning out to be way more complicated than I thought. Might not hear much from me today. Not that I don't want to be near you, just that life is fucked up and messing with me.*

Looking at the time the message was sent, I realized that it was fairly early in the day, and he probably thought I was completely blowing him off since I didn't respond. While I was starting to get that freak out, I made my brain shut it down, and just respond. Can't go backward in time, so just start where I was. Another thing therapy had taught me.

*Sorry I didn't respond earlier. Shop got busy. While it went by quickly, I still thought about you today.*

I sent it, then read what it was, and lord have mercy, did I sound desperate. The phone buzzed right away, but it was a notification for another app.

"Well?" Mai asked when I came back out.

"He told me not to worry if I didn't hear from him," I said.

"Good thing," she said. "We were too busy for you to connect, anyway. Not that I wouldn't have covered if he'd wanted to come by and take you somewhere to fuck your brains out."

"Mai," I said. "Can we not talk like that?"

"What?" she said. "Don't tell me you don't want to. I mean, he looks like he'd be fun. Like make up sex with him would probably be wild and crazy."

"Is that all you think about?" I asked her.

"I mean," she said with a shrug. "I'm not getting any, so I need to find an outlet, and your new man is just the outlet that will inspire my mind."

"Go get a hookup," I said. "I know it's not really your thing so much, but you need it, because you're driving me crazy with not getting any."

"Are you telling me to have meaningless sex with some rando?"

"Yes," I said emphatically. "I am absolutely telling you to just go get laid."

"Bossy, ain'tcha," she said.

"Well," I said. "What do you expect?"

"I expect a better report from tonight," she said. "Did you message him back?"

"I did," I said. "But it kinda sounds desperate."

"Lemme see," she said, holding her hand out for my phone.

I handed it over and she read the text, then looked at me.

"What?" I asked.

"It's a good start," she said, then started typing.

"Give me that," I said, but she was quick, moving into the bathroom and locking the door. "Mai, you give me back my fucking phone."

I heard her giggle, then the door unlocked and she came out, handing the phone back. I opened the texting app and read what she sent.

*Been thinking about you since you left. When do you think you can come back over?*

Okay, that wasn't bad, but then I looked at the next one.

*Gonna need you to be ready to rock my world tonight. None of that halfway business tonight. No, we're going all the way and then some. When do you think you can get here?*

I tried to delete the message, but it was already gone. Then I saw the little bubble come up that showed he was typing, and I kind of just slid down the wall and sat on the floor, thankful it had been behind me and caught me. The bubble went away, and I looked up at Mai, my face likely showing a mixture of terror, anger, and excitement in equal measures.

"He answer?" she asked, her smug smile still there, but there was some concern highlighting the edges.

I shook my head, not trusting my voice. The bubbles came back, and I watched, waiting for what I wasn't sure. When the chime went off, I closed my eyes and just handed the phone to Mai. She'd tell me if it was bad, and if it was, she'd know how to respond.

"Oh, yeah," she said and I could hear her typing away on the screen.

"Give it," I said, but she shook her head, replying, "I got you."

When she was done, she handed it to me and I looked at what he said and what she sent back.

*I'm ready, willing, and able if you're up for it.*

Okay, that was a good sign. Then I read what she said.

*Just let me know and I'll be waiting. Shop's closed, so I can either meet you at your hotel or you can come here. Just let me know.*

Still not awful. At least she wasn't as lewd this time. The bubbles were back, so I waited, anxiously anticipating what he was gonna say.

*I'm good with either, but figured you'd feel more comfortable at yours. We can do my hotel if you want. Just let me know and I'll give you the details.*

Instead of letting Mai speak for me, I typed a response.

*Mine would be great. Got a time in mind?*

"Look at you go with your bad self," Mai said, having slid down the wall to sit next to me. "You're actually doing it and doing a great job. Now, when I see you in the morning, I either need so many details I'll go off from your description, or you're just gonna have to not be able to walk straight."

"Oh. My. God," I said. "You never give up."

"And I'll Rick roll you if you ever think I will," she said with a laugh. "You want me to stay?"

"I don't think you need to," I said. "We've already done all the closing stuff, so there really isn't much else to do."

"I think we should go up to your apartment and pick something sexy out for you to wear," she said. "Really set the mood for a wild night."

"I am not letting you pick out my underwear," I said, pushing up from the floor. "I have a fine set on, thank you very much."

"You *are* gonna shower, right?" she asked. "I mean, you want to be fresh and clean when he goes down to eat you out. Don't want any of that stanky smell going on."

"Are you saying I stink?"

"No," she said. "But I don't want you to risk it, either. Nothing says gross like a body that hasn't been primed and pumped and is ready to go. Get that engine revved up so when he gets here, you can climb that ride and take it all the way to the stratosphere."

"You know I'm not a car, right?" I asked.

"Same principle," she said. "Gas that baby up, no wait, don't gas it up. But fuel up. Yeah, that's a better way to put it. Make sure you've got lots of hydration so you don't dry up. If you get a chance, get yourself primed for action with a toy or something. Take it into the shower and get yourself in the right headspace for it. Maybe then it'll happen even faster than before and you won't have to wait, or let your brain fuck it up again."

"You're ridiculous," I said. "You know that, right?"

"Oh, I know," she said, standing up herself. "Now, I'm gonna head out, and see if I can find someone to fuck. You get this all locked up, head upstairs and clean up and get ready, then when he says he's on his way, come down with a robe over your sexy outfit so he knows what's gonna happen."

"Now I know you need to get it," I said with a laugh. "Go find something else to occupy your mind and keep you out of my business."

"I'm gonna need to know all about your business," she said. "Tomorrow, when you get down here – because I expect you to sleep in after being worn out tonight – you can tell me every single detail. I'm talking size, width, piercings, tatts, hair, positions…"

"I get it," I said, unlocking the door.

"I hope you do," she said, pulling the gate across the front of the shop.

"Get out of here," I said, but it was obvious that I was being silly at that point. "I have to go prime my engine, or whatever."

"That's my girl," she said.

I locked the gate, then closed the door, locking it as well. The lights were turned off, the alarm set, and I headed up the back stairs to my apartment, wondering whether I should heed her advice, and get myself going in the shower or not.

# CHAPTER THIRTY-SEVEN

*J*ohn...

The texts were a little spicier than I expected from her, but I had to think that someone was helping her with them, because they just didn't sound like they were coming from her. Either way, I was happy with it, and was looking forward to getting back over to her place so we could try to continue what we started the night before.

My day had been filled with calls to everyone and their cousin, then going to pick up my car so I had something to get me between my apartment, the hotel, and anywhere else I needed to get to. Once I had my car, I went to my apartment to meet the guys from the cleaning company, and boy did I get the scoop on what had gone on in the apartment above me. I couldn't wait to share with Skye, although I was gonna wait until after any fun we got to, which I hoped would happen sooner rather than later.

Fortunately, my apartment didn't quite smell as bad as it had before, and the guys had suggested that, since I was on the third floor, and the fact that some of my windows didn't have a fire escape attached to them, that I open it up a bit, at least enough to get some air flow going, so that the remnants of the smell could go away. They even suggested I pick up a couple of fans to help in that manner, so I'd gone to get them after talking to the guys, and them getting what they would need to do an estimate.

From what I could tell, the coffee table was gonna be a total loss. They'd given me some ideas on what to do to keep the ick that had come through my ceiling where it was. I'd even gotten them to help me take the table down, and out of the apartment and into the dumpster outside, so at least there was that. They had taken pictures of it before we did anything, too, so that was good. Not like the apartment building could try to claim it wasn't there since the table had been removed.

Much later than I wanted, I was finally on my way back to the hotel to park my car before heading over to Skye's. I'd wanted to get a shower before going over, but maybe we could make that as part of our evening plans.

*Finally finished with everything. Heading that direction. Have to drop the car at the hotel. Should I shower before I get there? Or should we do that together?*

Taking the elevator down to the garage, I climbed into my car and started it up, plugging my phone into the system so it would be charged, and if she decided to call, I could answer through the car's stereo instead of trying to answer while driving. Pulling out onto the street, I turned and headed toward downtown. It wasn't that far, and thankfully it was after the main rush hour of traffic, although some-times I wondered whether there really was downtime when it came to the roads in Seattle.

Pulling up in front of the hotel, and thankfully they had a valet service, which I was definitely going to take advantage of. I got out of the car, and met the young man standing at the stand, who came over to me as I stepped out.

"You checked in already?" he asked.

"I am," I said.

"What's your room number? I can charge it to your room," he said.

I gave him my room number and left the keys in the ignition. He handed me a card and climbed in to take it to their parking garage. Heading into the building, I walked to the elevator, and pressed the up button, waiting for it to show up. The doors opened, and I waited to see if anyone was coming out. When no one did, I stepped in and the door began to close, when a woman's voice called out to hold the door. Hitting the button, the doors opened, and the woman from the other night stepped in.

"I guess we're destined to meet up again," she said. "Must mean you should come up to my room so we can get the night going in the right direction."

"Sorry," I said, punching the button for my floor, and the one for the top floor she had pressed when we were in the elevator before.

The door closed and she moved closer to me. I stepped back and against the wall, but she had turned and was damn near prowling toward me, like a cat stalking its prey. Sliding along the wall toward the back of the space, trying to get away from her, but she kept on moving, following me around it. When I was in front of the doors, I hit the button to open them, not caring whether I'd made it to my floor or not.

I almost fell out of the small space when the doors opened, scrambling to keep my feet under me. I backed away from her and walked to the other wall, waiting for the doors to close on her, hoping she wouldn't step out and follow me further.

"Your loss," she said, and the snide way she said it told me exactly what kind of woman she was, one who used men to fulfill her fantasies, and nothing more.

I let out a breath in a rush once she was gone, and turned to walk down to my room. Keying my way in with the card on the reader, I opened the door and stepped inside. I hadn't gotten a response from Skye, but I wanted to get to her sooner rather than later, so I grabbed my small duffle bag that I used to go to the gym when I was on the road and stuffed a spare pair of socks and jeans, along with a tee shirt and some boxers into it, then grabbed the box of condoms I had in the suitcase, just in case. Then I zipped it up. I was almost out the door when I realized I should take my charger with me so I wouldn't end up with a dead phone in the morning. Once that was stuffed into the bag as well, I headed out.

Not wanting to risk meeting the woman in the elevator again, I made my way toward the stairs, and opened the door to head down to the lobby. Walking across the space, I went out the door, and saw the same valet guy standing at the podium.

"You need your car?" he asked, a confused look on his face.

"Nah, man," I said. "I'm walking to meet a friend. There's no place to park near their place."

"Okay," he said. "'Cause if you did, I'd suggest you let us know when you drop it off, and we'll keep it here."

"If I need that, I'll make sure I do it," I said. "Thanks."

"No problem," he said. "Enjoy your night."

"You, too," I said, walking down the sidewalk.

It was cool, but the sun was still up, so I knew it would get cold before long. Thankfully, I had a warm place to go, and with luck, I'd have a warm body against mine sooner rather than later. The walk to the Market was easy, and it didn't take long before I was heading down the alley toward the front of her shop.

I pulled out my phone to check and see if she'd responded to my text, but there wasn't any. Hopefully, she was just distracted, so when I got to her place, I looked up to the windows above the shop that I knew were in her living room area. I could see lights on, but not super bright, which made me think they were just coming from her bedroom rather than the living room itself.

Wondering whether I'd gotten the signals mixed up, I decided on just calling her. I pressed the button to make the call and the phone rang several times before going to voicemail. I tried again, hoping she'd answer it, but again it rang, then went to voicemail. Pulling up the messages, just to make sure I hadn't got it wrong, and that she did, in fact, want me at her place tonight, I reread them.

*I'm ready, willing, and able if you're up for it.*

This was the first one, which seemed fine.

*Just let me know and I'll be waiting. Shop's closed, so I can either meet you at your hotel or you can come here. Just let me know.*

It clearly said she wanted me there, and that I should let her know.

*I'm good with either, but figured you'd feel more comfortable at yours. We can do my hotel if you want, just let me know and I'll give you the details.*

My response was what I'd asked about her desires.

*Mine would be great. Got a time in mind?*

Okay, so she definitely wanted me to come over, and asked about a time. My next response was much later, letting her know I was on my way. Maybe when she didn't get an answer right away, she thought I wasn't coming, so I checked the bottom to see if it had been read, which it hadn't. Checking the times on the messages, I sent mine only about half an hour or so after she'd sent hers, so I didn't think it would be an issue, but obviously there was something going on. I had no other way to get in touch with her, and I didn't want to go back to my hotel, because I was sure she was gonna be here. I tried one more time to call her, and got the exact same response, with the call going to voicemail after a few rings. This time, though, I decided to leave a message.

"Hey," I said. "It's John. I thought you were cool with me coming over. I'm going into the bar next door to grab some food. If you get this, and still want me to come over, send me a text or call me, although text would be better with the noise in the bar. Hope to see you soon."

Maybe that was enough that it would let her know I was here and ready when she was. Now, I just had to wait.

# CHAPTER THIRTY-EIGHT

*S*kye...
          When I walked into my apartment, everything was quiet, and it really felt peaceful. I had to figure out what all I needed to do before John came over, so I checked the phone, and he hadn't sent a response asking for a time. Guessing he was busy, as he had been earlier, I just plugged my phone in, and set it on my nightstand. The drawer was just slightly open, which was a bit odd, but not the end of the world. Sometimes I forgot to shut it all the way. Opening it, I saw that my toy was indeed plugged in, and the light indicated it was fully charged, so, taking a page out of Mai's book, I pulled it out, and set it on my bed.

Pulling my sweater over my head, I dropped it on the cedar chest at the end of the bed. The rest of my clothes followed it, and I was completely naked in just a couple of minutes. Picking up the toy, I headed into the bathroom, setting the toy on the stool next to the tub. I grabbed a towel and a washcloth, putting the towel under the toy, and throwing the cloth over the bar of the curtain.

Showers were usually done as a necessity and not as something enjoyable, but maybe this might change my perception of them. I turned on the water, letting it heat up before pulling the plunger thing up to send the water out of the shower head. I slipped into the tub, testing the water with my foot before stepping directly into the spray. The heat felt good as it ran down my body, and I ducked my head under it to wet my hair.

Grabbing the bottle for my shampoo, I squeezed a little into my hand. It seemed to last much longer now that I'd cut my hair again. At first, I hadn't understood why Dylan wanted me to grow it long, but then he started using it against me. Wrapping it around his hand as he held me where he wanted me to be, pulling it this way or that to get me to move, and dragging me by it into his bedroom at his apartment when he wanted to use my body.

An involuntary shudder went through my body as the thought crossed my mind. It hadn't started like that, but it happened faster than I would have imagined. From him asking me to do something I wasn't comfortable with, to using his manipulative words to convince me it was wrong to deny it, then simply taking it, using me as his ultimate fuck toy. A sob left my mouth, and I cried, letting the water wash the tears away. After a bit, when I was about as cried out as I could be, I finished washing my hair, then washed my face before putting conditioner into my hair. It wasn't much, but without it, my hair tended to just kind of lay there, so I added it to my routine at the suggestion of my friend, Alexis. She'd done wonders for my self-esteem when she'd cut every last long lock off my head. It was just as freeing as walking away from Dylan.

I really needed to do another girls night. It had been ages, and now that I had help at the shop, and the fact that it was going really well there, what with all the publicity I'd gotten from a freaking social media post, I had extra cash I could spend on my best friends. Mai had quickly become a part of our posse, adding another voice to the merry band of ladies who made up my found family. Of course, she and Britta were the only ones who knew about John, unless they'd spread the news around. Mai wouldn't, because the only people she could tell were her parents, and the others who worked with them, which would mean the word would get back to my parents, which we both knew would be bad.

"Focus girl," I said out loud, hoping it would bring me back to the here and now.

I reached out the side of the shower, and grabbed the toy, pressing the button to turn it on. The vibration was low, and I really couldn't hear it, but I could feel it. God, it had been so long since I'd done anything that I wondered if I'd closed up. Considering I was still getting my period, I assumed it was still in working order, just had to check things out, and make sure nothing got broken.

"Yeah, clinical thoughts are exactly how to turn you on, girl," I said to myself. "Nothing gets you all hot and bothered like thinking that way."

I laughed. I couldn't help it. It was so ridiculous to be talking to myself in my shower while trying to turn myself on. All I wanted was for John to be in there with me. Maybe with him beside me, moving his hands and his lips along my body, I could get revved up, as Mai had so succinctly put it.

Thinking about him, though, did make my breath catch, shuddering out in a rumble of air. And to think of how close we came to consummating the relationship on the first day we met felt somehow thrilling. Like, doing so would be naughty on so many levels. I didn't hook up. Never had. The fact that I kept Dylan around longer than the night I met him was a testament to how manipulative he was. But tonight was *not* about him. No, tonight was all about banishing any memory of him from my entire world.

Closing my eyes, I pictured John. The tall, imposing figure that he was, and how gentle he'd been with me, even from the beginning. While he terrified me initially, he took the time to make sure that I knew he meant me no harm. Not only that, but that he was more than just a little bit interested in me. Taking me to lunch in the middle of my day was a delight. Dinner was even better, in that he let me lead things on that front. The only thing marring that memory was the fact that Tony didn't take too kindly to me being out with a man that wasn't him. But even with that, John had been kind in his reprimand of the kid.

Then, after he'd left me in my shop, he went back to his hotel. He could have pushed, insisted that I let him in, but he didn't. Instead, he told me, in words and through texts, that he was there for me in whatever capacity I needed. Of course, I fell apart, called him back to me, and he was willing to come out in the middle of the night to rescue me. Nothing about that felt like it was a temporary thing. No, everything he'd done had been clearly meant to tell me that he was in it for the long haul.

The water rushing over my body was helping me to relax, and the suds from the soap I'd put onto my hand was making moving them along my skin that much easier. I still had the toy in one hand, vibrating in that low tone that I could feel but not hear. I slicked the silicone along my body, letting it hum along my skin as I moved it lower, and lower still, to the very center of myself. It was slick as it slid along my pussy lips, humming me up into a bit more of that excited feeling.

In the entirety of time I spent with my ex, had he let me fall over the top of that high hill and into the bliss that was supposed to be there? No, he'd always held me just on the edge, always in control of me, no matter what. I honestly wondered whether I could orgasm, since I never had in my life. Maybe it wasn't something I could do, which made me sad, because the way the girls talked, it was one of the best things to happen to a person.

Determined to figure out what it was all about, I pressed further, letting my hands just kind of take control, trying to shut my brain down and to just feel. It was hard at first, but then I thought about the way John had been when he came into my apartment. The teasing he did with me, working to get me to take my clothes off, while doing the same himself. How he'd managed to stay dressed when I was naked, still confused me, but I didn't think about that.

Instead, I thought about his chest, the way the muscles moved underneath his skin. The emotions he showed when I asked about the tattoo he'd gotten for his friend. How he'd smiled, just a little, with each piece of clothing I took off, and how he willingly played the game with me without any complaints, even when he was pushing me to go faster. Then there was the awe I saw in his eyes when I dropped my bra to the floor, and how he'd scooped me up and pinned me to the door. Not in a way that was dominating, but more of a way to make sure I was safe while we kissed.

Each of those moments were imprinted on my brain, and the emotions, the feelings, that they pulled from me helped get me to move with my toy and my hands. Picking up my foot, I placed it on the edge of the tub, allowing myself to have better access to my pussy, and the sliding of the toy along my lips was really making me breathe in halting, quick breaths. I slid the toy inside me, slowly at first, just the tip, to make sure it wasn't gonna hurt. Considering every time something went in there it hurt, it was wise to be cautious. Thankfully, no pain came, and I let it hum right at the edge of my innermost place.

The motion felt better than just good, and I kind of threw my head back, allowing myself to be immersed in the moment. Moving on its own, my hand slid the toy out, then back in, farther this time, but still not completely inside me, and wow, that hum was making things feel very good. Again, I pulled it out, then moved it back in, even further this time, and it was even better. Feeling brave, I pushed it even further in, and the little thing that stuck out the side came in contact with my clit, and I nearly fell, grabbing the bar on the side of the shower for support. Maybe doing this in the shower wasn't such a good idea, but I didn't want to stop. But it wasn't safe to stay standing if that was going to be the reaction I was going to have.

Pulling the toy out, I felt the loss, and it was an odd thing. I'd never felt that way after having sex before, and even though this wasn't technically sex, it was still an odd thing to experience. Rinsing the conditioner out of my hair, I shut the shower off, and slid the curtain back, grabbing up the towel I'd set out. I quickly dried off, wanting to get back to what I'd been doing, and dropped the towel on the floor, taking the toy with me back to my bed.

I flipped the covers back, the white sheet shining in the little light from the bedside table I'd turned on. I sat down, sliding over so I was flat on my back, and pulled my feet up, making my knees rise up and fall open. That allowed me easy access to myself, the place I wanted to be, and I slid the toy back down along my lips. While I'd dried off, I was still wet enough that it slid along my pussy easily. After only a couple of strokes, I shifted so that I could slide it inside myself, and the way I did put my face right near the pillow John had used the night before.

Whoever said that men don't have a distinct odor were idiots. I'd been up close and personal with him for just a short amount of time, but I was sure that his scent was something that would likely cause me to become intoxicated every time I smelled it. Leaning more toward the pillow, I inhaled his scent while simultaneously impaling myself with a piece of silicone surrounding a motor and other electronics. I was sure it wasn't anywhere near what it would feel like to have the actual man inside me, what I did know was that this was something I wanted.

Pressing the toy as deep as I could, the little extra bit right against my clit, my body kind of just fell apart. I could feel my insides pulsating around the foreign object, squeezing it as if it could pull it deeper inside. My whole body kind of tightened up, pulsating around that one small portion, that little piece of me that had been so abused it wasn't sure what it was supposed to do, until finally, I saw stars and felt like I'd been blown to pieces, left to scatter along the winds with no rhyme or reason as to where the pieces would land.

As I came back together, I could hear a noise, as if it were trying to intrude on the peaceful space I'd found. It went away, thankfully, but then started up again. Blocking the sound out, I concentrated on my body, the way it felt, the joy that was within my soul. Nothing could have prepared me to feel this, and I was so sad that I'd missed out on it for so long.

MY PHONE RINGING WOKE ME, AND I WASN'T SURE WHEN I'D GONE TO sleep. I rolled over only to realize that I'd left the toy inside me, and it kind of just slid out with this sickening sound. I pushed it away and looked at the phone. The call had ended, but I saw that I had several missed calls. Swiping the screen up and unlocking it, I pulled down the top to look at my notifications. I'd definitely missed a call, or more like a dozen. All of them from John.

"Oh, no," I said, realizing that I'd told him to come over.

Looking at the time, and the last call, I wondered if he'd left a message at all. Instead of listening to those, I just pressed the button to return the call. It only rang once, then he answered, but I could barely hear him from the noise in the background.

"I can't hear you," I shouted into the phone, standing up and grabbing the toy from the bed.

The noise slowly went down, and I finally heard him.

"I tried to call," he said. "I've actually called a few times. I didn't want to wake you up if you were sleeping, but I was worried."

"Sorry," I said, moving to the bathroom to set the toy in the sink. "I must have fallen asleep and not heard the phone. Did you go back to your hotel?"

"I'm next door," he said. "Well, actually, I'm right outside. Do you want me to stay here?"

"Yes," I nearly shouted. "I mean, if you want."

God, I was an embarrassment, even to myself.

"I would love to stay," he said, and I couldn't help but feel the smile tug at my lips.

"Give me about ten minutes and I'll let you in," I said.

"Front or back?" he asked.

"Front," I said.

"Okay," he replied. "I'll go in and settle up my tab, then be back out."

"Okay," I replied. "See you soon."

"Not soon enough," he said, then disconnected the call.

"Fuck," I said, then looked at my reflection in the mirror.

I had a glow about me, something I'd never seen before. My cheeks were pink, and my lips held that smile that said I'd done something wonderful, but it was a secret I wasn't going to share. I lifted the lid to the toilet and sat to go, wondering at the odd sensation I got. Guess it had been too long since anything had been up in there, but boy did I miss it.

After flushing, I washed my hands, along with the toy, then picked up the towel from the floor, and hung it over the bar to let it dry. I stuck the toy back in the drawer, connecting the little magnetic charger to its ports before shutting the drawer. Looking at the bed, I was impressed that it wasn't a mess. I picked up my clothes, and dropped them into the hamper, then pulled the robe I had on the bathroom door off and wrapped myself in it. After another quick look around, I figured it was as clean as it was gonna get, so I walked out into the living room to find my flats I used when I wasn't going anywhere but felt the need to have shoes on.

I grabbed my keys, slid my feet into my flats, and unbolted the door, turning the knob to head down the stairs. Opening the door to my shop, I turned the light on, pressed the passcode into the alarm panel, then went to the front where I anticipated seeing John. He wasn't there initially, but then he stepped from the bar next door to stand in front of my shop. I'd already unlocked the door, so all I had to do was undo the gate to let him in.

"You look comfy," he said when he stepped through the portal.

"Oh, yeah," I said and could feel the blush rush to my cheeks.

"Not at all complaining," he said after pulling the gate shut.

His presence at my back was warm and enticing, and I couldn't wait to get him upstairs to see what he could do to me. Pressing the keypad, I turned the alarm on, and opened the door to the hallway in the back, holding it as he came through behind me. The door shut, and I started up the stairs.

"Hey," he said when I was just a step up.

I turned around, and we were nearly eye to eye, which was a nice thing.

"You sure about this?" he asked, and it was odd that he was so hesitant.

"Absolutely," I said with as big a smile as I could muster.

"I don't want to push you too far," he said.

Reaching my arms out, I wrapped them around his neck, pulling him up against me, so I could kiss him. It was slow at first, just lips against each other, but it deepened quickly when he wrapped his own arms around my middle, hauling me against his hard front. I gasped at the motion, and he took the initiative to dive into my mouth with his tongue, sliding it along my own, twisting with mine in a dance I hoped would be repeated with other body parts sooner rather than later.

"I guess you're sure," he said when we finally came up for air.

"More than sure," I said and turned to continue up the steps to my apartment.

# CHAPTER THIRTY-NINE

*J*ohn...

"More than sure," she said before heading the rest of the way up the stairs.

The night before had left me wanting, and while I didn't want to push her, I wanted to at the same time. It didn't make sense in my head, but I knew she would be receptive to it if her outfit was any indication. What I wanted to do once she opened the door to her apartment, was shut it behind me, and pull the cord on her robe to let the fabric fall away from her beautiful frame. I wasn't gonna do it, but I wanted to.

Instead, I just kept my hands to myself, waiting for her to take the lead, and get us to where we were going. To my surprise, she stepped in and held the door as I walked through, then shut it behind her, and did what I wanted to, which was to pull that cord and drop the robe.

I swear my jaw hit the floor as her entire body was on display for me, and for me alone. I was a possessive son of a bitch when it came to certain things—my bats, my gloves, my car, and now, this woman. I wanted to keep her all to myself, and I intended to start right then.

"Is this a look but don't touch thing?" I asked, wanting to make sure she was comfortable before I pounced.

"Please touch me," she said in hushed tones, just barely above a whisper, and so desperate it was painful.

"My absolute pleasure," I replied, then took two steps to get to her.

Hands shot out from her sides as she pulled me in, backing herself up against the door behind her, her fingers through the loops on my jeans. I reached up and locked the deadbolt before letting my hand slide up along her arm to her shoulder, then the side of her neck to the back where I could hold her, and look at her before diving, mouth first, into a deep and languid kiss.

Her hands were at my back, pulling my shirt out of the waistband of my jeans, then sliding along the skin she'd found, pressing up and into my back as she held me fast against her. Both my hands were on either side of her face, holding her as I kissed her, letting her do the exploring while I just held on. A little mew came from her, and I pulled away, looking down into her eyes.

"Touch me," she begged, and it was so desperate, like she'd been starved of touch for entirely too long.

I let my hand slide down onto her shoulders as she pulled her own away from my skin and back to her side. I stepped back, taking my hands off her and the look I saw in her eyes was so sad.

"I just wanna take my clothes off," I said. "I'm not going anywhere. I promise."

The sigh of relief she let out was solemn, like she wasn't sure she believed me. Quick as I could, I let my jacket come off, unbuttoning my shirt as soon as it was on the back of the couch while simultaneously kicking off my shoes. I slid my feet back to pull the socks off as I laid my shirt on top of my jacket, then went to unbuckle my belt.

"Let me," she said, and I hadn't realized she'd come over to me.

Her hands were shaking, just a little bit, and I marveled as she focused enough to get the task done, finally pulling the lever out of the leather hole, sliding the rest of it through the ring. Then, she reached for the button at the top of my jeans, struggling to get it loose.

"Can I help?" I asked, and she looked up at me. "I'm not in a rush," I added, seeing the look on her face. "You just look like you're struggling."

She pulled her lower lip into her mouth, biting the edge of it as if deciding what she wanted to do. Finally, she nodded, and pulled her hands away. I undid the button, and she was back, quickly unzipping the jeans, and sliding her hands along the edge, delving down and under my balls, her eyes sliding closed as she smiled at her find. I wanted to take the jeans off, but I was captured, held in place by her soft hand on my most tender place.

"Mmm," she hummed, sliding her hand around the bottom to slip up along my shaft.

I was up against the back of the couch where she had me pinned with just one hand on me, and I didn't want to be anywhere else. My hands went up to the top of the couch to steady myself, trying desperately to control my reaction, not wanting to lose my load like a virgin at first touch.

"So soft," she murmured. "Steel wrapped in velvet."

I'd never heard the phrase, but the way she said it made me want to live up to whatever her fantasies were. My hips bucked as she pulled hard on my cock after sliding her hand up to the top. Her eyes popped open, fear clear in their brilliant blue.

"Just startled me," I said, and she let out a breath in a rush, clearly afraid of my reaction. "Mind if I get these off?"

She shook her head, stepping back and pulling her hand from my jeans. I missed the touch so much that I damn near tore my jeans when I pulled them down, stepping on the hems to get them off my feet. No sooner were they off than she was right there, holding my cock in her hand as she slid it up and down the shaft.

"God, you feel good," I said, the words coming out in a near growl. "Don't know how long I'll last if you keep that up."

She turned her eyes up to me, a smile playing on her lips, as she slowly knelt in front of me, sliding me through her perfect lips, and I swear I saw stars. Working me in and out, it was like she was a professional at blow jobs, because she pulled me right to the edge and over, and it was extremely embarrassing with how quickly she made me come.

"Oh, baby," I said when she'd sucked me dry. "That was fucking amazing."

"You like that?" she said, and the playful look in her eyes was something I hadn't seen.

"Very much," I replied, still working to stay upright. "I think I should return the favor, though. Where shall we start?"

She stood up, taking my hand to help, and turned and walked toward her room. That ass was one of the finest I'd seen, and my God did I want to hold it, kiss it, just slide my dick through her cheeks. The light on her bedside table was on and the room was cast in a soft glow. I hadn't realized it, but the kitchen light had been on, which was how I had been able to see her in the living room. Now, though, the light was more muted, a soft glow that mostly fell on the edge of the bed.

As she walked over to the bed, she looked back over her shoulder, and I wasn't sure whether she was making sure I was still there or trying to tease me with that shy look she had going on, and I had to call her out on it.

"I just want to eat you up," I said. "You good with that?"

She nodded, turning to sit on the edge of the bed.

"Stay right there," I said. "Lean back a little bit," I said, kind of pressing against her shoulder.

She leaned back on her elbows, her feet still on the floor, her knees tightly together. I slid my hand from her shoulder down her body, making it slow and as sensual as I could, as I dipped my fingers between her breasts, not touching the nipples as I had the night before. I wanted to get further down, making sure she was fine with everything. She was watching me, fixated on the way my hand moved along her skin.

I knelt in front of her, my hand finally making it to her hips, where I placed the other. With her knees so tight, there was no way to get between them, so I had to do something to get her to loosen up.

"You doing okay, baby?" I asked, keeping my tone low. She nodded, but I stopped and said, "Gonna need to hear it."

"I'm okay," she said, more a squeak than anything.

"If you want me to stop, you just say the word," I said, one hand going up to tip her eyes to mine. She nodded again, but I held her there until she said, "Okay."

"Anything I should know that you don't like?" I asked. "I don't want to push you into something you don't want to do. Remember, you're in charge here. When you say stop, I stop. No matter what's going on."

She pressed her lips together, rolling them between her teeth. I waited, wanting her to know I was a safe person, someone she could trust to take her word as if my life depended on it. Finally, after entirely too long, she sort of just blew a breath out and closed her eyes, sniffing in a bit.

"Hey, baby," I said. "It's okay."

Moving my hands back up, I pulled her to me, wrapping her in my arms as she just kind of went limp.

"I'm sorry," she said through a sob. "I'm so fucked up it's not even funny."

"Come on, baby," I said. "You've just been hurt. It's all good. I'm here. Let it out. When you're ready, we can try some more."

"I just want to let you love me, but I can't because I'm so fucking broken," she said, the last word coming out in a harsh breaking of her whole being.

Instead of just holding her like I was, at this awkward angle of me on the floor, and her on the bed, I pulled her down into my lap, letting my feet go out from under me, so I could sit on my ass, and hold her like she deserved.

"I don't know why you're still here," she said after she'd let most of the emotion out.

She'd pulled back some, still sitting on me, which put our faces at the same level.

"Because you're beautiful," I said. "And smart and capable and all the things I have wanted to find in one package. You're not needy, but you aren't so into self-sufficiency that you push me away. You've let me hold you, help you, even when you said I shouldn't. Every other woman I've met has wanted something from me, but not you. No, you have everything you could ever need. I'm just an extra."

She laughed, and I wasn't sure exactly what was so funny, so I asked her.

"I do not, at all, have everything I need," she said, shifting on my lap. "In fact, I am missing something very important in my life."

"What's that?" I asked.

"Someone who actually gives a fuck about me," she said.

"Mai seems to like you," I said.

"That's not what I mean," she retorted, sitting back even further. "I want someone to choose me. Someone who puts me ahead of everyone else. I don't mean I want a servant or a slave or anything like that. No, I want someone who wants what's best for me. Someone I can want what's best for them, too."

"Who wouldn't want that?" I asked.

"You'd be amazed," she said. "The asshole I was with before you…"

"Nope," I said, cutting her off. "He doesn't deserve even a moment's thought from you. I don't want you to think about him at all. I want all of your experiences to be in the moment, not the past. Whatever he did, whoever he was, it was nothing compared to the amazing person you are. You deserve to be treated like a queen, no, fuck that. You deserve to be treated like a goddess. I bow down to you, and all that you are. I will worship at your feet, show you the reverence of my love to your body, and build that beautiful mind up so much that you'll completely forget who he was. You deserve that."

"How are you real?" she asked in a whisper. "How do you even exist in this world?"

"I'm as real as they come," I said. "I'm also a fucked-up person, so I'm gonna make mistakes. I want you to call me out on them. Every fucking time, too. Don't let me slide just 'cause you like me."

"Okay," she said. "Then you're fucking up."

I looked at her, completely confused.

"What did I do?" I asked.

"It's what you haven't done," she said, and that smile slid onto her luscious lips.

"Okay," I said, drawing word out. "What haven't I done?"

"Whatever it was you were planning to do before I fucked it up," she said. "I assume it had something to do with me sitting on the side of the bed and you on the floor in front of me, right?"

"Now you're talking," I said, sliding her off my lap so I could get up.

She landed with an, "Oof," sort of sound and I was on my knees beside her, sliding one arm under her legs, the other around her back, and hoisting her up and onto the bed, back to where she started. I must have surprised her, because she just kind of let me do it, manhandling her like I was, which was both wonderful and terrible. She'd likely been manipulated both emotionally and physically in her past, and I didn't want that to be something she had to worry about with me.

"You good?" I asked, making sure before I moved further.

"Yeah," she said after a pause, looking up at me. I kind of gave her that look that said I wanted the truth, and she added, "It was a little much, honestly, but I'm good now."

"If you're sure," I said.

She actually took the time to assess herself, then nodded again, smiling up at me with that smile that just struck me as movie star perfect.

"God, you're exquisite," I said, moving closer to her, my hands on her knees. "I just want to kiss and taste every inch of you. I want to see if you taste as good as you look, because if you do, I'm likely to just keep going until I consume all of you."

She leaned back again, resting on her elbows behind her, but this time, she wasn't nearly as tense, and as I slid my hands down to her hips, she leaned back just a little more, thrusting her tits up, and I had to lean down and take one of her perfect nipples into my mouth, and my God, she was just as delicious as I remembered.

# CHAPTER FORTY

S kye...
Between his words, and then his mouth, I was quickly feeling that pressure inside me. The one that I'd never felt before until just a few hours earlier and wanted to dive back into headfirst. I'd thought I'd fucked it up, but he was kind and gentle, letting me fall apart, holding me until I could gather all my pieces. I wondered whether it would be the same if he toppled me over that cliff.

"Mmm," he hummed against my breast. "So good."

He continued to kiss down my body, and I just closed my eyes, and let my body experience it. The butterfly kisses along my abdomen made me shudder, then I realized where he was kissing me and I sat up, sort of knocking him back with my body. I wrapped my arms around my middle, feeling like an idiot for not realizing that he'd probably seen the scars along there. I mean, he likely saw them the night before, but this was just, I don't know, worse or something.

"He do that to you?" he asked, his voice pitched low like he was afraid I'd skitter away. I nodded and he reached out, his calloused palm against the soft flesh of the back of my hand that was covering it. "Let me see how strong you were," he said, and it kind of just threw me.

I relaxed a bit, and he moved my hand off my side, sliding it out of the way before doing the same with the other arm. Once he'd done that, he could see the entirety of my failure, the mark on my body that said I'd been used and abused, and left with nothing but my life, just the bare minimum.

"You are so brave," he said, laying a kiss on the deepest scar. "So strong to withstand all that the monster tried to do to you. I don't know anyone as remarkable as you."

Each sentence was punctuated with another kiss, and then he looked up at me, his eyes wide with something I'd never seen aimed at me before. It was awe, plain and simple. Like he was seeing something that blew his mind, and he couldn't believe he got to see it.

"I'm sure my words won't mean much," he said. "But I really am proud of you. I'm so glad you fought to stay here, that you stuck around long enough for me to meet you. And I know it's fast, and I know it's just been a few days, but I don't think I'll ever not be impressed with you. If you'll have me, I'll treat you like what you are —amazing."

This time, when tears threatened to spill, I let them because they were happy tears. Tears that I'd waited for forever to shed. Something I didn't think would happen just did. He loved me. Not like he wanted to fuck me, but like I was something impressive, something worthwhile. Like I mattered in this great, big, horrible, wonderful world.

His thumb traced the tears away, but I think he knew they weren't shed in sorrow. I think he understood exactly what had happened in that small moment in time. Somehow, even better than all the doctors that worked on me, he healed me. He made me whole. It was something I would forever be grateful for, and I didn't know how to tell him.

"Let's see if we can make you fly," he said, and the growl in his voice rumbled through my entire body.

Licking my lips, I watched as he kept going down my body, paying extra attention to the place where my body had been ripped to shreds by the careless work of a madman. He'd left me in ruins, but this man, the man kneeling before me, was carefully and perfectly putting me back together again.

I leaned back on my arms, opening myself up to his touch. His lips slid lower, down to my hips, and his hands slid further down my legs, sliding over my knees, pressing them apart. It wasn't like he was forcing me, just guiding me the way he wanted me to move. If I'd resisted, I was sure he'd stop, but I didn't want to resist him. No, I wanted to let him have control. I was more than willing to give up control to someone who would respect my decision to stop, and John had proven he would do that.

I shifted my legs so they were on either side of John's shoulders. He looked up at me, a smile on his lips that spoke volumes in the quiet hush of my room. Shifting up onto his knees, he laid a kiss on my lips, his body hovering over mine, hands on either side of my hips. It was intimate and close, but not quite touching. I arched my back, working to get in contact with him, but he was just out of reach.

"I want to take my time," he whispered against my lips. "I want to show you how beautiful you are. How remarkable you are. Exactly what I think of you. Are you okay with that?"

Looking into his eyes, even in the muted light of my room, I saw the truth in what he said. As much as I wanted him to take his time, I'd felt that fall, and I craved to climb the cliff again, just so I could tumble over the edge.

"Would you hate me if I said no?" I asked, terrified he'd be mad.

"You're driving, remember?" he asked. "What you say goes, and if you want fast and furious, then we'll do just that. It's gonna take me a minute to get back into shape, though, and I was hopeful I could get you to fly before we got into the full meal deal."

"We don't have to," I said.

"Nope," he replied, his voice firm. "You want it now, that's what you'll get. I just want to set expectations on what I'm capable of, okay?"

I nodded, then looked at the nightstand. He saw my glance, and looked at himself, obviously not understanding what I was meaning.

"I have something there that can get things going until you're ready," I said, all but a whisper.

"I like toys," he said with a smile, and slid back onto his heels beside the bed. "Which drawer?" he asked and I pointed to the top one.

Sliding the drawer open, he looked confused.

"Just the one?" he asked.

"Yeah," I said, turning away.

"Not shaming you," he said. "Just asking so I know whether I should keep digging."

I didn't turn back and kept my face away from him. His hand slid along my jaw as he turned my face so I was looking at him. I kept my eyes down, trying to not look without actually shutting them, but he moved so that he was in my line of sight.

"I know you've been hurt," he said. "But that wasn't me. I won't hurt you. I won't push you. But I may ask questions that are hard to answer, and I'm only asking because I want to know how to love you the best way possible."

I swallowed hard, trying to get rid of the lump in my throat that wouldn't go away. He kissed me then, slow and sweet, just his lips moving against mine. I sighed, opening my mouth to allow him in, and when his tongue collided with mine, I relaxed just that little bit more. His hands were on my body, just along my hips, and I could feel him moving them up and down my sides.

"I'll need to get my bag," he said when he pulled back, and I looked at him utterly confused. "Unless you have condoms hidden somewhere, I'll need to get mine."

"Oh," I said, realization dawning on me.

"You good for me to go now?"

"Yeah," I said, trying hard not to show how much I missed his touch when he was still touching me.

He got up and walked away from me, and that whole saying of loving to watch them leave even when you didn't want them to go was absolutely true in that instant. Mai had been right about how fine an ass he had, and I kind of giggled, stuffing my hand into my mouth to keep the noise down.

When he came back in, he was holding a box, and it wasn't one of those little ones, either. No, it looked to be entirely too big for what I expected. He caught me staring at it and smiled.

"Not planning to use them all tonight," he said. "But I didn't want to be without."

I nodded, unsure what the actual plan was. He set the box on my nightstand next to the light, opened it up, then just left it there. He didn't pull one out, didn't get anything ready, just had them available if the need should arise.

"Now," he said as he knelt in front of me. "Where were we?"

"I think we were kissing," I said.

He slid his hands up my legs and body, then pressed into me so that his entire torso was against mine. I shuddered with the touch, loving the way his warmth felt on my skin. His lips touched mine, gentle and soft, and I opened my mouth, wanting more of him, which he gave willingly. It was a heady rush to feel his dick start to stiffen as he kissed me.

I didn't know much about the time it took for someone to go from having come to being ready again, because it wasn't something I cared about. Now, though, I was anxious for him to get to the point he was ready, and it was obvious it was happening, his cock sitting right against my pussy. Pushing forward on the bed, I tried to get a better feel, get that friction going that worked in the shower earlier to get me going, then when I was here, in this same bed, just a little while before.

God, it was like waiting for molasses to run the way this was going. I felt like a petulant child wanting their goodies without having to wait for them. One of my hands came up and wrapped around his shoulders, holding myself up against him as I tried again to get closer, with even more contact between us.

When he pulled back, his eyes were hooded, his lips lush, and I wanted them on me. I didn't care if it took forever for him to fuck me at this point. I wanted him to do whatever he wanted, and I wasn't at all going to argue.

My head rolled back, and I pulled my arm off from around his shoulders, leaning back again on the bed, only this time, I let myself fall completely flat. I missed the heat from his body against me, but I wanted him to enjoy my body, one I was willing to give to him without reservation.

"What do you want, baby?" he asked in hushed tones.

"Make me fly," I said. "However you want, just get me there."

"You sure?" he asked.

"Yes," I said, turning my eyes up to him. "I want you to get me there however you can. I'm letting you take control because I don't know how to do it."

"You've never..." he left the word unsaid, but I nodded. I mean it was barely a lie. I had, but just a little bit earlier. "Okay, baby. I'll get you there. I'll get you there several times if I can."

I nodded, my head rubbing against the sheets underneath it. Trusting him more than I'd trusted anyone in my life, I closed my eyes and tried to relax, and just enjoy everything.

# CHAPTER FORTY-ONE

*J*ohn...

My heart broke when she'd implied she'd never had an orgasm. I didn't know, couldn't guarantee, but if I could help it, I'd try my best to give her as many as possible, at least until she was worn the fuck out. She'd closed her eyes and opened her legs even more, giving me full access to her entirely, and my God was she beautiful.

One would think I would have just gone straight in, but I wanted to draw her out, and build her up along the way. I rose up onto my feet, moving up so I covered her completely, while not actually touching her. I wanted her to feel my heat, but I didn't want to smother her. I kissed her gently, just a touch of my lips against her. She sighed at the touch, opening her mouth, and I let my tongue slide inside, moving against her own as I tasted her. I knew I'd get to taste even more of her as well, since she had pretty much given me permission. I wouldn't push, but she smelled divine, and I definitely wanted to get my fill of every part of her.

Moving my mouth away from hers, I kissed along her jaw, and up under her ear, feeling her breathing hitch as I hit that spot just so. Continuing my travels, I kissed down her delicate neck and along her collarbone, continuing along her soft skin until I reached the top of her breast, where I again felt that quick intake of air.

"I got you," I said, and could both feel and see her body relax just a bit.

I kissed the top of her breast, moving slowly to her nipple where I let my lips part ever so slightly, my tongue slipping out to lick the hard nub as it rose. She moaned, arching her back, and I took it as a good sign, pulling the nipple into my mouth, letting my warmth wrap around her. Not wanting to hurt her, I kept it to just lips and tongue before moving to the other breast to give it the same attention, enjoying every little noise she made.

Once I felt she was in a state of relaxation, I left her breasts to kiss my way further down her body, pressing my lips along her flat stomach, caressing the scars along the one side. She shuddered when my mouth first touched there, but relaxed as I paused, letting her get accustomed to it. I didn't want to push her, didn't want her uncomfortable, but wanted her to know that I wouldn't hurt her.

Moving slowly, giving her time to resist if she wanted, I finally got to the bottom of her abdomen, right at the top of the lighter than light hair there. I was thankful she wasn't one of those women who shaved everything off, because that was creepy as fuck. I didn't do kids, so didn't want a woman who was bare.

I could smell her, and she was more than just a little aroused, which turned me the fuck on. My cock had already stirred to life earlier, and it was now rising to the occasion, which suited me just fine. Kissing along the hairline, her stomach quivered, and I wasn't sure whether it was in anticipation or fear, but she didn't shut me down, didn't push me away, didn't move to close her legs, so I assumed it was excitement causing the movement.

Instead of heading right to her pussy, I kissed the top of her thigh, going along the inside edge of it and toward her knee. She made a mewling sound as I moved farther away from her opening, so took that as a clue to move back to my desired location. I took my time, though, and her legs shifted along with her body, pressing me to get to where she wanted me, and boy did I want to get there.

Finally, I let my lips press against the outside of her pussy, just laying a kiss along the lips that were there. Arching her back, she pressed herself closer to me, and I opened my mouth, letting my tongue slide all the way from her cunt to her clit in one swift line, and felt her shudder again, another moan releasing from her. Again, I licked her, opening to that nub of nerves at the apex.

"Yes," she sighed, and I accepted that invitation to continue.

My hands had been mostly just sliding along her sides, but I brought them up and over to lay atop her thighs, not pushing them out or anything, just kind of holding them steady. I continued using my tongue on her pussy, licking and sucking on all the parts, enjoying her moans as I did something she liked.

I wanted to make her come with just my mouth, but I wasn't sure I'd get there. Sticking my tongue inside her, I grazed my teeth along her clit, and she tensed, her legs tightening up under my palms, and her breathing increased in quick pants until she cried out in a long oh sound that just sent my heart racing.

Once she'd settled some, I pulled back, looking up across her beautiful body, hoping she'd open her eyes and look at me, but she didn't.

"Baby," I said, low so I didn't startle her, but she wouldn't move. "Baby, look at me," I said, this time with a bit more force.

Her eyes opened slowly, and she looked down her body at me, a smile playing on her lips.

"You good?" I asked.

"Mmhmm," she hummed.

"You want some more?"

"Mmhmm," came again.

"Fingers good for now?" I asked. "Or you want my cock buried deep inside you?"

Her eyes popped wide, and I stilled.

"Easy, baby," I said. "I'll do whatever you want. You want me to keep on keeping on with my mouth, I'm good with that. You just gotta let me know. Remember what I said? You're driving this bus, so what you say goes."

She nodded, her eyes still wide.

"Talk to me, baby," I said, trying to keep my voice low and even without being too demanding. "Tell me what you want. If you don't know, just let me know that, too. We can try something, see if you like it, and keep it up or switch it up."

She pulled her bottom lip into her mouth, biting it, and it made me want to climb her body and kiss her. Then I saw the first tear slip out and I did exactly that. Placing my hands on the bed on either side of her hips, I shifted up out of my seat, and eased up over her, watching her eyes to see if there was fear in them.

"It's okay, baby," I said, hoping my words soothed her. "We can stop if you want."

"I don't want to stop," she said, her tone soft. "I just don't know what I want. I've never had anyone ask me that, and I don't know what to do."

"That's okay," I said as I settled over her, keeping my weight on my arms and off her.

"Can you just do something?" she asked.

"Do you want me to lead?"

"Yeah," she said, her eyes still wide, but there was hope in them.

"I'm happy to do that," I said. "If something bothers you, tell me. I don't want you to go along because you think you have to. I want you to enjoy this ride, feel all the things, and if it isn't working, to tell me so I'll stop. I promise I won't get mad, and if you say stop, I'll stop."

"But what if…"

"Nope," I said, cutting her off. "I don't want you to think about me at all. I want this to be all about you. You gave me a great gift earlier. Now it's my turn to give back to you. I start something, and you don't like it, tell me. I do something you do like, you can tell me that, too. We'll learn this dance together, okay?"

She nodded and I pierced her with my eyes until she finally said, "Okay."

"That's my girl," I said. "You're so beautiful, and I want only the best for you."

Her smile lit me up, and I leaned down, and laid my lips on her. She opened hers, letting me into her in such an intimate way I couldn't help but devour her. Everything about her was perfect, even her scars. Nothing could have made me believe I'd fall head over heels for someone I'd just met, but my God did she draw me in. I was sure we'd get into some things at some point, but for now she was mine, and I would treasure her, and show her how amazing she was. That was a vow I made in that moment. Nothing would stop me from that task, no matter how long it took for her to believe it.

# CHAPTER FORTY-TWO

*S*kye...

"That's my girl," he said.

Those words made me feel some type of way, and I wasn't sure why. His praise meant everything to me, and I wanted to do whatever he wanted, even if it wasn't something I enjoyed.

"You're so beautiful, and I want only the best for you," he added, and it was just perfect.

The kiss he began was slow, but I opened my mouth, wanting this more than almost anything. Arching my back, I pressed my body against his, wanting to feel his warm skin on my own, which was cooler. He moaned into my mouth, then pulled away.

"Baby," he said, breathless. "You have no idea what you're doing to me. I want you so bad, I want to bury myself deep inside you."

"Do it," I said, without hesitation.

"You sure?"

"Yes," I said, sounding desperate, even to myself. "Please, for the love of God, fuck me."

"As you wish," he said, shifting to the side and reaching behind him to my nightstand.

I could hear the condoms come out of the box, the whisper of the foil packets as they rubbed against the cardboard. The way we were settled was awkward, so I shifted, pulling myself up onto the bed fully, and swinging my legs around, using my feet to shove the blankets down further on the bed. He watched me move, but didn't follow me, just sort of stood there, eyes trained on my body as it settled.

"You comfy?" he asked, holding a foil packet in one hand.

I nodded and he stood up to his full height, lording over me, but I wasn't afraid. In fact, I didn't think I'd been afraid of him since we had officially met. He was scary looking, for sure, but his kindness had made me see past the harsh and solid exterior to the gentle giant he hid inside.

I smiled as I watched him roll the condom down his length, which was much bigger than I'd ever seen. I knew how big he was from the blow job I'd given him earlier, but seeing it in this context, without having myself lined up to him, was just delightful. Once he was ready, he leaned down onto the bed, one hand next to my body, his face coming to mine, and he kissed me again, and I'd like to think I could die happy having had his kisses.

Once he pulled back, his lips were plump, and I just wanted to keep kissing them, but he moved over me, one knee going between my legs as I opened for him. Moving slowly, my guess was, for me to have time to stop him, he pulled the other leg up, and placed it between my own as well.

"You say stop, we stop," he said, and I nodded. "I'm serious," he added, looking deep into my eyes with his own. "I want you to enjoy this, but if I do something you don't like, you tell me. I need to know you're gonna do that before we start."

"Okay," I said, feeling a bit odd about having this conversation while he was poised to enter me.

"Promise me," he said, and the seriousness was almost overwhelming.

"I promise," I said.

Again, he leaned down and kissed me, his lips against mine, moving slowly as he lowered his body. I could feel his cock sliding against my pussy, rubbing up and down, and it was just enough friction to ramp me up again. With Dylan, it was always just, "bend over, I'm gonna fuck you," but that wasn't what John did. He was patient, caring, made sure I was ready, and was just so kind about it all.

"Hey," he said as he pulled away. "You good?"

"Sorry," I said.

"Nope," he replied. "What's going on in that beautiful head of yours?"

"Just that you're so nice," I said. "I've never had that before."

"Fuck," he said, looking away.

"I'm sorry," I said, apologizing again.

"No," he said, looking back at me, his expression serious. "It's not that. I'm just pissed you've never had anyone care for you like this. Everyone in your life should worship you, pay homage to you, and treat you with reverence. It's the least you deserve."

"I don't know what any of that means," I said.

"It means you're a goddess and deserve to be treated as such," he said. "I aim to make up for the entire male species if you'll let me. Starting right now."

With that, he pressed another kiss against my lips, nearly forcing my mouth open so he could make me lose my mind with the tangle of tongues. When he finally pulled away, I was breathless, and I didn't even mind. Holding himself up above me, he took one hand and slid it down my body, slowly tracing a line his lips had earlier, between my breasts, along my scars, and slowly down between my legs.

He hadn't mentioned that I hadn't shaved, which was a nice change to what Dylan wanted. When he slid his hand between my pussy lips, all thought of anyone else went out the window, and all I could think about was his hand, sliding between my folds, and his finger sliding inside me. He pulled his hips back and pressed his thumb against the bundle of nerves at the apex of my sex, pressing hard enough for me to roll my eyes back and see stars.

"That's it, baby," he said. "Just feel it, let it consume you. Let go and fly."

And I did. Stars erupted all around, and I felt weightless, like I was floating among them. Wave after wave rolled through me, my body bucking and shattering, until I was falling hard, landing in the warm embrace of a man who seemed to care more for me than anyone on the entire planet.

"I got you," he whispered in my ear. "God, you're beautiful when you fall apart."

My breathing slowed, but I could tell I'd been panting. I wanted something to drink but didn't want to move from where I was.

"What do you need?" he asked, sensing it without me saying anything.

"Drink," I said.

"Water or something stronger?"

"Water," I said, licking my lips.

"Be right back," he said, kissing my temple before he left me.

I wanted him to stay with me, but needed to drink, so suffered the silent moments he was gone.

"Here we go," he said, sitting beside me, and raising my head, holding a glass of cool water to my lips.

I swallowed, nearly gulping it down, almost choking on it as I got my fill. He pulled the glass away, turning to set it on the table beside my bed, then coming back to wrap me up in his warmth. He made soothing sounds as he held me, one hand behind and around my back, the other running up and down my arm. I was safe in that cocoon, away from any harm that might try to find me.

"How are you doing?" he asked after a bit.

"Good," I said, but had to try a couple times to get the word out.

"More water?"

"More you," I said, turning my face up to look at him.

With the light behind him, I couldn't see the expression on his face, but his body language told me he was more than willing to fulfill my request. Slowly, he brought his head down, his lips touching mine in a soft caress. I twined my arms around him, one going between the mattress and his body, the other wrapping around his shoulders. I shifted, lying down, pulling him on top of me, and he moved carefully, but purposefully, to do my bidding.

Pressing his leg between mine, I opened for him, wanting him there. He shifted, his other leg moving into position between mine as well. Never stopping the kiss, he just deepened it, sliding his tongue along mine in a mimic of what I hoped he'd do with his cock. I could feel it, not yet firm, between us, and I pulled one hand from around him, and slid it down between us. He rose up just slightly, and I found my mark, sliding my hand along the length of him, stroking him to firmness once again.

The condom he'd put on must have come off, because all I could feel was the velvet skin wrapping his firm cock. Pulling back from the kiss, he looked down at me, and I could feel the questions rumbling around in his mind.

"I think we need another one," I said, stroking him to his full stiffness. "Will you get me one?"

Again, he shifted, pressing up with his hand on the far side of me while reaching toward the nightstand. Turning to watch, he pulled another strip from the box and tore the strip apart with his teeth, dropping the bundle on the bed, and handing me the one he'd separated from the rest. I took the slick disk and let my hands figure out where they needed to be, not taking my eyes off his. Even though the room was dark, our eyes had adjusted, and I assumed we could both see each other sufficiently, and he was gorgeous. I hadn't really thought about his looks, but now I could see the rugged beauty he had. He was strong, with arms as big as my thighs, and a chest that was more solid than the walls of my apartment.

It wasn't just his looks that drew me to him, either. No, the way he treated me, even before we actually met, was that of a man who cared about his fellow human. Something you just didn't see these days.

When my hand found his dick, I slid the rubber down the length, making sure it was on good and solid before shifting my hips to try to line myself up with him. Both his hands were pressed into the mattress, one on either side of my head, and he held himself up, but I could see the toll it was taking on him. Instead of initiating things, I shifted again, placing a hand along his bicep.

"Lie back," I said, hoping he'd let me be on top for this.

He did as I asked, turning, and almost falling onto the other side of the bed, giving me room to move before shifting over onto his back. I slid my leg over his, moving so I was straddling him, then slid myself up and down his cock, sliding it with my pussy lips as he'd done when he was on top earlier. He was firm, but not quite rock hard, so I was hopeful I'd be able to make that happen sooner rather than later. I wanted him, and I wanted him bad, and it wasn't something I was used to experiencing.

"That's it, baby," he said, his hands on my hips as I moved along him. "Use me however you want. I want to see you fall apart again, this time on top of me."

I let my eyes slide closed, concentrating on the feel of him underneath me, until I couldn't stand it any longer, and shifted up, sliding my hand between us to lift him up, trying to line him up with my entrance. The way we were together, though, I couldn't make it work, and it was beginning to piss me off.

"Here," he said, his hand going over mine that was on him. "Let me do that part. You just enjoy the ride."

As if by magic, he shifted it so that he slid right into me, almost to the hilt, and I had to hold myself up just enough to not be completely impaled by him. He was thick, which I'd known, but wasn't prepared for the fullness I'd experience, and boy did I like that feeling.

Raising up, I let him slide nearly out of me before sliding down, just a little further this time, and again, that fullness was such an endorphin rush. Again, sliding up and off him nearly completely before sliding down again, still not quite all the way, but much closer this time.

"Good girl," he said, his hands on my hips, not forcing me, just holding me steady. "You keep doing that, just like that. You're so beautiful."

Those words, that praise, made my whole body shudder, completely from the inside all the out to the tips of my fingers and toes, all the way to the top of my head, and it was such a good feeling. Again, up and down, slow and steady, him guiding me along the way, praising me with each stroke, until I just kind of exploded, sliding all the way down until he was fully inside me, blowing apart at the seams while he held onto me and kept me steady.

"Wow," I said when I'd come back to myself. "Is it always like this?"

"Like what, baby?"

"With you," I said. "Does everyone you're with see stars over and over again?"

He chuckled, the movement of his dick inside me making me shiver.

"I try to be a generous lover," he said. "But I think you're just touch starved, love starved."

"Well, I'm definitely the latter," I said, sitting on top of him, his cock buried deep inside me.

"Pretty sure that needs to change," he said, shifting his hips so he moved further into me. "You should get all the loving you deserve. I want you to have trouble walking. I want you to dream about me when I'm not next to you, not inside you."

"Not gonna lie," I said, sliding myself up, and feeling the quiver of my pussy around him. "I want to feel this a whole lot more."

Sliding back down, I pressed until he was fully inside me, all the way to the hilt, and I felt him press against my cervix. I could do this for a long time, and not get tired, but I wondered whether he'd be on board for my crazy life. Then I thought about who he was, and what he did, and figured he likely had a much crazier one than I did.

"Get out of your head," he said, holding me in place, squeezing my hips with his strong fingers.

I looked at him, realizing that I'd likely been far off in another place without moving for too long. It was what I did with Dylan. I had grown to hate sex, but John had erased those memories, but not the automatic body responses.

"Sorry," I said, and meant it. "Old habits die hard."

"I know," he said. "But I want you to enjoy this."

"I am," I insisted. "Really, I am. It's just…"

I let the word trail off, not wanting to piss him off.

"Hey," he said. "I get it. Same thing was happening to me at the dish. I was all up in my head where nothing good could come. This break is perfect for me, and this," he said, waving his hand between us. "This, I hope, will be as good for you as it is for me."

I smiled at him, and said, "It's been very good so far."

"Let's keep it going," he said, his smile matching mine.

Taking the cue he gave me, I started to move above him again. Slowly at first, just a shifting of my hips, but then I could feel him slide in and out of me, his hips pulling back and driving up into me, and damn did it feel good. My knees were resting on the bed on either side of his hips, and I pushed myself up, allowing him to slide out of me some, then settled back down, taking him deep inside me, hitting my cervix before I rose up again, making the same stroke, letting him out, then taking him back in.

"Oh yeah," he said, and I watched him watch me. "Dance to that beautiful heartbeat, baby. Get yourself there. Let me know how I can help."

"Touch me," I said, not really knowing what I wanted, but knowing his hands on me in any manner was at least a good beginning.

Pulling his hands from my hips, he slid them up and down my side in slow movements to match my own. I leaned forward some, pressing my hands on his chest, and I could feel the muscles beneath the skin as his arms moved. The shift in my body made the movement of him sliding in and out of me just different enough that it messed with my rhythm, making it not quite as good as it had been. I sighed, then pushed myself back up to sitting on top of him. I knew I wouldn't be able to keep this going, but it was a better feeling than leaning forward.

"You want me on top?" he asked and I nodded, moving to get off so we could change places. Instead, he held me where I was, with him deep inside me, hands on my hips. "Tuck your leg up and over me," he said. "Don't want to break it."

Doing what he said, I leaned one direction, pulling my leg up and kind of stretching it back, which forced me to lean forward and onto his chest. With his arms around me, he flipped us over in one smooth motion, one knee between mine, the other on the outside of my thigh.

Lifting that leg up, he sort of scooted my legs apart, settling between them.

"Better?" he asked and I thought, then nodded, saying, "Yeah."

"Good," he said. "Now, let me move and you tell me what works, okay?"

"Okay," I said, knowing he would stop if it was too much.

Slowly, he began to move in and out of me, just short strokes at first, his arms on either side of me, holding himself above me without pressing his entire weight onto me. I moved my legs out a bit, opening myself more, and pulling my knees further up, and all of a sudden it was just right and he was rubbing the right spot inside me to make me feel that warm glow starting again.

"How?" I asked as he moved in me.

"How what?" he asked back, stopping his movement.

"Don't stop," I said, and he began moving again. "How does it feel so good with you?"

"Because you're in charge," he said. "You're letting yourself actually feel the good things without worrying about something going wrong."

His movements continued at that slow and steady pace, in and out, over and over that spot inside. I took a deep breath, wanting something more, but not knowing what it was. He shifted, just a little, and took one hand to slide up my body, finally capturing my breast, massaging the soft skin with his calloused palms. That friction against my nipples made me arch my back, pressing myself further into his hand.

"You like that?" he asked.

"Mmhmm," I said.

He kept going, but it wasn't quite enough. There was still something missing, and I was frustrated with not knowing what it was.

"Touch yourself," he said and my eyes went wide. "Press on your clit. It'll help, I promise."

Trusting him, I slid my hand down between us, finding the spot he'd directed me, feeling the slick fluids from my own body, and pressing my fingers into the nub at the top, rubbing it in circles, feeling the nerve endings come to life, bringing me up and over that cliff in just a few strokes. I was aware of him moving in me, stiffening, and his rhythm halting and stuttering, until my name caressed my ear in a hush of his exhale. He let himself down, leaning on his arm at the side of me, pulling himself out while holding the condom onto the base of his cock.

"That was incredible," he said, lying next to me. "Give me a minute, and I'll get you cleaned up."

"You don't have to," I said.

"I want to," he said. "I just need a minute."

"It's okay," I said.

I moved to get up, but he pinned me down to the bed, and growled. Like, full on growl.

"Stay," he said, and I didn't move. "I don't mean to be bossy, but I want to take care of you. Please let me do that."

The sincerity in his voice, and the look he gave me, held me where I was. It wasn't a fight I was going to win, and it really wasn't one I wanted to.

# CHAPTER FORTY-THREE

*J*ohn...
   I didn't want to scare her, but I wanted to take care of her, and she was just too used to having to do everything all on her own. I didn't want that for her, so I used my power against her. I wasn't proud of it, but it was what I knew would work. Finally, after I felt like I could get up without falling over, I slid down her bed to the foot of it and over the bench that sat at the end, padding into the bathroom.

I'd held the condom on my dick, not wanting to drip on anything along the way. Tossing it into the trash can she had in there, I washed my hands, and grabbed a cloth from the basket she had on a shelf in there, wetting it down with some warm water. Picking up the hand towel from the ring it was in on the wall, I went back to the room, and the side of her bed.

"Hi," she said when I knelt next to her.

"Hey, baby," I said, my tone low. "Let me clean you up, okay?"

"Mmhmm," she said, her eyes drifting closed.

I took the warm cloth, and slid it down between her legs, being careful to watch for anything that indicated she was uncomfortable. Instead, she opened herself up to me, giving me full access to her pussy, and I was thankful she was trusting me. I was gentle, wiping her carefully from front to back. She dozed, and I was glad she was worn out, but knew I needed to get her into the bathroom to pee before I let her sleep.

Once I felt she'd been cleaned enough, I set the cloth on the floor on top of the hand towel I'd brought, then pushed my arm underneath her.

"Come on, baby," I said.

"No," she whined.

"You gotta pee," I said. "Don't want you to get an infection. Let me help you, okay?"

She groaned, but rolled to me, letting me help her up to a sitting position on the edge of her bed. Standing up, I slipped my arm behind her back, the other under her legs, and lifted her up, carrying her to the bathroom. She wrapped her arms around my neck, clinging to me as she dozed off again. When we got to the smaller room, I set her carefully on her feet in front of the closed toilet, reaching behind her to lift the lid, helping her to sit.

"Go away," she said, her tone icy.

"You gonna be okay?"

"Yeah," she said. "Just go. And close the door."

She added the last as I was walking through the portal. I closed the door behind me, giving her the privacy she wanted. I went to the bed and picked up the rags I'd set on the floor. I checked the bed and picked up the condoms that ended up on the floor, tucking them into the box on the nightstand. I fixed the blankets, pulling them up from the end of the bed and setting it up so she could get into bed easily.

When the door opened, she looked sheepish, like she was embarrassed about something.

"You good?" I asked, and she nodded. "Ready to sleep?"

"Yeah," she said, looking at the floor.

"Hey, baby," I said, going to her and wrapping her in my arms. "Talk to me."

She shook her head, but I just held her, kind of rocking her back and forth, waiting her out. I didn't have to wait long until she shuddered in my arms.

"Oh, baby," I said. "It's okay. Just talk to me. You're not gonna hurt my feelings, but I need you to tell me what's wrong."

"I'm afraid," she said and I waited for more, but she didn't continue.

"Afraid of me?" I asked and she shook her head no. "Then what are you afraid of?"

"This is all so fast," she said. "I don't want it to end."

"I'm not going anywhere," I said. "Not until you kick me out. I'm in it for the long haul."

"How can you say that?" she asked, her voice strong as she pulled away from me. "You have known me for all of five fucking minutes. You don't know me or what my life is. You've seen a tiny snapshot of it, so how can you stand there and say you're in it for the long haul?"

"I know it's fast," I admitted. "And to be honest, it's kinda freaking me out, too."

"See," she said, pushing me away.

I held her fast, pulling her back to me.

"Baby," I said as she struggled. "Baby, stop."

My voice was harsh, but I wanted her to be still and actually listen to me.

"What?" she shouted.

"I know it's fast," I said again. "But I also know what I feel, and I feel like I've been looking for you my whole life. It's like everything else has been leading me to you."

"Really?" she asked, looking up at me. Even in the dark I could tell her eyes were wide.

"Yeah," I said. "You have no idea how long I waited to find someone like you. You're perfect in every way that matters."

She started to protest, but I kissed her to keep it from coming out.

"I know you're not," I said once I pulled back. "But here's the deal. We're both messed up, and we will probably piss each other off more often than we should. But I don't want you to ever think that you're not the absolute best thing that ever happened to me."

I waited for her to argue, just so I could kiss her again, but she kind of just stood there.

"Thank you," she said, more a whisper than an actual spoken word.

"For what?" I asked.

"For being you," she said. "For being willing to help me. To make me realize that I'm not unlovable. And for giving me orgasms that I didn't realize were so wonderful."

"I'll happily keep doing that," I said. "Any time you want one, you just let me know and I'll get right to it."

"I think you mean that," she said with a laugh.

"I do," I replied. "I mean, if I'm on the road, it's gonna be hard. But if I have to, I'll fly home just to fuck you senseless."

This time her laugh was full, loud, and long, and it filled my heart with more joy than anything. I could listen to her laugh like this for days, hell, years. Yeah, this was fast, but it was right, and I knew that.

# CHAPTER FORTY-FOUR

$\mathcal{S}$ kye...
   He was kinder than anyone I knew, and the fact that he wouldn't let me argue about it just proved that he wanted me to be happy, which was a far cry from anything I'd ever experienced in my entire life. We'd snuggled into bed, him behind me, his arm wrapped securely around me, holding me tight against his body. It was warm and safe, and I didn't want to be anywhere else.

The rain pattering on the window in the living room woke me before my alarm, and I didn't want to leave him, but I had to pee, and I needed to start getting ready for work soon, so I tried to untangle myself, but he pulled me closer, his strength something I couldn't match, even if I wanted to.

"Gotta pee," I said, hoping I wouldn't wake him.

"Five more minutes," he mumbled.

"I'm gonna wet the bed," I said and he released me, but I could tell he didn't want to.

I was quick in the bathroom, finishing without turning on the light. When I opened the door, I could see him in the dim filtered light from the windows in the living room. He was lying there on his back, eyes open, and he raised his hands to me, making that grabby-hands motion. I obliged him and walked back to the bed.

"Stay with me in bed all day," he mumbled, pulling me to him.

"I can't," I said, but moving into his arms. "I have to work."

"No you don't," he said. "I'll pay for everything, just stay with me."

"I can't do that," I said. "I love my job. It makes me happy. It's the only thing that's been a constant, and I won't give it up."

I was probably harsher than I needed to be, but I wasn't gonna let him take it away from me. Dylan tried that, and it was the only thing I wouldn't fucking give in on.

"I'm sorry," he said. "I just don't want you to go."

"I know," I said. "But this isn't a discussion we're gonna have. It is a no go in every way. I will keep this store and continue to work, no matter how much you want it. This is mine, and no one is going to take it away from me."

"Baby," he said, his voice soothing, as he rubbed his hand up and down my back. "I said I was sorry, and I know you love it. I just wanted to spend more time with you."

"I know," I said. "But I can't have you trying to make me late or make me not go to work. This is who I am, and if that isn't gonna work for you, then we need to end this right now. I can't get invested in you if you're gonna turn out to be a controlling asshole."

"I'll admit I'm an asshole," he said. "And I like to be in control. But I won't do it again. Now, kiss me before you get ready. Please."

I took a deep breath, held it for a moment, then let it out. He was right. I was comparing him to someone else, and that wasn't fair of me. But I was determined to be myself, no matter the cost. I was glad it was dark enough that he couldn't see that all I wanted to do was break down when I told him he had to leave if he thought that way. Now, though, I let him hold me, and finally, kissed him before grabbing some stuff to get myself ready to work.

Closing the bathroom door, I turned the light and fan on before grabbing a towel. The water warmed quickly, and I got in, letting it run along my body. I was sore, but it felt good, so I enjoyed it, hoping it would be a regular thing. I damn near fell when the curtain moved and he climbed in.

"Judas Priest," I said. "Don't do that."

"Sorry," he said, sliding his hands around my waist. "I just couldn't pass up the chance to shower with you. I mean, you fucking turn me on just existing, so the thought of you all wet and slippery just made me hard."

"I can see that," I said, looking at his cock standing damn near straight up. "You should probably do something about that. Looks painful."

"I was hoping you'd help me out with it," he said, the smirk on his face charming.

"Oh, yeah?"

"Definitely," he said, pulling me closer. "You want to let me fuck your mouth?"

"Not a chance I'm getting on my knees in here," I said.

"Shit," he said, then slipped out of the shower.

"Fuck," I mumbled. "Figures."

I thought he was pissed, but he was back quickly, slipping a condom onto himself.

"Now I can fuck that pussy," he said, his voice so low it was almost a growl. "You want to turn around, or should I lift you up and pin you to the wall?"

While I knew he could hold me, and I really did trust him, I opted for the first option and turned in his arms, leaning forward just enough that my ass was pushed back toward him.

"God, that ass is fine," he said, smoothing his hand down and over one of the globes.

I could feel him moving behind me, then felt his cock slide up and down against my pussy before he shifted a bit more, his feet far apart against the sides of the tub. My legs were between his, but it worked with the height difference, and then he was pressing my entrance, slow and steady, sliding in and out, inch by inch, and my God, did it feel good.

"Hang on, baby," he said, and reached one arm around to push my hand against the wall.

I mirrored the movement with my other arm, holding myself up so he could press into me with more ease. In and out, one arm wrapped around my hips, holding me still as he worked his way in until I felt him hit my cervix. That tap made me clench and I heard him inhale sharply. Relaxing, he pulled back and pushed in again, and again, involuntarily, my body clenched around him, and again, he sucked in a breath. Letting go, he groaned.

"You keep doing that, I'm not gonna last long," he said. "But please, keep doing that."

His words made me clench again, and it felt good. Slow and steady, in and out, a rhythm that I found not quite enough.

"Faster," I said as he pulled out.

"You sure?"

"Yes," I said. "I want you to go faster and harder."

"It gets too much, you tell me," he said.

"I will," I said. "Now, fuck me hard."

That was all it took, and he slammed into me hard and fast, nearly pushing me into the wall. I held my hands still, not wanting to lock my arms, but needing to make sure I was protected. He pulled out, but this time he held my waist, his strong forearm tight against my pelvic bone, and he literally hauled me back and onto him, slamming into me with a greater force than he'd done before, and I saw stars.

Big explosions, lights, shivers, the whole thing, and it kept going. He punished my pussy with fast and hard strokes, slamming into me over and over and over until I couldn't stand, and had to rely on him to hold me up. There was pain, but it was quick and sharp, and relieved by the pleasure he wrung out of me. Finally, after eons, his rhythm faltered, stuttered, and then one final push before I could feel him come, and it was a glorious thing. He was pulsing inside me, and I could feel it against my raw nerve endings, my pussy squeezing and sucking it out of him. His hand went above my own against the shower wall as he finished, breathing hard against my back.

"Holy fuck," he said.

"It was of the gods," I replied.

"You're not kidding," he said. "Hang on, I gotta move."

My hands were against the wall, but I concentrated on staying upright as he slipped out of me, and that movement caused another ripple through my core. There was a sucking sound as he pulled the condom off, and set it on the edge of the tub, then I was once again wrapped in his arms, the warm water sliding down my front, his heat at my back.

"I'd wake up early to do this every day," he said in my ear, a rush of air against my skin.

"I wouldn't complain," I said, leaning back into him.

"Then it's a date," he said, kissing my temple softly. "But I don't want you to be late, so I should let you finish."

"Stay," I said, looking back over my shoulder at him.

His hazel eyes with their gold flecks boring into my own blue ones told me that he would, and it wouldn't just be for the here and now, but they held a promise of much longer. I was okay with that and could likely get used to him being in my sacred space. He was the only man I'd ever let in, and he had proven, so far, to be worthy of that gesture.

# EPILOGUE

## OCTOBER

*J*ohn...

"I can't believe you're done," she said.

"I wish I wasn't," I replied. "But we didn't play hard enough. We came so close, but those fucking Dragons beat us out. I would take the loss from anyone but them."

"I know what you mean," she said, kissing me.

"Thank you for coming," I said.

"Wouldn't miss it for the world," she replied.

Our season had actually ended before the last game was played, but it still felt like a letdown that we were done for the year. Anything could happen during the offseason. I could be traded, we could lose our coach, anything. Most of the guys would likely stay, but some would end up either retiring, going elsewhere due to free agency, or being traded. I hoped with all my heart that I wouldn't have to leave Seattle, but if I did, I'd still make this my home.

I'd thought about selling my house in Denver, but Skye talked me out of it, promising that we could take a vacation there during the offseason so I could introduce her to my family. She'd already introduced me to hers, which was small. But the other thing she did was help me see that family wasn't just blood. No, she had a huge family within the Market, one that helped each other out any time they needed. It was how Mai had ended up at her shop the day we met.

Now, Mai was the manager, and they had to hire a couple more people. I got to go on a couple of her ghost tours around the Market, and it was very interesting. Not that I believed in any of that shit, but she did, and it made her happy, so that's all that mattered. We were scheduled to go to Denver in a couple of weeks, and she'd been a hot mess, worried about the shop, and how it would hold up, but Mai had put her mind at ease, promising to call her if anything went sideways.

"What'cha thinking?" she asked.

"About life," I said, kissing her. "How this whole crazy world lined everything up just so you and I could meet. Who would have thought getting hit by a pitch would lead me to the best thing that ever happened to me."

"I'm not gonna say I'm sorry," she said. "Best pizza I ever ordered."

"It was really good, too," I said.

She'd come to watch the last game, sitting in the stands with the rest of the families, and it just made me so happy to see her there. It wasn't the first game she'd come to, but this one was special.

"Ready to go home?" I asked.

"Only if that means you and I get to have some fun," she replied, her eyebrows going up and down in the most ridiculous manner.

"I'll drive down the sidewalk if it gets me there faster," I said, holding her tight.

"Can't get there if we don't go get in your car," she said.

"You're right," I replied.

We'd been standing outside the locker room, just kind of waiting for everyone to file out of the building. It was always interesting to get out of the garage inside the stadium, and onto whatever surface streets or highways we needed to use to get home. The fans were awesome, but there were always so many of them that it was kind of clogged up.

Most of the guys just sat around shooting the shit, but some of us headed out as soon as we could.

Walking through the corridors of the underbelly of the stadium, we made our way to the parking area for players and coaches. Some of the cars were gone, but most were still here.

"Hey," Decker shouted to us as we entered. "We're all going to hit a pub. You guys wanna come?"

I looked at Skye and could tell she didn't want to, but also didn't want to be rude.

"Maybe," I said, then pulled her to me. "You say no, we don't go. I'm good with whatever you want. Honestly, I'd love to get you back to our place and fuck your brains out, but that's just me."

"But they're your friends," she said.

"And you're my girlfriend," I countered. "You are far more important than the rest of these fuckers. I'll take you over the whole crew."

"Half an hour," she said. "We get a little booze, we have a little fun, then we go home to have the best time."

"Your call," I said. "If that's what you want, that's what we'll do."

She'd been good about meeting up after games with the crew, and had actually become really good friends with Kylie, Decker's fiancée. They had a lot in common, turns out, at least from a trauma point of view, so I was okay with it. She'd brought her into the fold of her friend group, and the girl had blossomed. She was still shy to the point of tears, but after hanging out with Fi and Skye, she was beginning to hold her own.

"Who's on babysitting duty?" I asked as we got closer.

"You," Hennings said. "You're the only one they're afraid of."

"Not gonna happen, Becky," I said, using the nickname I'd given to him when he finally came back after his injury.

"My fucking name is *not* Becky," he shouted, but Fi just laughed. "Shut up," he said to her. "It's not fucking funny."

"But it is," she said through tears. "If you didn't react, he'd quit. He does it 'cause it pisses you off. Can't you see that?"

"He needs to fucking stop," he said, then turned to me. "You need to fucking knock it the fuck off."

"Or what?" I asked, pulling myself up right to my full height, which was at least a foot taller than the shortstop. "You gonna punch me in the knee?"

"Fucking asshole," he said, and I laughed. "I fucking hate him," he said to Fi, but she just looked at me over his head, shaking hers, which just made me laugh even more.

"Let's play nice," Skye said, and I saw she was looking at Kylie.

"Fuck," I said. "Sorry. Didn't mean to upset you."

"It's okay," she said.

"Nah, it ain't," I replied. "I should try to be better. Thankfully, Skye makes me want to even more than I did before. So, I'm sorry I upset you, and I'll try to keep that in mind."

"Thanks," she said.

"Thanks," Decker said, holding his woman to his side.

"Where's the party?" Adams asked when he came up to us.

"Fuck," Hennings said.

"You just pissed 'cause we get to go home with a new girl any time we want?" Swift asked.

"No woman can match Fi," he said. "And no, that's not why. It's 'cause you two make every fucking outing feel like we have to watch over you to make sure you don't end up pissing some guy off 'cause you're hitting on his woman."

"If she wants us, we can't make her want just one guy," Adams said. "Besides, how can any woman resist the two of us?"

"I can," Fi said. "Never even wanted to look your way."

Hennings puffed out his chest like he was the biggest dog in the room, but he just gave off that small dick energy, which got me to laughing again.

"Shut the fuck up," he said.

"Hey," Cameron said as he walked up. "We going out?"

"Yeah," I said. "You coming with?"

"Duh," he said. "Invited Jefferson to come with, too."

"Good times," Decker said.

"The more the merrier," Adams added and I just shook my head.

"Not everyone wants to share," I said.

"Don't know what you're missing," Swift said, giving a fist bump to Adams.

"Hey, mates," Tanner said as he came to the group. "We all popping to a pub?"

"Sure thing," Adams said. "You coming with?"

"Aw, yeah," he said, that Australian accent making the words sound just different enough that it was odd.

"Where we going?" I asked the group.

"Not Fado's," Hennings and Fi said in unison.

"Okay," I said, drawing the word out. "Bad memories?"

"Something like that," Hennings said, but didn't elaborate.

"Let's do Kell's," Skye said, and I looked at her.

She didn't want anyone to know where she lived, but the fact that she suggested the bar right next door surprised me.

"You sure?" I asked her.

"Yeah," she said. "They have great music, and they aren't too busy on Sunday nights. It'd be perfect."

"Let's go," Swift said, and the rest of the group agreed.

"I love you," I said, kissing her forehead. "You know that, right?"

"I do," she said. "And I love you, too."

"Would you two knock it the fuck off," Hennings said. "We wanna party, not watch you two fuck."

"Speak for yourself," Swift said. "I'd watch that in a heartbeat."

"Not an exhibitionist," Skye said. "Not gonna happen."

"Damn," Adams said. "'Cause his ass is great."

"I know," she said, her smile reaching her eyes. "Why do you think I walk behind him?"

The whole crew started laughing, and I couldn't help but join in. Yeah, this was what I'd been searching for, and the universe sent her to me, and I couldn't be happier.

# NOTE FROM AUTHOR

**Images and Blurbs available upon request.**
I would ask that you obtain high quality headshots and cover art images directly through me, rather than taking them from either my website or Amazon, however, blurbs are readily available through both places.

# ABOUT THE AUTHOR

Born and raised in the Pacific Northwest, CM Kane was fed a steady diet of sports, particularly baseball. Having this love of the game instilled in her at an early age, she found that nothing was better than getting lost in the game. Storytelling was another gift that was encouraged in her youth, and she's taking to the written word to explore a new aspect to the game she loves.

**Social Media and Website Links:**

Website:
https://www.authorcmkane.com

Facebook:
https://www.facebook.com/AuthorCMKane

Instagram:
https://www.instagram.com/authorcmkane/

Amazon:
https://www.amazon.com/author/cmkane

BlueSky:
https://bsky.app/profile/authorcmkane.bsky.social

# ALSO BY C.M. KANE

**Seattle Cascades**

1. Extra Innings

2. Caught Stealing

3. Backstop

4. Power Hitter

5. Double Play

6. Find a Gap

7. Sweet Spot (Coming Soon)

8. 7th Inning Stretch (Coming Soon)

**New Orleans Magicians**

1. Choke Up

2. Caught in a Pickle

3. Brand New Ballgame (Coming Soon)

4. Fan Interference (Coming Soon)

5. Flashing the Leather (Coming Soon)

**Austin Aces Hockey Club (Shared World)**

Power Play

**Anthologies**

Unnerving: Eclipse

Street Justice (Limited Time)

Fooling Around (Coming April 1, 2025)

Neon Lights & Country Nights (Coming June 1, 2025)

**Stand Alone Titles**

A Switch in Time

www.ingramcontent.com/pod-product-compliance
Lightning Source LLC
Chambersburg PA
CBHW051526260626
47170CB00003B/809